T0208524

John Lee Johnson in the Valley of the Sun:

Along Came Jones

CONN HAMLETT

authorHOUSE®

AuthorHouse™
1663 Liberty Drive
Bloomington, IN 47403
www.authorhouse.com
Phone: 833-262-8899

Published by AuthorHouse 11/19/2021

ISBN: 978-1-6655-4452-8 (sc)
ISBN: 978-1-6655-4451-1 (hc)
ISBN: 978-1-6655-4453-5 (e)

Library of Congress Control Number: 2021923393

Print information available on the last page.

This book is printed on acid-free paper.

To Linda Kay Whitehead,
a wounded angel who trod the earth with gentle footsteps

CHAPTER 1

It was midnight. The thick yellow light of the coal oil lantern on the wall spread its buttery rays over the features of four men gathered around a green felt table in the backroom of a West Texas saloon. The hole-in-the-road establishment where these men had gathered was just a hundred miles from Baileysboro, Texas. This was no coincidence. The location had been well thought out. The meeting had not been hastily called together. It had been meticulously planned by the current supreme power in 1866 Texas, Sheriff Robert Lang. Lang once had been the autocratic sheriff in Austin but then promoted himself to high sheriff of the whole state of Texas. Although he was actively involved in punishing former officials of the Confederacy (and legally robbing them), his main mission was to eliminate by any means possible the powerful West Texas rancher, John Lee Johnson.

Lang's agent, Tim Slater, swarthy and rangy and sporting a pencil-thin mustache, was one of the men situated around the table. Facing him were three gang leaders from the western part of the Nations.

Slater leaned inwards, his lupine eyes canvassing the faces of the bandit chieftains, as if his words were not only informative but secretive. Although Slater's face was partially shadowed by his dark hat brim, his intense eyes captured the attention of the men scrutinizing him before he laid out his plan. The three large leather pokes filled with gold coins that had been placed before them piqued their interest as well.

To Slater's immediate left was Lucky Wheeler, a large red-faced man who always had an annoying smirk on his face. He was in charge of the Wheeler gang, with its twenty members. He robbed banks on the average of one every two weeks. On the opposite side of the table from Slater sat Cephus Green, a cautious-looking individual wearing a looped earring and a ponytail hanging down his back. His gang totaled twelve members, and they specialized in stagecoach holdups. To Slater's right sat a well-built man, a skeptical-looking individual named Guy Morris. He was the newest and youngest gang leader. His gang numbers did not match Wheeler's and Green's, but they were handy at robberies and rustling. Morris looked wary and uncomfortable. Slater's eyes stayed on Guy longer than usual, wondering what was troubling him.

Slater, disregarding Morris's demeanor but seeing he at least had his attention, began talking. "Here is the deal," he said, indicating he was talking to all of them. "We chose you because you have always cooperated with each other in the Nations." He let a mirthless smile move across his thin face, made more menacing by his thin mustache. His eyes took on a cunning look when he added in an oily voice, "That's why we didn't bring in Turk Larsen."

It was true the three gang leaders did work together. They respected the agreed-on boundaries and often cooperated on joint ventures that were too large for one gang. When an aggressive posse ventured into another outlawry's domain, a neighboring gang would come to assist their owlhoot brethren.

And it was true that the new interloper in the Nations, Turk Larsen, known for being a maverick, was notoriously disrespectful toward established territories and other outlaw protocol. Thus he was shunned by the outlaw brotherhood.

Slater once more panned their facial expressions before he continued, "All you men have to do is go to Baileysboro and rob the bank, and then head down to Hawkshaw and rob that one, and then circle back and hit that cracker-box bank in Roxy, and then head on back to the Nations." He lifted his gloved hands out so as to emphasize the piece-of-cake job. Then, as though the thought just hit him, he added, "One of your gangs will need to burn down a ranch house as a diversion while the other two rob the bank in Baileysboro." He paused to catch any reaction and saw none. "After you burn down the ranch house and rob the bank, link back up with each other at the landmark on the map I'm goin' to give you and head on down to Hawkshaw." His cunning, thin-lipped smile again appeared. "You won't be hindered by the Texas state government. We'll stay out of it until you are safely back in the Nations, countin' your money." With that same smile, he added, "Once you're out of sight, we'll come in and act all officially indignant ... but do nothin'."

Pleased by his own words, Slater pushed an individual bag of gold toward each gang leader. "Here's five thousand dollars for each of you, based on good faith that we have a deal." He paused and gave an evaluating look at each leader. "Now I'm goin' to step outside the room, and you let me know when you come to a decision." He gave each one of them an optimistic look with a nod.

He pushed his chair back soundlessly, disappeared into the umbra of the room, and exited the door quietly into the main saloon area.

Lucky Wheeler looked at the bag of gold enticingly close by. He smugly shrugged as though he liked the plan and saw no reason to turn down such a compelling offer. But before he reached out and raked in the large leather poke, he turned to Cephus Green, raising his eyebrows and appraising his old friend's mood, anxious for his response.

Cephus caught Lucky's look and gave back a quick nod of approval. But as he extended his own hands to pull in his leather bag, he took a quick glance at the stern-faced Guy Morris. Seeing Guy's negative expression, Cephus froze, refraining from pulling the bag in. "What's eatin' on you, Guy?"

Guy pushed up the brim of his hat and said thoughtfully, "Has it ever occurred to you two to wonder why the head man in Texas wants you to rob banks in his state and burn down a ranch house?"

Cephus did not want to admit that this thought had not occurred to him. His head now dawdled over that bothersome question. His eyes narrowed as awaited Guy's explanation. He cautiously withdrew his hands from the bag of gold earmarked for him. "Keep talkin', Guy," he said gruffly before turning to see whether Lucky was also affected by Morris's words. He saw that he was. Lucky slowly nodded; he too wanted to hear Guy's concerns. Both Cephus and Lucky knew that if Morris, a gang leader in good standing, was balking, there had to be a reasonable explanation.

Guy's eyes narrowed as he peered around the darkened room as though looking for an eavesdropper. Seeing no one and hearing only the faint sounds of the rinky-dink piano coming from the main saloon, he began, "A little over a year ago, I came through the Nations with a man named Sabbath Sam. There was twenty-one of us. We were army veterans, and all of us were capable men. We were hired to kill a man named John Lee Johnson." He inhaled and met both sets of eyes keenly on him. "Oh, Sabbath Sam was a bad man, all right, and was skilled with a gun. We were about as good of a unit as you could put together. But John Lee Johnson met and braced Sabbath Sam and put him out of action. He personally killed many of the rest of us. Those of us who survived ran for our lives.

"Baileysboro is the home of John Lee Johnson. The ranch house that Slater fella is asking you to burn belongs to him. Sheriff Lang, the bigwig outta Austin, works for a fella in Pennsylvania named General McGrew. For some reason going back to the late war, this general hates John Lee Johnson and is hell-bent on killing him." Guy slowly shook his head side to side in an admonishing way. "I like you two birds and respect you; hope you listen to me. But there is no way in hell you can go there and burn his ranch house down and escape with your lives." He exhaled audibly and hissed, "You don't mess with John Lee Johnson."

Cephus contemplated Guy's compelling words and nod. "All right, I clearly understand he's a bad man. I get the point. But *why* are they hirin' us to rob them banks and burn his house?"

Guy leaned back in his chair and shrugged. "Probably to get that mean bastard chasing you. They are hopin' to use us as pawns to draw him into an ambush and keep Lang's hands and his men's hands lily-white of the robberies. Even they couldn't get away with that. I would imagine they have skilled gunmen set up on this journey from Baileysboro to Hawkshaw to Roxy covered in killers, while he's chasing our asses—make that your asses. They hope to catch him vulnerable and find a chance to bring him down"—he paused dramatically—"and blame his death on outlaws, all the while keeping the Texas state government in the clear."

Cephus, disturbed, rubbed his whisker-stubbled chin. He sent the edge of his eyes toward Lucky. "What do you think, Lucky?"

Lucky snorted and impulsively reached out to pull in one of the bags of gold. "I don't know nothin' about this John Lee Johnson. If he wants to chase after me, let him have at it." He seconded his own remark by adding, "Hell, I can kill too."

Cephus, emboldened by Lucky's pluck, reached over and pulled in the second bag.

Guy Morris looked at both expectant faces observing him, trying to gauge his move. He slowly and disdainfully pushed the bag of gold away, eased back his chair, and then stood. Adjusting his hat, he matter-of-factly stated, "It was nice knowing you birds. You're as good as dead."

The two bandit leaders gave him a bemused smile but remained silent. Guy took his gaze away from them and quickly exited the same door that Tim Slater had used.

One week later, in early April, Cephus Green, given the assignment of burning down John Lee Johnson's ranch house and creating as much mayhem as he could while torching it, was riding point, leading six mounted men. They were headed toward the same saloon where he had met with Tim Slater. He was a mile away from Gorham's place. He and his men were cognizant of the roiling sky with its lead- and pewter-colored clouds. They were hoping to beat the rain that he knew was surely going to cut loose.

He wanted some vittles, along with something to drink and cigars. He and his men needed a night's lodging. He needed a secluded place to stay until the second unit of his gang could meet up with him. They had been sent days earlier to rob the stagecoach that went from Roxy to Hawkshaw, Texas. If things went as planned, they were en route to meet him at Gorham's saloon.

Gorham's saloon sat at a crossroads. Everyone called the location "Four Ways." But it had no official name. It had a dinky barn separate from the large mercantile store. The store itself was situated on a small hillock to avoid the spring rain flooding from the fresh water stream that ran behind it. The saloon was affixed to the emporium but was built on the low side of the rise. The saloon had no front door or batwings. Patrons had to enter the emporium and then descend down a four-step stairway into the saloon itself.

Big Ben Gorham had been paid in advance for Cephus Green's stay. He had been given strict instructions to make sure there were no other customers. Witnesses were bad enough, but unwitting witnesses were the most troublesome and unforgiven of all. He had earlier shushed a few reluctant barflies from the saloon area with dire threats about their personal safety if they remained. Since the steady patrons had firsthand knowledge of outlaw gangs seeking refuge at the emporium in the past, they departed wordlessly. Gorham had made a small fortune in dealing with the various outlaw gangs and was well acquainted with all of them, except Turk Larsen's bunch. He was strict about observing protocol and following orders. He knew he was alive and reasonably wealthy from staying on their good side.

Big Ben, in his late fifties, had gone to seed. He was a large-framed man with an oversized paunch. His frayed derby covered a bald spot, leaving wispy, gray hair dangling beneath the hat's curled brim. He moved slowly around the merchant's counter, headed to the front door. He stopped and fumbled for his pocket watch; satisfied with the time, he knew he was ready to meet and greet Cephus Green and his outlaw friends. He tiredly made his way out the main entrance. He now stood on a crude, uneven planked deck, surveying the barren countryside. His eyes moved up to the undulating, darkening clouds and knew rain was only minutes away.

As he was about to return inside, he caught sight of a solitary horseman out of the peripheral of his vision. Ben, now focusing on the rider, sensed he was not one of Cephus's men because of his apparel. The mounted man was close enough to make out he was wearing a black duster. He noticed the man's posture. He sat tall in the saddle and had all the appearance of being someone ominous, a person he did not want to deal with, especially at this time. He watched the rider walk his horse into the stable and dismount.

Ben inhaled uneasily; telling some toady customers to hit the trail was one thing, but he imagined telling this man his business was closed was going to be a sight more difficult. He folded his arms and tried to decide what to say and how to get out of this unforeseen jam.

Ben thought he heard hoofbeats to his left, and when he turned to look, he saw another rider approaching on a huge black horse. If the first rider left him nettled and bothered, this rider scared the hell out of him. The rider's tan duster could not disguise the mammoth breadth of his shoulders. Ben nervously gulped as the rider drew closer. It was John Lee Johnson, and to the seedy merchant, he seemed almost unworldly.

Ben's eyebrows shot up like a window shade as he watched the powerful-looking man ride past him toward the stable. He had no idea of why the two men had appeared at this inauspicious moment. He licked his lips nervously as he began backpedaling guardedly to his doorway.

After entering, he shut the door and conspicuously placed the "Closed" sign outwards against the large glass pane; then he locked the door. He made his way behind the counter and pulled out his .10 gauge shotgun, placing it on the countertop. He was hoping to bluff the two dangerous men but he was unsure that he would be successful.

Ben's eyes were on the large glass pane of the broad door. He saw the faint outline of the first man appear and then he saw more clearly the black duster. He heard the doorknob rattle, and then there was a pregnant period of silence. He watched in incredulity as the doorway burst open, followed by the booted foot of the gunman.

Homer Timms entered. Homer was a skilled gunsmith from Gandy, Texas, and worked with John Lee Johnson. He walked straight to the counter, and his sky-blue eyes shaded somewhat by his expansive black brim took in the shotgun. Then his vision raised and locked with Big Ben's watery eyes. Homer gave a short smile and said, "You have to be kidding me."

Big Ben gulped as he gingerly removed the shotgun, placing it under the counter. He placed up two wavering palms of protest. "I'm closed and don't want no trouble."

Homer gave an inscrutable face to the nervous merchant. "Too late for that." He added mirthlessly, "It's already here."

Ben dropped his protesting palms. He began appraising his interloper. Homer's arresting blue eyes and stoic look caught Ben's attention first, but as he perused the gunman, he could see a .44 jutting from his well-used holster and a calm attitude that indicated he was no stranger to danger.

Homer moved his eyes to his right and saw the four-step stairway leading down to the saloon. "How about you and I take a little walk," he said, "and you set up two beers for me and my friend?"

Ben shuddered thinking of the gunman's friend. He swallowed audibly once more and nodded his acquiescence.

Homer indicated by the canting his head that he wanted Ben to walk first. Ben hesitated momentarily until he caught the impatient glint in Homer's eye. He stepped it off and walked down the steps and around the bar. Homer followed and stationed himself at the customer side of the zinc-covered counter.

As Ben began drawing two beers, he looked over his shoulder at the gunman. "Now I got to warn you, Mister, trouble's on its way." Seeing that his words had little effect, he added, breaking his own rule of confidentiality, "Cephus Green's probably not far from here, and he don't cotton to unwanted company."

Homer tossed two dimes on the bar top and said nonchalantly, "The hell you say."

Ben, not knowing the interpretation of Homer's statement, asked, "Do you know Cephus, by the way?"

Homer took a swig of his beer and looked over Ben's head as if he were glancing beyond the back wall and the door that led to the meeting room where Cephus had accepted his assignment. "Never met the man, but I sure hope to."

Ben nervously ran his tongue over his dry lips. "He ain't a man to be trifled with." Seeing his words had little effect on Homer, he continued in a stronger tone, "I guarantee you that."

Homer sighed and reached for a cigar. "I reckon we'll find out, won't we?"

Ben realized not only were Homer's words grim but the tone indicated a complete lack of fear. Ben's eyes widened considerably when John Lee Johnson walked down the steps. The big Texan gave a nod of thanks to Homer as he took his schooner from the bar, moved into the shadowy corners to their left, and took a seat.

Ben shuddered when he saw John go by. He had never witnessed a man who looked like he did. He had the strange appearance of an avenging angel and pagan god all rolled into one but draped in a western duster. He wondered who in the hell he was, but he sure was not going to ask.

It was becoming obvious to Ben that these men did not come to his place by accident but rather by intent. He concluded they were waiting on Cephus. Ben mulled over the situation. He realized that the bandit leader had the numbers on his side, but he also knew he had never faced this sort of adversary, either. He did not know the names of the man with the solemn face standing at the bar and the mind-warping beast of a man sitting at the corner table. He just knew it was going to be a bloodbath. Ben was sweating profusely, and he could hear the distant rumble of thunder from outside. He pulled his pocket watch out. It was straight up noon. It was at that time he heard the sky-ripping sizzle of lightning and the resounding boom of thunder.

As the rumbling noises subsided, he heard the secondary noises of hoofbeats. He did not feel any exhilaration. He knew the moment was close at hand, and it scared the hell out of him. He sent an edge-of-the-eye look toward John Lee Johnson. Neither the thunder boom nor the crackling lightning seemed to faze him. The big man just sat there with those gray eyes that seemed to have an inner light, looking in the direction of the steps that led into the saloon.

Cephus and his men rode straight to the stable and dismounted. The impending rain and the fear of lightning caused them to overlook the two horses already stalled. They tied off quickly and began a soft trot toward the steps that led to the raised deck of the general store. Upon reaching the front entrance, Cephus did take note of the splintered door facing, indicating the door had been forced. He gave a curious look at it and would have investigated further, but the rain began to pelt down in thick drops. He shrugged it off, and he and his men hastened inside and down toward the steps that would lead to the saloon.

As their heavy spurs jangled, he and his men tromped toward the steps; Cephus shouted out, "Get them beers out, you old sumbitch."

The leader maintained his toothy grin as he quick stepped the stoop to floor level. But that grin quickly evaporated when he reached the saloon itself. His eyes took in the portentous gunman at the bar, studying him silently. Cephus stepped warily into the saloon, with his men grouped behind him. The bandit leader shot Ben an accusatory glance. He received an apologetic look in return.

As Cephus moved away from Homer, he saw John Lee Johnson out of the corner of his eye. He slowly moved his thick neck and saw the immense outline of a man slowly standing from his table. Cephus's eyes moved slowly back and forth. That frightful glance at John Lee Johnson caused a shiver of fear to course through him. In a split-second, he knew this was the man Guy Morris had alluded to. Although no description had been given, he realized this formidable man had to be John Lee Johnson.

Cephus's men normally would have been overjoyed by having the numbers, but they too were affected by the deadly aura of the two men.

Their flittering vision moved from one frightful man to the other, over and over.

Cephus began inexplicably nodding his head, as though fear and indecision were battling in his skull. He turned and faced the big devil, now standing, in the darkened corner. "Before we get it on, who ratted me out?"

John ignored the question. He grimly pushed aside his duster, exposing the twin gun belts and two ivory-gripped Navy .36s.

Cephus, irritated that he had walked into a trap, gritted his thick yellow teeth in an angry snarl. His gold-looped earring jiggled with each frenetic turn of his neck as he took in the two ominous gunmen with alternating glances. He realized there was no wiggle room. He understood it was showtime. He and his men were mentally on the same page, and they simultaneously made a downward swoop for their .44s. While their hands were moving, John Lee Johnson responded. His Navy Colts began spitting orange flames a foot long.

Homer, too, was wreaking havoc, dropping bandits like dominos with his Colt. Homer had his reserve pistol in his left hand and did a quick crossover when he fired the last shot from the first pistol.

Cephus took a shot high in the chest and fired his half-raised revolver into the floor. He fell forward, losing his grip on his pistol but still having the resolve to roll over onto his back. He awaited the two men who had unmercifully destroyed his gang. As he lie there, Cephus silently cussed as he felt the strangulation from his own blood. The overflow now moving over his lips and down to his neck and chest. Out of the corner of his eye, Cephus saw that all his men were dead and not only dead, but lying in all kinds of gruesome postures.

His dying eyes looked up at John Lee Johnson, who was reloading his Navy sixes with a workmanlike expression. Cephus tried to spit the excess blood from his lips to frame his last words. "You're John Lee Johnson, ain't you?"

John nodded.

Cephus painfully sighed before uttering, "Damn my luck." His eyes glazed over as he breathed his last ragged breath.

Behind the bar, Ben Gorham gulped in a fearful shock. His wary eyes darted back and forth at the two dangerous gunmen. He then took a look at the piles of dead men, lying on his floor in gruesome twisted shapes.

Capturing some courage and hoping to curry some favor with the deadly shootists, Ben eked out the words, "More of 'em is comin', you know."

Homer moved from the bar and went over to the corpses. He looked over the back of his shoulder and said, "No, they're not." He knelt and began pilfering through the bandits' pockets. "If things went as planned, they are all dead just outside of Hawkshaw."

John Lee Johnson walked around Homer and headed up the crude steps, with his destination the stable. They had agreed that John got the horses and Homer got the money.

Ben watched the extraordinary man pass and then focused his attention on Homer, who had just found a motherlode of money on Cephus's body. Ben, mustering his courage and saying with a hint in his voice, "They owed me five hundred dollars."

Homer matter-of-factly answered, "They owed you—I don't." Still bent over rummaging through pockets, he added, "You can have their gun belts and weapons." Seeing that he had fleeced the dead outlaws, he stood and faced Ben. "And you can bury them too."

Ben nodded. He knew he had been outfoxed, and he knew that if he played with verbal fire long enough, he would get burned. He sighed and continued nodding as though to shake loose his predicament and make sense of it all. Their belts, weapons, and boots would somewhat cover his loss of revenue. As far as burying them, he would feed them to the pigs he kept behind the saloon.

Six days later, at nine thirty in the morning, Lucky Wheeler and five of his gang members were making ready to ride out of an arroyo that was a mile from the backside of Baileysboro. It was their intention to come in from the north and join up with their other gang members.

The rest of the Wheeler gang was divided into three units of five men. They had been instructed to come in from the other three directions: one group would enter from the east and seal off the town. Another division of the gang would ride in from the west and secure the other end of the street. Coming in from a southerly direction, the remaining unit would ride down empty alleys and meet Lucky's group as they simultaneously emerged from the northern opposite alleyways, thus effectively choking the town in all directions.

Lucky's five-man crew had been hidden from sight since three o'clock in the morning. Getting an affirmative nod from Lucky, they crow-hopped their mounts up the soft dirt incline. Everything was going as planned, and the conditions could not have been better. A mild sandstorm had started blowing at sunrise and had served as a smoke screen to mask their arrival. However, that same sandstorm hindered their vision as well. They could make out the sketchy outlines of the backs of the buildings that fronted the main drag of the town. But any other crucial details were impossible.

Once they crested the top of the ravine, Lucky raised a hand and halted his gang. He nodded for his men to take their positions on each side of him. With expectant eyes, he looked through the yellow haze of dust, hoping to catch sight of his brother, Jack, who had been scouting the area. Lucky, always conscious of time, meticulously looked at his pocket watch. His brother was five minutes late. Snapping the watch casings together, he searched the expanse, hoping to catch sight of his brother.

Concerned that Jack was late, a relieved Lucky soon saw a shadowy outline of a rider emerging through the veil of yellow dust from the sand-shrouded line of structures. He approvingly took note that Jack cantered his horse instead of galloping, which was textbook surveillance. He did not want to draw undue attention, even in a sandstorm.

Jack, large framed and ruddy complexioned like his brother, saw his fellow gang members ahead; he could tell they were huddled closer than normal due to the abrasive windstorm.

When he reined up beside Lucky, he gave a backwards glance toward the town, as though something was rankling him.

Lucky knew that look well and gave his brother an inquiring look. Jack, knowing time was of essence, forked a thumb over his shoulder toward the backs of the stores. "I didn't see anything out of the ordinary." He paused and added, "except."

Lucky studied his brother's features and mulled over the word "except." Lucky trusted his brother's judgment. But the word "except" niggled him. He was wanting a more optimistic outlook from his brother. And not the word "except."

Jack, catching that prickly look in his brother's eyes, started talking. "Every thang looks fine, except there's nine horses in the corral." Not waiting for Lucky's response, he continued, "That's too many horses in a livery corral for a burg this small." He turned toward Baileysboro and added, "The owner of the livery has his front doors closed too." He shook his head in agitation. "Ain't nobody goin' to close livery stable doors in this warm weather and suffer all them damn smells."

Lucky deliberated Jack's words but chose to be optimistic. He tilted his head one way and then another as he mulled over decision. "Did you see anything else that would cause us to call this thing off?"

Jack, seeing his brother was not overly deterred with his report, shook his head. "I didn't see anyone scurryin' around with a rifle. And the sheriff came out on his porch and threw out a pan of shave water." He went on to say that there did not seem to be any out-of-the-ordinary horse traffic or shadowy movements along the roofline.

That information seemed to please Lucky, but that "thumb stuck in a Christmas pie" look slowly transitioned into a more thoughtful mien. "I ain't spooked by them horses in the corral. I ain't worried about the livery stable door being closed. Hell, the ol' boy that runs livery might have a stopped-up nose." He thoughtfully paused. "The only thing that spooks me is the fact we ain't heard from Cephus."

Jack shrugged as though that information was of no consequence. "We've worked with him before, and he generally does whatever he pleases."

Those words seemed to mollify Lucky. He once more pulled out his pocket watch and checked the time. He decided he was going to hit the bank. He had heard for over a year that the Baileysboro bank was loaded. The temptation of getting his hands on all that money overrode any reservation he might have had.

The men mounted on both sides of Lucky and his brother had heard only bits and pieces of their conversation due to the noisy wind, but they could tell the attack and robbery were on. The impending excitement was infectious; hitting that rich bank and shooting the hell out of a few store windows altered their tired looks. They were ready and adjusted themselves in their saddles for the anxious ride toward the shadowy lines of buildings that lie ahead.

However, they stayed in their positions until it was ten thirty. After Lucky gave them a nod, they began a soft trot to the blurry outlines of the backside buildings. They deliberately began to pan out as to ride down the individual dust-filled alleys.

The wind whistled, and the loose sand beat at their faces as they made their way to the store buildings. The exposed sun shining through the heavy dust clouds outlined the Wheeler gang in thick, yellow-orange tints. Each man rode down a singular alley, passing a rain barrel or two. They spotted little or no etched footprints in the sand. Each rider, experienced in their craft, observed nothing out of the ordinary.

As though choreographed, all twenty gang members now simultaneously appeared from the four directions. They effectively had the town in their clutches.

At first, Lucky looked at the vestiges of hoofprints in the street becoming fainter with the whistling force of the wind. His eyes moved over the buildings and windows as if to see who might be watching or hiding.

Seeing nothing, he viewed the bank itself. It was made of brick and mortar and looked worthy of robbing. There was one horse tethered to one of the two sturdy-looking hitchracks. The horse looked swayback but that fact was more amusing than pertinent.

What did catch his eye were the two covered wagons, each at the opposite ends of the town. Covered wagons were not unusual in themselves. But that style of wagon was used in long-distance freight hauling, and seeing two of this sort in this cattle community seemed odd. That matter held his interest for a moment. One seemed plausible, but two did not.

Putting the Conestoga wagons on the back burner of his mind, he moved his eyes to the sheriff's office and the empty porch and the slanted wood tile roof that covered it. It looked as though the sheriff was still napping or ignorant of the present danger. Once more, he glanced suspiciously both ways at the bulky covered wagons at the opposite ends of town, but the lure of the bank's rich money-trove outweighed his suspicions. He pulled his Army .44 from his holster and waved the barrel high in the air. This obvious signal caused the riders at each end of the street to move in a hundred feet closer, passing the wagons and leaving them in their wake.

Seeing he had the usual successful formation he had used on past robberies, Lucky gently trotted from the line of his men toward the bank. He was joined by his brother and a tall gangly hombre named Otis from the other side. The three men leisurely rode toward the bank.

When Lucky was within ten feet of the bank, a strange thing happened. Men began pouring out of the Conestoga wagons located at the opposite ends of town. They were now situated behind his men, who had moved in at his signal.

These deputies and ranch hands were joined by many other unseen men who had been concealed. These men, previously hidden, pushed other wagons into the street that had been planted out of sight to block the Wheeler gang's exit.

The door to Chili's Livery barn, located four buildings down from the bank, suddenly flung open, and more than two dozen federal agents hurried to the covered wagon that housed premade wooden barricades now being pulled to shield them from the outlaws' gunfire as well as serving as effective blockades.

At the other end of the town, the exact same process was taking place. Additional men were pouring out of the feed store and were stretched across the street, protected by barrels and crude wooden barriers.

Lucky had picked up on this movement from his peripheral vision. He clenched his nicotine-stained teeth in a snarling grimace at the trap he found himself in. Hoping to be pragmatic in his predicament, he swiveled his head in each direction, aware that it would be difficult to escape. Then his eyes immediately went to the once-empty, dust-strewn alleyways. But to his chagrin, those alleys, vacant moments ago, were now filled with a lot of ominous-looking armed men, ensconced behind wooden barrels; all holding rifles or pistols.

Jack, mounted next to Lucky, seethed out some cuss words. He too recognized they were in a serious bind. He turned to give recommendations to Lucky, who was still twisting his neck around appraising himself of what action to take. Jack had his mouth open ready to give counsel when he received another shock.

The bank's twin doors opened dramatically, as if it were a stage play. Five men came through the doors, three of them holding sawed-off .10 gauge shotguns. Jack watched as Seth Johnson, the bank president, came out first, followed by Floyd Maccabee, the vice president. A dumpy-looking teller, Merle Tadlock, followed. All three men carried ominous greeners pointed in their direction. The fourth man caught Jack's attention, and not in a good way. Homer Timms looked like a dark and dangerous man. He did not even have a pistol leveled at them, but he still bothered the hell out of Jack.

When Jack and Lucky's eyes moved to the fifth man, both brothers fought back fear. Their mouths dropped open as they saw the unearthly John Lee Johnson come through the door and move toward the end of the lineup of the bank cadre. He looked like someone from another world. The outlaw brothers realized they were in dangerous depths.

Of the five men who had exited the bank, now spread out on the wooden boardwalk, it was John Lee Johnson and Homer Timms that held their attention.

Lucky, still digesting the clear and present danger, heard a stentorian voice behind him coming from the once-vacant porch of the sheriff's office: "Drop your guns, Lucky."

Lucky did not turn in his saddle to acknowledge the sheriff. The lawman behind him was the least of his worries. Still shaken at seeing the man he knew had to be John Lee Johnson, he could not mask the fatalistic feelings in his chest and the worry on his face.

It quickly ran through his mind that Guy Morris had been correct when he said, "You don't mess with John Lee Johnson." Initially, when the town had sprung the trap, he realized he was boxed in and even outgunned, but he still thought he might have a chance, but seeing this imposing man standing there, he knew they had two choices, and both were bad: Turn and ride east and try to escape through the few gaps in the wagons blocking their way, hoping to endure the enfilading gunfire, or drop their weapons and resign themselves to the rope.

Lucky made his decision quickly. He roughly reined his horse around. The heavy neck jerk to the mount sent a viscous rope of horse saliva into the wind. The churning dust of departing horses and the present sandstorm created several yellow clouds. The outlaws appeared like milky silhouettes as they made ready to gallop down the street toward the east. The Wheeler gang was shooting in desperation. Orange and yellow flashes jetted from their .44s. As Lucky was readying himself for his getaway, he pointed his revolver in the direction of John Lee Johnson.

John Lee Johnson had anticipated Lucky's course of action. The yellow-dust fog was more of an annoyance than an actual hindrance. While Lucky turned his horse around, the big Texan already had his two Navy sixes drawn and leveled. He fired two roaring rounds. The pistol balls thudded simultaneously: one lodged in the outlaw's right shoulder, and the second one caught him lower in the chest. Lucky, mortally tagged, dropped his pistol and fell next to his horse in a billow of dust.

Jack didn't have time to grieve for his brother. He instinctively drew his weapon as he made a quick turn on his horse. Homer Timms already had him in his sights and fired three successive rounds that rocked the thick outlaw. Jack jerked painfully with each shot. He fell soddenly forward in a grotesque sprawl on the ground.

The Wheeler gang, now leaderless, had the presence of mind to head east toward the string of armed men located near Chili's barn. Unfortunately for the outlaws, these entrenched men were US Army cavalrymen. The gunfire from behind and the fusillade of rifle fire facing them left all of them dead in minutes.

John Lee Johnson holstered his weapons and walked through the grisly death postures of the lifeless desperados. He made his way to the dying Lucky Wheeler. He stood over him, not in arrogance but to ask him where Tim Slater was.

Lucky Wheeler, lying in the yellow dust with outstretched arms, was wheezing in labored breaths. His blue eyes, narrowed in anguish, took in the looming shadow of the unusual man. He eked out, "You John Lee Johnson?"

John nodded and then opened the side-gate of his Navy .36 and began reloading. All the while, his eyes were on Lucky Wheeler.

Lucky watched John Lee Johnson as he finished loading his weapon and replacing it into his holster. "You know something, big man?"

John gave a negative shake of his head.

Lucky continued, his voice laboring in pain, "I am dyin' here in this street." Lucky gave a long pause with a tear running from his right eye down his cheek. "I never thought it would end like this." He managed to point his finger from his extended hand to make what he dying remark. "You too will end up like me, dyin' in the street like a dog."

John Lee Johnson could see by Lucky's condition that he would not get the chance to ask him any questions. John merely looked off as he made ready to leave. "Lucky, I am twenty-six years old. In my lifetime, I've never met a prophet." He looked down and met Lucky's eyes. As he walked away, Lucky could hear John Lee Johnson's trailing words, "And I still haven't met one."

Seeing his words had no effect on the big Texan, Lucky gritted his teeth in pain and humiliation. He took in one last gasp of air and died.

Ten miles from Baileysboro, alongside the road to Hawkshaw, Tim Slater sat concealed in a small cottonwood grove near a gurgling stream. Behind the lanky leader was a sizeable group of riflemen and gunslingers. If things went as planned, Tim figured that both Lucky and Cephus would meet up five miles north from his present position and ride past him on their way to Hawkshaw to hit the bank there.

He felt that John Lee Johnson and a ragtag posse would soon be in pursuit. He sensed that he had the men and firepower finally to destroy the man who had bedeviled so many.

Two of the most capable of his experienced crew were Utah Jimmy Pruett and Memphis Mayford, both highly reputed gunmen. Slater could tell that Utah Jimmy and Memphis Mayford disliked each other. They both were accustomed to working alone and did not cotton to working with others. Each man considered himself an alpha male. They had been together for over a month and shunned each other as much as possible.

Utah Jimmy was six feet tall with lake blue eyes. He had a horseback rider's physique: lean but not skinny. He wore a beige Texas-style hat. The crown shot up forever and a wide brim that stretched out far. He wore a low-slung holster with a walnut-gripped Army .44. It was obvious he knew how to use it.

Memphis Mayford was short, thin, and pale. He wore all black, which seemed to match his dour personality. His hat, like Utah Jimmy's, had a tall crown and wide brim that sat atop his rounded face. He had a cud of tobacco in his jaw that made him look like a squirrel storing a nut for the winter. His dark eyes always seemed suspicious that someone was out to cheat him.

Tim noticed that folks tended to call Utah Jimmy Pruett by different versions of his name. Some called him "Utah," others "Jimmy," some just said "Pruett."

But not so with Memphis Mayford. He was known as "Memphis Mayford." No exceptions. He would not entertain any conversation unless he was called by both names. Memphis Mayford wore twin black gun belts. His ivory-gripped .44s were placed backwards for a crossover draw. As he walked away from Tim and Utah Jimmy Pruett, he carried a seven-shot

Spencer rifle in his right hand. He eventually made his way toward the bole of a cottonwood tree and concealed himself, awaiting John Lee Johnson and the posse they believed he'd be heading his way.

The time went slowly, with Tim frequently checking his turnip-shaped pocket watch. He did not mention it to his group, who by this time were all well-hidden in the small grove. But he was concerned. According to his calculations, if the attack had taken place at ten thirty, the two gangs should have passed his hiding place fifteen minutes ago. He maintained a calm exterior, but inside he was feeling anxious.

It was Utah Jimmy who broke the silence. Speaking behind a nearby tree, his voice, low-leveled and whispery but sounding urgent all the same, asked, "Hell, Slater, shouldn't they be by here by now?"

Tim shushed his hand at Pruett, trying to quiet him. He did not want to reveal his personal worry to the others. He tried to mask his feelings by appearing unruffled, but he knew Utah Jimmy was correct.

Ten minutes later, Tim concluded the jig was up. There was no more pretense. He stood from his squatting position. He knew his scout would be along shortly to inform him about the bank holdup, but at this point, it was not much of a mystery. Something bad had happened. He knew it, and the seasoned veterans standing behind him knew it as well. Slater made a half-turn and waved to the men to break cover. They edged closer, forming a respectful semicircle behind him.

Tim and his crew remained silent, but their silence spoke volumes in abject disappointment. They stood with concerned quietude as they viewed the road. Their emotions went even flatter when they saw a solitary rider rawhiding his horse down the tawny-colored road. They knew it was Shotgun Stevens, their scout. The fact that Shotgun was flaying his horse with his rein straps indicated that he was the bearer of bad news. Shotgun, florid-faced and agitated, rode up to the group and quickly dismounted. He handed the reins of his foam-covered horse to Utah Jimmy Pruett, who immediately led the jaded horse to the brook situated behind them.

Stevens wiped the sweat from his flushed face, all the while shaking his head in an exaggerated negative manner. Looking Tim in the eyes, he said, "Damn, Wheeler and all his men are dead. The townsmen and what looked deputies from other counties were there. I was a quarter-mile away, like you told me to be. It sounded like a small war goin' on."

Slater rubbed his chin thoughtfully with his gloved left hand. "Wheeler?"

Stevens shrugged as though he had already answered the question. "Dead."

"What about Cephus and his group?"

Stevens again shook his head. "I have no idea, boss, but I got me an idea that they're dead too."

Slater continued to rub his chin. "What about John Lee Johnson?"

Stevens looked off as though the following revelation pained him. "I took it on myself to ride into town later, after all the commotion had settled down. I rode in all casual like and heard some deputies talkin', and the word was that John Lee Johnson hisself killed Wheeler." Shotgun looked at all the expectant eyes on him as he was talking. Feeling he might need to be more discreet, he took Tim aside and said in a low voice. "Boss, someone sold us out."

Tim appreciated Shotgun's prudence in not expressing that to his fellow gang members; he took his scout by the elbow and led him even farther away so no one could overhear them.

"Shotgun, get you a fresh mount. You ride to Tucker's Station and use the telegraph there—send the coded message to Austin we agreed on." Tim paused and looked behind himself as though safeguarding his words. "After that, go to the Pipton Ranch, thirty miles south of Gandy."

He gave the scout a searching look, a look needing to know that Shotgun not only understood the message but would act on it faithfully.

Shotgun, whether he liked the assignment or not, nodded slowly and headed to the remuda located slightly behind the trees. Tim thoughtfully watched him walked away.

He dwelt on what the scout had said and knew he was correct. They were set up. Tim knew he'd end up being the fall guy, even though he was not responsible for this fiasco. He knew that Sheriff Lang would cuss a blue streak, and his fawning coterie would join in blaming him for the setback.

But Tim was not particularly worried about being the scapegoat. He was aware that the inner circle around Sheriff Lang would know he was not at fault. They would endure Lang's anger but not act on it. These insiders already knew about the leak and realized who was really accountable. He also knew his job was safe, simply because he was the best man in the field.

What bothered Tim more than being held culpable for something he was not guilty of was the knowledge that a lot of money and manpower had gone down the drain because their security was lacking.

For some time, he and the others (with the exception of Sheriff Lang) had suspected someone in his inner circle was tipping off Lieutenant Bragg. The lieutenant was the second in command at the federal garrison in Austin. Slater was well-acquainted with Lieutenant Bragg's reputation. He knew him to be an outspoken critic of the present administration in Austin and their brazen and illegal actions taken against former Confederate sympathizers.

Lieutenant Bragg did not approve of the stringent Reconstruction policies being enforced by the radical element now ruling Texas. Tim was aware that the lieutenant regularly sent coded messages to Washington. The lieutenant was known for keeping close tabs on Sheriff Lang's rough-and-ready tactics. Tim had accurately supposed that those wires were severe grievances against the sheriff and his radical friends. He had a good idea that those coded telegrams demanded a quick investigation into the shenanigans of the carpetbagger government now in power in Austin.

He had heard it mentioned but never confirmed the lieutenant was fast friends with John Lee Johnson. But now he knew it. Tim saw the ambush of the Wheeler gang in Baileysboro as evidence that Lieutenant Bragg and Johnson were acting hand in glove.

He placed that subject in another part of his brain as he turned his vision to the empty, sinuous road. He did not see any trail dust of an ensuing posse and realized why no was following him. Undoubtedly, his intended ambush of John Lee Johnson was known by his adversaries. After all, the Lieutenant Bragg/John Lee Johnson crowd knew every facet of the so-called secret plan. His one down card was that his place of ambush was unknown. He had purposely kept that fact a secret. Regardless, he knew he and his men needed to make tracks before they were discovered. He wanted one more chance to bring down the big Texan, only this time he would keep his destination a secret, even from Sheriff Lang.

Tim turned his back to the road once more, observing Shotgun as he saddled a fresh mount. His eyes then moved over to Utah Jimmy Pruett and Memphis Mayford as they returned to the tree line to await his further orders. He called each man by name and waved for them to join him.

The two men looked questioningly at each other, as though they might be in for a verbal dressing down, but seeing the amenable look on Slater's face, they approached him more confidently.

Once they were close and out of earshot from their curious compadres, Tim gathered them even closer. Before he confided in them, he watched Shotgun ride off toward Tucker's Station.

Satisfied that he had his plan in gear, he turned his full attention toward the two gunmen. Trying to remain optimistic due to the present and depressing setback, Slater sighed and said, "I realize you two birds are high-dollar gunmen. I recognize today was a bust. But there's still money to be made, and I want you to listen to me and listen well."

Memphis Mayford glanced at Utah Jimmy, who was watching him from the corner of his eye, as Slater added, "The information I'm about to give you has not been divulged to anyone, so it can't be compromised." Slater pulled a cigar from his pocket, put it in the corner of his mouth, and snapped a match against his thumbnail, bringing it to life. He took a draw and continued, "In six weeks, Homer Timms, the gunman who runs with John Lee Johnson, is getting married in Gandy. That's a long ways from here. If you go to his wedding and kill that bastard, there's twenty-five hundred bucks to the man who brings him down."

Before Memphis Mayford and Utah Jimmy could respond, he reached into his pants pocket and pulled out a thick roll of greenbacks. He peeled off a thousand dollars, giving each man five hundred and remarked that was for expenses. He puffed his smoke thoughtfully, and then his eyes moved back and forth, looking each man in the eye. "We got a deal?"

Utah Jimmy and Memphis Mayford accepted the money and nodded. And then Utah Jimmy replied aloud, "You got a deal." He paused and met the level gaze of Slater. "I've heard you mention this Homer Timms fella runs with John Lee Johnson before." Utah Jimmy let a half-smile cross his face as he continued, "It sounds by your voice and this dinero that this Homer person's pretty damn salty hisself."

Slater did not respond right away, choosing his words carefully. "He's one damn dangerous man. I paid you both well. But I can tell you truthfully that you'll earn your damn money and at the same time put a feather in your cap if you can bring that bastard down."

A confident Slater felt the two gunmen could kill Timms. It was very logical to Slater that Timms's death would lure John Lee Johnson on the vengeance trail. Slater believed that the big Texan would be filled with emotion, leaving himself vulnerable. And that would open the door for his men to settle his hash once and for all.

Slater returned his attention to the two gunmen and said, "After you get the job done, ride to the Pipton Ranch, south of Gandy, and get your bonus money." He added, "With Timms out of the way, you can reckon who's next. And that'll be one hell of a payday."

Slater spent as much time as he could afford with the two pistoleros; he walked back to the rest of the men. As he walked toward his crew, he pulled out his roll of greenbacks once more. He knew once he paid them, they would forget today's failure, and their morale would shoot up dramatically. And not only that, the laborious ride to the Pipton Ranch would not seem as long. He was satisfied that his new plan would be successful, mainly because he'd be keeping it secret from Sheriff Lang's inner circle. He made a promise to himself that when he did return to Austin, he personally would put an end to the spy's life.

Utah Jimmy Pruett and Memphis Mayford watched the Slater outfit mount up and ride southeast. They silently observed them for a few minutes, and then Utah Jimmy Pruett broke the stillness: "Memphis Mayford, I want to propose somethin' to you."

Memphis Mayford gave him a suspicious narrow-eyed look and growled, "What?"

Utah Jimmy, seeing this was not going to be an easy task, pushed his hat brim up with a gloved finger and looked off to the south. "If this Homer Timms fella is as tough as we hear, we might ought to work together and make a pact."

Memphis Mayford canted his head back and forth, still eyeballing Utah Jimmy. "What in the hell does 'pact' mean?"

"An agreement." Utah Jimmy wanted to add the word "Blockhead" but decided to forgo that response. "What I'm sayin' is that we join up instead of goin' it alone."

"Why?"

That "why" offered up by Memphis Mayford fried Utah Jimmy's liver. He had to fight the anger that flashed through him. He knew Memphis Mayford was good with a gun and would be invaluable, but he felt the man in black was stupid as hell. Jimmy's first inclination was just to walk off and tell Memphis Mayford to kiss his ass, but he fought that impulse and let the anger slowly subside. "This Homer Timms is one damn tough gunman. I've heard of him all over Texas."

Seeing Memphis Mayford still regarding him suspiciously, Utah Jimmy continued, "If we make a pact ..." Seeing Memphis Mayford's puzzled expression trying to process the word "pact" again, Jimmy quickly substituted "agreement."

Utah inhaled and began anew, "Now, Memphis Mayford, if we agree to work together, we're good enough to bring him down. Hell, he might be fast, but both of us are fast too. He might get one of us, but the other one will shut down his lights."

Memphis Mayford rubbed his jaw as he contemplated on Utah Jimmy's words. "So what you're sayin', Jimmy, is that we work as a team and that we share the bonus money for killin' this Homer Timms?"

Utah Jimmy gave a surprised but sarcastic smile that his comrade had finally gotten the message. He tiredly answered, "Yes, Memphis Mayford. We split it right down the middle."

Memphis Mayford frowned and looked off at nothing in particular. His thick tobacco chaw looked like he had small apple in his cheek. He uttered, "I don't trust you, Jimmy."

Utah Jimmy audibly sighed all the while shaking his head in exasperation. "Listen, Memphis Mayford, I've lied to you before, and chances are I'll lie to you again, but this time, I'm tellin' you the truth."

When Utah Jimmy said that, Memphis Mayford shot out his hand and sought Utah Jimmy's hand. He said out of the corner of his mouth, "Why didn't you say that in the first place? We got a deal."

CHAPTER 2

FOUR MEN STOOD IN A SOMEWHAT-RELAXED SEMICIRCLE FACING the empty desk in Sheriff Henry Nelson's small office in Baileysboro: John Lee Johnson, Homer Timms, Sergeant Joe Brewer, and Sheriff Nelson himself.

Sergeant Brewer, a blocky but well-built man, had the floor because soon he and his cavalry unit would be moving out of town before they were recognized as federal troopers. If word of their unauthorized participation in quelling the outlaws reached the wrong ears in Austin, there would be hell to pay. They were using a nearby ranch as headquarters; once there, they would change back into their official uniforms. They had ridden to Baileysboro surreptitiously. Their publicly declared orders were to seek and find a certain band of Comanche renegades (that never existed) when, in fact, they were sent to protect John Lee Johnson and the bank at Baileysboro.

Sergeant Brewer scanned each of the three faces looking at him as he talked. "We need to get out of here fast as you all know." After making that statement, his eyes locked with the big Texan. "Before I go, John, you need to know that Tim Slater has got two very fast gunmen working with him: Memphis Mayford and Utah Jimmy Pruett." He described them as well as possible due to the sketchy information he had available. After completing that task, he nodded farewell to each of the three and whirled around and headed to the back door. Soon the departing hoofbeats of the troopers' horses could be heard as they headed north to Johnny Conner's ranch.

With the hoofbeats of the departing troopers in the background, Sheriff Nelson, the wiry and leathery-skinned sheriff, looked at Homer Timms and pointed to a large leather bag on his desk. "Homer, that's blood money paid for ..." He paused and caustically added, "... by our good friends in Austin." Exchanging the contempt in his voice to a solemn, respectful voice, he continued, "John says you're getting married and that you get the money."

Homer graciously nodded at his two friends and started to express his thanks when the door of the sheriff's office was suddenly opened by a thin, older man who looked worse for the wear: dust-covered Texas-style hat, dirty pants covered in deeply scarred chaps. He had a dreary-looking hoary mustache that hung down, lining his sunburnt lips. He looked out of sorts until his vision landed on Homer Timms.

It was obvious that Homer not only knew the man but liked him. It was also obvious that the old cowhand was troubled. Homer, sparing the distressed man the pain of verbalizing his problems in front of the sheriff and John Lee Johnson, led him quietly to the front porch of the jail, closing the door behind him.

Rufus, the old cowman, looked curiously at the street scene. He saw men carrying bodies and loading them on wagons. As he had ridden into town, his need to see Homer had captured his attention, and he had mentally bypassed all the commotion on the street.

Homer could see the puzzled look on Rufus's face but wanted to get to the reason he looked so desperate; he quickly informed him that he was looking at the aftermath of a failed bank robbery. Homer hoped the brief description would spur Rufus to relate his mission.

Rufus numbly nodded at Homer's explanation but still swiveled his head around, looking up and down the street at the number of armed men carrying corpses. Pulling his eyes from this unusual scene, he met the inquiring blue eyes of Homer Timms and said quickly, "Miss Jessie is in a heap of trouble."

Homer knew that Miss Jessie was the first cousin of Big Ruby, his bride-to-be. An exhausted and frustrated Homer stepped closer to old Rufus. Homer knew by the statement that he was expected to go immediately and aid the lady.

Feeling more inconvenience than he intended to show, Homer stated, "Rufus, I aim to marry up with Big Ruby in six weeks." He knew that Jessie and many others depended on him for justice. It was just that the timing could not have been worse. With immense self-control, he gently placed his large hands on the wrangler's shoulders. The moment of annoyance coursed through the gunman veins and then subsided.

Homer closed his eyes and calmed down after reminding himself how hard the journey must have been on the old-timer ... the loneliness and dangers he must have faced, not knowing for sure whether he would even find him.

Homer forced himself to give a courteous smile to the humble-looking man and asked, "What's going on, Rufus?"

Rufus, considering not only Homer's words but his obvious weary body English, began to understand the difficult request he had tendered. Rufus could see by the aftermath of the bloody street scene that Homer had been involved in thwarting the bank robbery. All these factors caused the old cowhand to look down shamefacedly at his own boots. It suddenly dawned on him that he was asking too much.

His voice took on an apologetic tone as answered Homer's question. "Well, Homer, the Russell brothers have rustled Mrs. Jessie's cattle ... four hundred head, thereabouts." He looked humbly down once more at his boots. "Since the sheriff ain't no count, we both turned to you. I'm sorry, I can see you've been helpin' other folks and ..."

Homer interrupted him. Seeing the humble look of his longtime acquaintance touched him. "You don't have to apologize to me, Rufus." Resigning himself to the task at hand, he sighed and said, "I'll saddle up, and we'll get going."

Suddenly a strong voice in the background overrode the moment. "Hell, no, you ain't goin' nowhere but to Gandy and marry up."

John Lee Johnson, having heard most of the conversation, stepped from the jailhouse door he had exited minutes after Homer had departed.

Rufus's mouth opened in wonder when he saw the powerful man walk up behind Homer. Like others, he had never seen a man who looked so unworldly.

John Lee placed a large paw on Homer's shoulders. "Go get your money and hit the trail. Get ready for that weddin'." Whatever this man needs, I'll take care of it."

Homer allowed himself a smile. He accepted the offer with a slight nod. He knew if the shoe were on the other foot, he would have done the same.

Three weeks later, Barto and Elmo Russell, the brothers who had rustled Jessie Jones's cattle, heard that the widow rancher had sent her foreman to fetch Homer Timms for assistance; the brothers dispatched three desperados to intercept and kill both men.

These three men were galloping their horses down a crude dirt road toward a distant, sandy hillock. The three men were in a hurry and were leaving a dust cloud behind them. They had been told in no certain terms "kill 'em or don't come back." They took those words very seriously.

The straw boss of this small group was a one-eyed man named Diamond Dee. He wore a prominent black patch over his offending eye. The other two were the Tilman brothers, Wally and Sid. Wally was fleshy, and Sid was slim. Each Tilman was nondescript and unimportant. All three wore high crowned hats and a cloth vest. Each had a Spencer rifle in their saddle scabbards and jutting .44s in their holsters. They were pushing their mounts hard because they wanted the high ground before Rufus and Homer arrived, thus giving them a decided observational advantage.

After reaching the sandy hillock, they tethered their mounts, pulled their rifles, and walked awkwardly up the incline before laying on their stomachs with a two-mile view of the winding road before them. Diamond Dee had a wolfish grin on his face. With the two Tilmans on each side of him, he gave quick gleeful looks back and forth to the two men. "This is goin' to be a damn turkey shoot, boys."

Wally began nodding in assent of Diamond Dee's appraisal. "They shore in hell ain't behind us, that's for damn shore."

Their enthusiasm was short-lived. The day was hot and the landscape bleak. After not seeing anything for six hours, their tedium led to passing a dark bottle of whiskey back and forth with increasingly lax vigilance on the road. At sundown, an intoxicated Wally Tilman was asleep; his body was curled in a fetal position, with his hat shielding the side of his face. Sid, half-asleep himself, thought he heard a rataplan of hooves behind him. He rolled over on his side and looked backwards, seeing two men approaching, each pulling a packhorse. He recognized the riders as Texas postal employees. He started to raise his hand in greeting but was halted by a firm grip on his hand. He turned his startled vision to the fierce looking eye of Diamond Dee.

The snarling Diamond Dee hissed, "Have you lost your cotton-pickin' mind?"

Sid nodded sheepishly and said, "I wasn't thinkin'."

Diamond Dee ignored his ignorant response and took a look-see himself at the two riders as they cantered their mounts down the road. He inhaled sharply, realizing that if he could see them, they could see him and the Tilmans. As they rode even with the hummock they were situated on, he removed his hat and slapped his leg with it in frustration. He then crawled with his Spencer cradled in his hands to the somewhat level crest and studied on the backs of the onward-bound mail carriers. He was mollified that they did not break into a gallop. He nodded that they might have seen him and his cronies, but likely interpreted his group as benign hunters rather than ambushers. In any case, it stood to reason that the passersby would more likely be concerned about performing their service than tipping off Homer Timms.

Diamond Dee was wrong on both counts. They did see him and the Tilmans. The mail carriers did not think it was a hunting party. They knew the three men were waiting on Rufus Williams and Homer Timms; hell, everyone and his brother knew that. The postal riders went out of their way to tell Rufus and the mysterious stranger about the ambush site, even though it cost them three hours of time.

At nine o'clock that very night, under the umbrella of millions of sparkling stars and a rustlers' moon, a discouraged Diamond Dee along with the two Tilmans walked slowly down the sandy incline, deciding to start a mesquite fire to make coffee and eat their meager rations.

Later, after eating some beef jerky, they stood around the low crackling fire with a metal tripod holding a coffee pot. The flickering orange flames revealed scintillating yellowish flashes of the three men. The flittering, brooding image of Diamond Dee's face was fixed on the fire. He pulled his .44 out of his holster and began running the gun cylinder in a metallic whirr. Soon out of boredom or frustration, he began talking. The two Tilmans on each side of him looked at his solemn profile as he began his vicious spate of words.

"I aim to tell you two birds something. I should've killed those two mail carriers whether they are innocent or not, just on general principles. That's not like me to make a mistake like that. Usually I'm just Johnny-on-the-spot."

He narrowed his one eye and continued thoughtfully, "I'm not a half-job type of hombre. When I start somethin', I finish it." Not waiting for any rebuttal, he continued, "I shore in hell would love to get my hands not only on Rufus but that damned Homer Timms."

Sid leaned in closer with his thin, inquisitive face and asked, "What would you do, Diamond Dee, if you had Homer Timms in your hands?"

Diamond Dee snorted disdainfully at the question. "What would I do if I had that gunfightin' bastard in my hands? Well, one thang I would do would be to overpower him. The next thang I would do would be to rip out his eyeballs and eat 'em like grapes. Then I would tear his arms and legs off his body like an insect." Gathering steam, he continued, "Yes sirree, when I got done with that Homer Timms, people all over West Texas would be talkin' about ol' Diamond Dee."

Sid nodded at the prophetic words. Wally, on the other hand, the elder brother, nodded briefly to keep peace but had reservations. He knew that Homer Timms would be a sight tougher than Diamond Dee was allowing for but kept his inner thoughts to himself.

As the two brothers looked at Diamond Dee, they noticed a strange metamorphosis beginning to take place. The angry, dour look slowly began to dissipate. As it evolved into a look of shock and then terror, his one good eye bulged out, as if it were on stalks. His mouth changed shape from a grim, menacing look to an incredulous open-mouth expression, and he screamed like a schoolgirl.

They followed the path of Dee's vision and saw a sight that caused them to freeze in fright.

A giant man was emerging from the shadows. He looked to them by the glow of the fire to be a bronzed god. The powerful figure was over six feet six inches and weighed 250. His neck was thick and corded, his shoulders a yard wide, and his powerful arms boasted prominent veins running up and down his biceps. His torn shirt revealed a deeply chiseled chest. Even though he had a dipped hat brim, they still could see his cold, dispassionate eyes. Around his iron-slab waist, they saw twin gun belts armed with Navy .36s, with two others edged into the belt straps. They took note he had no weapons in his hands, but he did not seem to care.

Diamond Dee instantly threw his pistol to the sand in total surrender and croaked, "Who are you, mister?"

John Lee Johnson, furrowing his eyebrows and ignoring the question, moved in closer, making the three men even more alarmed.

In a voice that sounded as though it came from a deep well, John Lee said, "Toss your rifles in front of me. Unload your pistols, get on your horses, and take off."

They immediately threw their rifles in front of him and began unloading their pistols.

Sid, finishing first, rashly asking, "Where do you want us to go?"

The big man replied, "If you go back to the Russells, I'll eventually kill you, so I recommend you just take off."

After they replaced their .44s, John Lee looked at Diamond Dee. "I thought I told you to unload your revolver."

Diamond Dee swallowed nervously but remained silent. He had purposely left one shot in his Walker Colt. John walked closer and pulled Diamond Dee's weapon from its holster and broke down the loading chamber. After tossing the offending shot to the ground, he grabbed Diamond Dee by the neck, turned him brusquely around, and kicked his ass, sending him several feet into the air. His hat shot from his head with the blow. The outlaw landed on his chest with his face mired in the sand.

Wally and Sid watched the complete disgrace of their leader with a mixed look of fascination and pity. Diamond Dee slowly climbed to his feet. He staggered, with his humiliated face tilted downward, refusing to make eye contact with the three men watching him. He timidly reached down for his hat and placed it on his head.

After seeing their leader emasculated and degraded, Wally now took command. He grabbed Diamond Dee by the arm and began to lead him to his horse. He gave a sidewise look at the big Texan and said, "We ain't returning to the Russells. They don't pay worth a damn, and besides that, we ain't got no quarrel with you. We were paid to git Homer Timms." He sighed, shrugged, and added, "But we don't want no part of him now."

John Lee gave them an unreadable look and watched them ride off into the darkness. There was a new pecking order: Wally took the lead; his brother Sid was second, and bringing up the rear was a slumped-over Diamond Dee.

John knew they would not be back. Into the orange glow of the fire emerged the tired, lined face of Rufus Williams, who came and stood next to John. He gave a sideways look at the big Texan and asked, "What's next?"

John gave a nod at the coffee pot.

Rufus made an about-face and went to retrieve two tin cups. Soon they were sitting at the base of the hill, basking by the light of the orange fire and drinking coffee. John's narrowed his eyes as he shared his thoughts with Rufus. He made a statement that caught the old foreman by surprise: "We got four men tailing us."

Rufus's eyebrows pitched upwards. It was obvious he had no clue about the four men. It was also obvious by his expression that he considered John Lee Johnson a powerful man of mystery, always knowing more than he allowed.

Rufus mulled over what John had just revealed. His cup stopped on the way up. "How do you know this stuff?"

"I had this feelin' we were bein' followed. Call it intuition or a mind itch. I just felt it, and two days ago, I confirmed it when I saw a gent in the far distance, tryin' to stay unseen. I never let on that I had seen him." John paused and took a thoughtful sip of coffee. "That night while you were asleep, I decided to do some reconnoitering. I backtracked until I saw a small campfire off to my right. I dismounted and crept as close as I could until I knew their horses would start nickerin.' I was near enough to hear the gist of their conversation." He let his cup lower to chest level as he continued, "Those birds seem to be followin' me to give me a message."

Rufus leaned in and asked, "So they are after you?"

John nodded and took another sip. "I guess in a manner of speakin', but they ain't gunnin' for me. It seems they just want to talk."

Rufus, unconvinced, shook his head. He gave a skeptical response. "Want to talk, hey?" He added, "That don't make no sense."

John smiled easily and said, "You're right, Rufus, it doesn't make any sense. All I know is that last night would have been bad timin'. I let the matter go. So I reckon I'll let them catch up to me at the right time."

Rufus gave a thoughtful look at the big Texan's handsome profile.

Deciding to change the subject to the matter at hand, Rufus stated, "Since we are goin' to face them rustlers around noon tomorrow, I reckon I need to tell you more about the Russell brothers."

"Get to talkin'."

"Barto and Elmo have always been bastards. They have made trouble for everyone for years, but about a year ago, they started rustlin'. They started off stealin' a little, and then they started stealin' a lot. They started changing brands and sellin' to out-of-county buyers. And the sheriff, Sheriff Dobbs, is scared of 'em and won't do nothin' about it."

John responded, still facing forward, "Why in hell is he afraid of the damn Russell brothers?"

Rufus finished his cup and reached to the pot to get a refill. "The Russell brothers hired this top gunman." He gave a quick look to John's profile to get his facial response. He received none and continued, "This bird he hired ain't like Diamond Dee who, as you saw, is all hot air and bluff." Rufus replaced the coffee pot in its holder and thoughtfully swiveled the fresh coffee around in his cup. "This gunman he hired is named Saddle Roy."

When he heard the unusual name, John raised his eyebrows and muttered to himself, "Saddle Roy?" He added in a neutral voice, "You wouldn't be joshin' me now, would you, Rufus?"

Rufus continued drinking his coffee. He gave a leathery smile and replied, "No, that's his name. Hell, it's just one of those West Texas names that nobody knows why." He paused a long time. "He has been with the Russells several months now; as I said, he ain't no Diamond Dee. He's the real deal." He paused and added with serious finality, "He's already killed several men while in their employ."

Rufus studied John's expression to see if his description of Saddle Roy had any effect on him. It didn't. It was as though Rufus had related how a bird flew over. This calm reaction spurred Rufus to ask, "You ain't a bit worried?"

John's expression stayed the same. "A pebble always feels bigger in your boot than it really is."

Rufus took that statement to mean that the big man didn't worry too much about impending showdowns.

Rufus had been on the trail with John Lee Johnson for several weeks. After seeing him up close and personal, he came to the conclusion that he was the "most" man he had ever encountered. He was the most confident man he had ever met, but he was in no way arrogant. He was the most powerful man he had ever seen, but never acted like a bully. He had a good sense of humor accompanied with a hearty laugh. But he avoided making fun of someone.

Rufus could see the big man had a solid character: honest, strong, and capable of mercy. It was obvious that he not only loved but was deeply devoted to his wife. He did not disparage women on any level, even if they were prostitutes. It was clear that he was very loyal to his friends, especially Homer Timms. The final thing that defined John Lee Johnson was that he was a just and upright man. But it was also very clear ... brook ice clear ... that he would kill if necessary.

Curious, Rufus asked, "How did you and Homer become friends?" When John did not reply, Rufus continued, "You both are kind of like legends in a different part of Texas, but how did you finally link up?"

John studied on his question and then said, "It was by accident, but to my good fortune. He's one of the best men and best friends I ever had."

Rufus could see that was all he was going to get from the taciturn giant. He changed the subject again and asked, "What's the plan?"

John nodded as if he had thought the whole thing through. "You told me how to get to the Russell ranch. In the morning, you head to Miss Jessie's place. Bring her up to date and then get all the hands you can find and head them to the property line of the Russells that connect with hers." He paused as he turned his thick neck toward Rufus and added matter-of-factly, "I'll take care of the rest."

At noon the following day, John Lee Johnson was riding down the caramel-colored road that fronted the Russell ranch property line. He saw the wagon trail off to his left that led to the ranch house. He kneed his 17-hands-tall black horse, taking the turn and beginning a steady canter. He rode almost a mile; up ahead, he saw a man standing by a poorly made gate that blocked free access to the ranch house, which lay ahead.

The scrawny-looking young man wore a scruffy derby, and the top of his union suit served as his shirt. He had an unshaven face and intense eyes. He was clutching his shotgun somewhat diagonally across his thin chest. He appeared defensive and hostile until he got a better look at the unwelcome visitor. His face suddenly blanched when he saw the powerful figure approaching him.

John rode up closer to him and shot the guard a menacing look beneath his dipped hat brim. He could tell the man looked uncomfortable, perplexed. John simply said, "Drop the weapon or use it." He paused and added, "One or the other."

The guard swallowed as he took in the intimidating figure before him.

It did not take long for him to make up his mind. He tossed the shotgun down like it was a scorpion and went without being told and opened the rickety road gate.

John rode up to the entrance, dismounted, picked up the shotgun, and broke it against the thick post that secured the gate. He grabbed the grubby man by his union suit top and pulled him upwards and toward him until they were nose to nose.

"I don't want to hurt you," John said, nodding his head toward the makeshift road he had just ridden on. "Just take off runnin'."

The frightened young man's eyes took on a look of sadness, a look that caused John to release his grip. The man did not attempt to straighten his recently rumpled union suit top. He nodded meekly and said helplessly, "I'll take off runnin' if you want me to." He looked down at his worn boots and added, "Trouble is … I don't know where to run to."

John, confused by his response, stepped back with softening eyes. "What's your name?"

"Hobie."

What's your last name?"

Hobie shook his head and answered, his eyes still on his boots, "I don't rightly know. I was the bastard son of a dance hall girl over in Pea Vine." His trembling frail body facing the prospects of nowhere to run caused John's face to mellow.

Moved by Hobie's lot in life, John asked in a thoughtful voice, "How much do the Russells pay you to work here?"

Hobie shook his head again, giving a faraway look as though it pained him to confess. "Nothin'." He shrugged his frail shoulders, moving his tear-rimmed eyes to meet the inquiring gray eyes of the intimidating stranger. He reluctantly finished the question. "Mister, I work for food and a bunk. The only thing I could call my own was that …" He paused as he pointed at the broken shotgun. He suddenly thought of another possession he had. "I got this picture of a saloon girl on the wall by my bed." He reached into his pocket and pulled out two extra shotgun shells. "And these number 9 shots that cost four cents apiece." He shrugged apologetically, as though he were ashamed.

John looked again at the ruined shotgun and back at the forlorn man. "The Russells treat you okay?"

Hobie toed the ground, sadly confessing, "No, they cuss me a lot, but at least I get food and a place to sleep."

Hobie inhaled a lung of air and asked in a quivering voice, "Do I still have to take off runnin'?"

John did not answer. He quickly mounted his huge horse and extended his hand downward. "C'mon, Hobie, just do what I say."

Hobie extended his arm and was pulled up effortlessly to sit behind the big man.

John slapped the reins, and his horse took off like a bat out of hell. He thundered down the road, leaving a trail of dust. He covered the short distance in no time. He reined up beside two rough, wooden structures fronted by six bedraggled, armed men standing in a menacing semicircle. He leapt from his saddle, confronting them in an aggressive posture.

The Russell brothers were as Rufus had described: ridiculously short … wearing Texas-style hats with high crowns that shot up to Mars. They had faces like chipmunks: full cheeks, prominent front teeth, large excitable-looking eyes.

Barto, who was older by one year, was apparently the alpha male. He let a smile move over his rodent-like features, looked at his brother, and said out the side of his mouth, "Well, Elmo, looky here, we got us a nosy busybody comin' in here, messin' in matters that don't concern him a-tall."

Elmo chuckled his chipmunk laugh and repeated, "Don't concern him a-tall."

Barto echoed the same rodentlike laughter. He looked John up and down and then cast a disdainful glance toward the subdued Hobie, sitting just to the back of the saddle on the black stallion horse. Returning his eyes to John, he asked, "All right, big man, what are you doin' here?" Not giving John a chance to answer, Barto added sarcastically, "As if I didn't know."

John chose not to respond, which resulted in Barto again breaking into another irritating laugh. He interrupted his weird giggle to ask, "Where's Homer?" He looked around, with his hand hovering over his eyes much like a burlesque Indian scout would make. He chuckled as he kept peering around John, as if mockingly searching for the lost Homer in the distance. After milking this caper for all its worth, he glanced over at his brother for moral support.

He then returned his accusing eyes toward the big man and asked, "Did he chicken out?"

Elmo chimed in, asking, "Yeah, where's Homer? I bet he chickened out."

Feeling they had the situation in hand, Barto reached down provocatively, pulling up his drooping gun belt as if he was properly addressing the moment and was just seconds from pulling iron. All the while, one brother would look at the other for encouragement. Those looks were accompanied by the infernal cackling.

Barto suddenly stopped his tittering laughter, and his face grew somber. He once again looked John over. He noticed the big man did not seem at all intimidated or amused by their laughter. Barto's face took on the same stern look of the giant who stood before them. "Mister, have you ever considered how you're going to get out of this yard alive? We got us six men here."

John let a half-smile escape and said, "I see four men and two sawed-off runts." He paused as his smile increased. "As far as gettin' out of here, it's funny, but I was thinkin' the same thing on how all of you would get out of this yard alive."

Barto quickly retorted, "Like I said, we got us six men here."

"You probably need about two more."

Barto, concerned by John's words and his indifferent behavior, rubbed his jaw. "What do you want, mister?"

"I want you two turds to get your men together and drive four hundred and fifty cattle to Miss Jessie's ranch."

Elmo started the silly laughter again but this time was not joined by his brother. Barto shouted out, "We only stole four hundred."

John answered, "You're goin' to pay a little extra for rustlin' them in the first place."

Barto's eyes widened as he thought on John's words. "No man can call the Russell brothers turds." His little face screwed up a scowl. "And there ain't no way in hell I'm going to drive four hundred and fifty cattle to that old woman."

John let his eyes pan the men who stood facing him. He stepped back, and they could see he was ready to meet their challenge. His large hands hovered over his holsters.

Barto quickly extended his arm in warning. "Hey, mister, it ain't that easy." He felt like he needed to say it one more time to magnify the impending drama. "It ain't that easy at all." He let a creepy smile move over his chipmunk face. He suddenly turned and shouted over his left shoulder, "Saddle Roy!"

John could see the ramshackle ranch house off to his right; still to his right but closer was a bunkhouse that looked like the carpenter had been on peyote when he built it. The building was what Texans called a shotgun house. It was long and narrow. Giving credence to the shotgun title, because if you shot a greener into the front door entrance, the pellets would go straight through the house and out the back door.

John thought he heard the faint sounds of creaking bedsprings. He could not see anyone because the windows were covered with burlap sacks. It was obvious that no window maker in the Southwest could frame glass to fit the poorly constructed apertures.

The bunkhouse had an extended porch with a poorly constructed roof held up by warped wooden posts. Soon John saw the man named Saddle Roy walk out on the porch and adjust his suspenders to his baggy pants. He used his underwear top as a shirt, like Hobie. His hat brim was frayed. He looked at first glance like a mountain man who had strayed westward. But belying that first impression were the worn cowman's boots and silver-dollar-sized spurs. Wrapped around his waist was an expensive gun belt, and in that gun belt was a shiny Army .44. He did not glance at John. He looked like he was bored and in a trance. He stepped off the low-level porch, took a sharp left, and walked toward the Russell brothers. He established his position between the two brothers.

Up close, Saddle Roy looked like a character from a carnival sideshow. He had a severe overbite that revealed his thick yellow teeth at all times. He had uneven eyes; one eye socket was higher than the other. He had one blue eye, and the other one was brown. Those uneven eyes were now locked on John Lee Johnson.

Barto and Elmo once more began the irritating laughter. Barto paused long enough to point an accusatory finger at John Lee Johnson and say, "Saddle Roy, that big galoot called me and Elmo 'turds.'" After saying that, he and Elmo once again began the silly chuckling. Deliberating yet again, Barto said, "Kill him, Saddle Roy; I want him dead. No one talks to the Russell brothers like that."

Saddle Roy indicated by his head that he wanted the Russell brothers to give him some space. The two brothers looked gleeful as they moved five or six steps away.

Saddle Roy's uneven eyes continued to be focused on the big man himself. Unlike many of John's opponents, he did not show any sign of fear. His eyes, projecting lunacy, actually twinkled at the prospect of killing. John detected a curling smile beneath his prominent overbite.

John watched Saddle Roy place his feet farther apart. He could see his fingers tense. He went for his .44 deftly and smoothly. It was one hell of a draw. It ranked up there with some of the good ones, but before his pistol barrel had elevated horizontally, Saddle Roy received a thudding shot in his forehead. His unleveled eyes momentarily crossed, and his mouth flew open, forming a painful oval as he was knocked backwards by the force of the pistol ball from the smoking Navy six in John's right hand.

John did not holster. He didn't wave his weapon around aggressively, but rather he slowly panned his .36 slowly side to side, letting the fearful yokels know he meant business.

Seeing that he had the hands under control, he fastened his deadly gray eyes on the two Russell brothers. But their disbelieving eyes were still focused on Saddle Roy's corpse. The two brothers were no longer laughing that annoying chortle. They stood dumbfounded. They looked like two kids who had just been told there was no Santa Claus.

However, Hobie, still situated on John Lee Johnson's horse, was not shocked. He had known Saddle Roy for three months and thought of him as a jackass but awfully good with a pistol. He had witnessed Saddle Roy callously kill three men. He figured he took pride in his craft to make up for being so damned ugly. Hobie intuited when he saw Saddle Roy brace the big man that even though he was considered the best for miles around, he was not in the same league as the seemingly invincible man who stood with his smoking revolver. He had watched the deadly results with a certain predictability.

With the blood drained from his face, the crestfallen Barto turned his attention to the big man with the looming pistol. He asked in a defeatist, low-level voice, "What do you want us two turds to do?"

"Like I said, I want you to drive 450 head over to Jessie Jones's ranch."

Barto sighed and said, "Can we make it 449 cattle so I can feel better about it?"

John gave him a wry look and motioned for Barto to get mounted. He turned to the other gawking ranch hands and commanded them to get on their horses and round up some quality beeves to deliver to Miss Jessie Jones.

John glanced at Hobie and told him to dismount. He instructed him to go through the dead gunfighter's pants and confiscate any money he might find and strip him of his gun belt and put it on. After Hobie did all that, he went to the bunkhouse and retrieved the saloon girl's picture from the wall near his bunk. When he returned, Elmo Russell was holding Saddle Roy's paint quarter horse. It could tell by Elmo's expression it was now his. Hobie did not ask permission to saddle up. He just did. He knew the otherworldly giant of a man was now running the show.

Jessie Jones, an attractive widow, stood on the uneven, sun-warped porch of her small house. She was tall with raven-dark hair streaked in silver. She had broad shoulders, and her dark eyes were shielded by a hand blocking the sunlight as she surveyed the landscape of her ranch.

She wore a severe black dress that covered black boots. With her free hand, she held a .10 gauge shotgun by the barrels, resting the stock on the crudely made porch. Her expression was grim. Although Rufus had told her that help was on the way, she still was skeptical.

She suddenly saw one of her young riders galloping toward her in the distance. He seemed to be bringing good news. A hesitant smile crept across her features. She did not want to get too optimistic, only to have her hopes dashed. She let her face grow solemn, hoping not to be disappointed.

The young cowhand had a smile etched on his round freckled face as he rode up to the porch. "John Lee Johnson just killed Saddle Roy," he said, breathing heavily, "and the Russells are driving 449 head of cattle to your property."

She couldn't believe it. She gasped and covered her mouth with her other hand. She had been frightened of Saddle Roy and the threat he posed to her cowhands. Knowing her cattle were returning plus some extra ones caused her to tear up, but she quickly regained her composure. She had been through hell but wanted to present herself as stolidly in control. She looked up the trail and spotted soft clouds of dust in the distance.

She quickly turned to Timmy, the young hand, and said good-naturedly, "Well, don't just sit there gawking. Git goin' and earn your keep."

Timmy gave a big smile, turned his roan, and said, "Yes, ma'am."

Soon, Rufus, John Lee Johnson, and the two Russell brothers, riding ahead of the herd, arrived at her porch. She nodded briefly at her old cowhand and John Lee but directed her attention at the despicable brothers. Her pleasant features hardened as she watched them ride straight up to the porch. They both looked chastened and humble, but she had no sympathy for them. She picked up the shotgun and held it across her body.

"Seein' your bald faces up close and personal makes me want me to blow your ornery carcasses out of your saddles."

Barto pushed up the brim of his oversized hat and spoke, trying without success to sound sincere: "We apologize, Miss Jessie."

Jessie's face reddened as she shouted out, "You apologize?" She inhaled an angry breath. "You're a damned rustler, Barto. I don't want your useless apology. I want you to hang."

Barto, unsure of where her anger would take her in the midst of John Lee Johnson and her crew, put up his hand and said, "I promise you on my sainted mother that we'll not steal any of your cattle for a year."

Jessie's face grew hotter as she retorted, "Best I remember, your sainted mother was sent to prison for murder."

Barto, caught off guard by her accurate statement, shrugged as he rolled his searching eyes upward, partially shadowed by hat brim. "I meant my grandmother."

Jessie ignored that statement. She was still focused on the one-year moratorium. "I swear, Barto, I've had enough of you and your mealymouth lies." She extended the shotgun up to a shooting level.

"Now, hold it, Miss Jessie," Barto exclaimed. His chipmunk face suddenly paled. "I've told a few lies in my time." He took a deep breath and continued, "But you can believe Elmo; he tells the truth at least 40 percent of the time."

Jessie shook her head in disgust and snapped, "The dangerous thing about a liar is that they don't always tell lies." She sighed audibly. "That's what makes you harmless, Barto; you always tell lies."

She let his vision moved to Elmo, who also had a hangdog look. "Elmo, you got anything to say?"

He glanced at his brother, sighed, and said, "Well, I reckon we can wait two years before we start rustlin' your cattle again." He sighed and looked to his brother for confirmation. "We can always steal Old Man Wallace's cattle for a change, I reckon."

Jessie slowly eased her shotgun down and placed it against her leg. "You two ain't worth the price of the buckshot. Get the hell outta my sight, and I mean never come back."

They gladly took that cue. They whirled their mounts around and started galloping away.

As John Lee Johnson turned sideways to watch the departing Russells, he asked Rufus, "What was the final count on the cattle we returned?"

Rufus pulled a slip of paper from his front pocket. "448."

John gave a twisted smile to himself. He thought he could hear the blasted Russell brothers cackling as they rode away.

Jessie, feeling safer, positioned her shotgun against the wall behind her. She turned to face John, who had stayed mounted.

She watched Hobie riding Saddle Roy's paint up next to the big man. Her narrowed eyes took in the underfed-looking youngster as he sat meekly beside the big Texan. She looked Hobie over with a slight frown and asked, "Don't you work for the Russells?"

Hobie audibly swallowed but answered, "I did work for 'em. But I don't no more."

Jessie nodded and said, "I'm hirin', if you need a job."

Hobie looked to John out of the corner of his eyes. "No offense, ma'am, but I work for him."

John was not surprised when he said those words. He just did not respond to them.

Jessie sighed as her face grew calm. "John Lee Johnson, you've been a blessin'." She turned her head and looked at the horizon, where she could still see the Russells riding like hell. "Any advice on how to handle them damn Russell brothers?"

John straightened up and asked, "You ever thought about rustlin' their cattle?"

Jessie stroked her jaw in thought. Her dark eyes took on a glint. She chuckled softly and said, "I like your style of thinkin'." She then straightened up and looked over at her foreman. "Rufus, fix them a packhorse laden with supplies. Can't you tell John Lee is champin' at the bit to get to Homer's weddin'?"

Later that day, John Lee Johnson and Hobie were riding due west. They continued to keep up the grueling pace John demanded. At first, John thought of Hobie much like a stray dog. He did not know what to make of him and thought it would take some time to figure out if he would hire him on at his ranch or find a suitable place for him to land along their journey.

Over the next several days, to John's surprise, Hobie showed that he was a good trail companion. He was a hard worker. He never complained. He tended to the horses like an experienced cowhand and made coffee as well as anyone he ever worked with. His conversation was short and to the point, and he did things without being told.

Hobie, on the other hand, found John Lee Johnson to be inexhaustible. At night, John would disappear and be gone for hours, and yet at five o'clock, he was up and helping Hobie saddle the horses and strapping on the heavy canvas gear for the packhorse. Hobie realized early on that John Lee Johnson was beyond extraordinary. He lifted things that would take at least two men to do. His stamina was beyond what Hobie had ever seen or even imagined.

They rode out before dawn and kept a steady pace until near dark. It was obvious that John was a driven man, a man with an unshakeable determination. And yet even though he had this inexorable devotion to duty, he often showed signs of kindness and understanding. Hobie was astounded that the big man never talked down to him, never belittled him like others had done. The thing about John Lee Johnson was that he made him feel important.

At the end of their fifth day, they made camp; after securing the horses, John sat with a coffee cup, looking into the small mesquite fire. Hobie had sensed all day long that John had something on his mind. He didn't want to initiate the conversation because he was thinking he might have done something wrong.

John looked over at Hobie and said matter-of-factly, "Hobie, I need to tell you somethin'. First of all, you've been a good help." John sighed out the trailing words, "really good." He sat for an interminable time, thinking, and then he just laid it all out to the young man. "But there's a real good chance that I might be leadin' you into danger."

Hobie nodded as if he understood, but he did not quite get the portent of the words. Danger to him was just an abstract concept, not anything specific. He knew there had to be more than what Big John was allowing. He gave a pensive look at the big man and said, "If there's goin' to be danger, I would rather be with you than the Russell brothers,"

John gave Hobie an appreciative look but ignored the compliment. Instead, he concluded, "I just wanted to give you a chance to saddle up and head on out while you still can."

Hobie looked down at the ground and sighed. His thoughtful face was dappled by shadows of the coruscating campfire. He gave a solemn glance at his new boss and said, "I ain't good with words, but the last few days have been better than all my previous days all put together. When I'm with you, I ain't afraid of nothin'." He returned his gaze to the fire as he concluded, "I ain't goin' nowhere."

John had not told Hobie yet, but he connected the dots and predicted that Memphis Mayford and Utah Jimmy Pruett would be in Gandy for the wedding. It just made sense. The Austin crowd wanted to separate him and Homer. He figured that by killing Homer, they would isolate him and come for him. He wanted to get there quickly and spoil their plans. His gray eyes narrowed as he peered into the orange licking flames. He estimated Memphis Mayford and Utah Jimmy Pruett's point of origin was just a few miles out of Baileysboro. He did some mental figuring, considering the angle they would travel toward Gandy. He also reasoned that his two-week trip to the Pea Vine area had not hindered him too much. He estimated they had a two-day advantage on him, maybe more. He knew he had to beat them there or come close to it, and determined he would.

After they departed the next morning, Hobie was pulling the packhorse when he saw John rein up and sit thoughtfully looking at something on the horizon.

Hobie, at first confused by his boss's action, raised his eyes and saw three mounted men wearing dusters, about a quarter-mile ahead, ride out of a cluster of mesquite trees and line themselves beside the tawny-colored road. It was as though they were queuing themselves up for a parade. They appeared relaxed and nonthreatening, more like a greeting party than menacing problem.

John noticed that one man was missing of the four men he had counted days earlier. This small group were the same ones who had doggedly followed him all the way from Baileysboro to Pea Vine. He turned and told Hobie not to come any further until he gave him a signal.

John rode slowly toward the three men. As he ambled toward them, he took note of their non-Texas-style hats. Their hats had smaller brims, and the crown was flattened, as commonly worn by cattlemen from territories west of Colorado. They all were clad in heavy beige dusters. He spotted gun belts with Army .44s. Although they were well-armed, with each rider possessing a seven-shot Spencer rifle jutting from their scabbards, they had a different look than men who were riding the owlhoot trail. They seemed like professionals or even military men.

John noticed they seemed amiable, even relieved to see him. They all smiled as they nodded in greeting. John rode up closer, and the riders all looked at each other, giving and receiving approving messages with their eyes. One of the men, a taller and older man, obviously used to the outdoors by his tanned skin, raised his hand and said, "Man, are we glad to see you."

John thought his comment strange. He gave all of them a curious but courteous nod. He leaned forward, placing his large hands over his saddle pommel, and abruptly asked, "Who in the hell are you?"

That brought smiles and some low-level chuckles. The leathery-looking man countered, "Before we answer that question, let me inform you that we have ridden well over a thousand miles to meet with you." Before John could reply, the tall man spread his hands out and continued in a sincere voice, "We are definitely your friends. We definitely are on your side."

John canted his head as he listened and then replied, "I feel like I'm in the middle of a conversation that I never even started."

The man nodded. "I imagine you do at that." He looked over his shoulder as though there was someone else in the background that would be better qualified to explain their mission. "My name's Tullis; would you ride back with me to meet Mr. Pemberton?"

Anticipating that John would probably ask him who Mr. Pemberton was, Tullis added quickly, "He's the man who can tell you why we're here."

John shrugged his massive shoulders in consent. He now knew who the fourth man was, at least. He followed Tullis for a short distance through a gap in the mesquite. There in a clearing, John saw a stocky, bespectacled man sitting in a chair under a lone hackberry tree, reading a book. John could tell by Tullis's demeanor that he had tremendous respect for Jim Pemberton. Tullis immediately sat straighter in the saddle, and his face grew more serious.

Pemberton's eyes moved up from his reading material. He caught sight of Tullis and the man who had muscles that moved over his body the size of moored ropes. Pemberton removed his spectacles and gave an approving nod that he had at last found the elusive John Lee Johnson.

John studied Pemberton. He was well dressed, neat in appearance, and handsome. It was obvious that he was a man of authority. As Pemberton stood, he motioned for both John and Tullis to join him.

Both men dismounted and walked toward the stout man with the pleasing smile. Pemberton motioned for John to take his now-vacated chair. John gave both Tullis and Pemberton an unreadable expression as he walked over and sat down, making considerable wood stress noises in the cane-bottomed chair.

Pemberton continued to smile as he looked at the seated Texas rancher. "You're exactly as you were described, except better."

John canted his head, considering Pemberton's comment, but chose not to respond to it. He asked again, "Who are all of you, and why are you followin' me?"

Pemberton raised the palms of his hand in supplication and said, "John, we are here to save your life and a man named Mike Jones as well." He added, "Before we go any further, I need to have your complete assurance that what is said here … stays here."

John's body leaned to one side as he thoughtfully processed what he had just heard. He nodded, adding, "I can do that."

Pemberton's hazel eyes narrowed as if he were forming words. He stood arms akimbo and looked toward the gray eyes intent on him. "Our boss has spent a great deal of money to make sure you are safe." Receiving no response from the big man, he continued, "We've come from California to give you a message personally."

John thought that remark was strange. He had no knowledge of someone from California who would be interested in his welfare.

Pemberton paused to give John a chance to respond; when he didn't, he added, "Over four months ago, an agent and lawyer in the employ of a former brigadier general named Frank McGrew met with my boss, seeking some sort of collusion resulting in your death."

Pemberton could see by John's intense gray eyes that he definitely had the big man's attention.

"This general apparently has a burning hatred of you and assumed my boss held the same views."

Pemberton suddenly straightened. "But my boss doesn't and recently learned that you've had some run-ins with McGrew already." He let his hazel eyes meet the gray ones to assess his response.

John replied, "I've had run-ins with his hired help, but strangely haven't ever met him." But in his own inimitable way, he added, "But I shore in hell intend to someday."

Pemberton looked at the powerful man sitting in the chair. He had never seen anyone who looked like him. John Lee reminded Pemberton of a huge lion, barely under control.

Brigadier General Frank McGrew was a powerful railroad magnate in Pennsylvania. Pemberton knew the general had money and lots of it. He could snap his finger and have all the women and creature comforts he could possibly summon. He had also heard that McGrew was one of the most arrogant, despicable men on the planet. He had learned that he hated John Lee Johnson for personal reasons dating back to the late war. He knew McGrew was fixated on the big Texan for being involved in his brother's death at Fort Pillow.

Pemberton smiled to himself momentarily because regardless of McGrew's wealth and power, he knew he should forget about revenge, especially revenge against this man. Pemberton knew the general faced a very formidable foe in the big Texan. It was a test of irresistible wealth and influence versus an inexorable force of a very powerful man.

Still Pemberton, a dutiful man obsessed with completing his mission, began relating things as if they were rote. "My boss is one of the wealthiest people in the state of California." He paused and then added, "She has gone along with McGrew's plans because she felt it would save you."

When the pronoun "she" caught John Lee's attention, Pemberton paused and stated, "My boss is Marilla Urmacher. I think you know her well."

Pemberton noticed the formerly impassive features of John Lee Johnson change. He suddenly looked shock. The powerful man reacted like an overheated prospector in the middle of a sunbaked desert who suddenly felt an unexpected blast of a harsh polar wind.

Two years ago, the beautiful Marilla had hired some killers to attack John Lee. He and his men killed or captured the whole lot, and then, he had found her, snake-bitten, several miles from an abandoned town.

When he found her, she was unconscious. He treated her wounds, and they spent several days and nights together, bonding and becoming friends; they even sang a song together, "Shall We Gather at the River?" He thought she was the most beautiful woman he had ever encountered.

After she was healed, he thought she was the most mesmerizing human he had ever met. She had shaken him down to his core. She was beautiful and charismatic. He knew if he spent any more time with her, she would have been as addictive as opium, someone you could not possibly live without. She was not an evil woman, just otherworldly charismatic. He thought he had shaken her spell, but hearing her name brought back feelings he had wanted to suppress.

John could see Pemberton staring at him with a curious expression and pulled himself together. He felt any reply might reveal things he did not want to share.

Pemberton had not expected this unusual reaction from such a seemingly controlled individual. He made a mental notation that there had to be more than a friendship connection.

"McGrew has hired a gunfighter from Mexico named Macro Cio," he explained. "He has the reputation of being the fastest and deadliest man in the world."

Pemberton could see he had John's full attention.

"McGrew has issued a challenge to you and has offered a prize of one hundred thousand dollars if you accept. But before you answer, let me inform you what Marilla has done. She has gone along with the McGrew faction to protect you. In the guise of doing her part in this unholy alliance, she hired the best gunman in California, ostensibly to join Macro Cio in killing you. But the truth is, this gunman, named Mike Jones, has been hired to kill Macro Cio on your behalf. Jones is currently at the Comancheros headquarters. That is why your silence on the matter is necessary. I have an idea the Comancheros already resent his being there. So don't breathe this to anyone, not even to your friend, Homer Timms; any hint or whisper of this plan will result in Jones being a dead man."

John's gray eyes seemed to glow with an inner light. He tilted his head as he processed what Pemberton had said. Finally, after thinking everything through, he said, "This matter will remain a secret." He paused and added with some emotion, "One hundred thousand dollars is a lot of money, but I'm not really motivated in meetin' someone to just have a gunfight." He stood up from the chair and asked, "Where's this so-called gunfight supposed to take place?"

Pemberton replied, "In the state of Chihuahua, Mexico, in the Valley of the Sun." These words seemed dramatically to hang in the air. For an interminable period of time, there was no trailing comments, just those previous words echoing in their minds.

Pemberton then filled in some gaps in their discourse that had gone unsaid. He informed John that if he refused this showdown, the Comancheros had been ordered to raid his ranch and kill him, his wife, and daughter. He concluded by saying, "You do it or else."

Pemberton allowed this chilling information to linger before continuing, "There is another story to this, and it might help you make up your mind. Earlier this year, a female assassin hired to kill you double-crossed McGrew's faction and stole $760,000 from their safe in Austin. She killed Judge Roy and removed these valuable funds from the McGrew stash; it would have been used to send an endless line of killers after you." He raised his eyebrows and pointed out, "That caused McGrew to have to reach into his personal savings and his business account to finance all these shenanigans against you."

Pemberton threw out his hands palm up as to emphasize a point. "The assassin's name was Judith Levy. She has never been found, even with a dozen private detectives on her case. That outlandish money she stole was duly noted by McGrew's business associates. McGrew has spent a fortune to have you killed. His stockholders are cognizant that his mission to kill you has been a financial disaster. They want him to stop this nonsense. It has been rumored that if you kill Marco Cio, he will leave you alone, fearing that he might be ousted as the president of their consortium. This hundred thousand dollars he is offering is his last gasp to rid the earth of you."

Pemberton added, "If you agree to meet him on July first of this year, I will get word to the Comancheros." To make that last sentence more trenchant, he again spread his hands, "After all, they think we're on their side."

John leaned forward, his eyebrows arched over his shaded gray eyes. "How can you be so shore the money will be there? I trust you, but how do you know those things?"

Pemberton nodded at the natural question. "We have spies and know that it will be en route to the Valley of the Sun three days before the event; there is a ruined mission with some of the exterior walls remaining. Just behind what used to be a church nave will be an old Aztec altar stacked with Mexican gold coins." He matter-of-factly added, "It's winner take all." He looked off momentarily, adding, "They have supreme confidence in Marco Cio."

John remained silent for several seconds. "And you?"

Pemberton gave a half-smile. "I have confidence in you." After another pause, he added, "This could be your last chance to rid yourself of Frank McGrew. You win and walk away with one hundred thousand dollars in gold, and he'll have a hard time convincing his associates to waste any more money on killing you."

John slowly stood. He loomed over Pemberton and Tullis. He gave them both a controlled smile and said, "I believe you." He thoughtfully added, "Tell the bastards I'll be there." What John wanted to say but would not publicly say was that he believed in Marilla. Their peculiar friendship was hard to explain, but it was strong.

Pemberton walked with John toward his black stallion, which was stomping the sand. "John, you probably need to take someone with you for a second. Mike Jones is good but going against this Marco Cio could be too much of a challenge, even for him."

John saddled up, all the while choosing not to reveal his own plans. He merely asked, "July first?"

Pemberton nodded yes to the question as he watched the big man mount his horse and head back toward the road that would lead him to Gandy, Texas.

Tullis leaned in and said, "Mr. Pemberton, I don't know much about Marco Cio, and I don't know much about Mike Jones, but I can tell you if I had a bet ..." He paused as he watched John riding toward his companion down the road. "I sure in hell would bet on that big Texan."

Pemberton nodded but did not answer. He was well aware and greatly relieved that he had performed most of his mission. He had to report to the Comancheros that the showdown was on, and then he could return to California, having done his duty. When John Lee Johnson was out of sight, Tullis picked up Pemberton's wooden chair, and they made ready to head to south Texas.

CHAPTER 3

Two nights later, John and Hobie made camp by a small creek. There were a few willow trees and a cottonwood tree that formed a small grove beside the stream. They utilized this copse as a wind shelter and a suitable place to tether their horseflesh. The starry night was clear but especially dark, as the moon was in the silver-sliver crescent phase.

Hobie had a small flickering campfire burning and the coffee pot heating in its metal tripod holder. John Lee had made another disappearance. It no longer bothered Hobie that the big man just vanished at times. He knew that was part of his obscure nature.

As Hobie tossed in several mesquite twigs into the rock-rimmed fire, he thought he heard noises coming north of his position. He knew it was not the boss because he never made a sound. He cocked his head and listened. He reasoned that it was at least three horses he could hear but could not see. He knew he had visitors … and probably unwelcome ones, at that. Hobie was well aware this part of Texas was thick with thieves and robbers. But he felt no worries. He knew the big Texan was around somewhere. He reached over, took the pot out of its tripod, and filled his tin cup.

He could sense some stealthy movement coming toward his left side. He turned to see a shrouded, shadowy figure become more visible due to the firelight.

A man standing about six feet tall with scraggly blond hair and a sunburned face, sporting a large black Texas hat, emerged from the darkness. He was brandishing a pistol, and it was aimed at Hobie.

Hobie nodded and nonchalantly asked him if he wanted some coffee.

The man seemed surprised at Hobie's calm demeanor. The outlaw looked down at his Walker Colt to see if it were invisible. Immediately wanting to establish his dominance of the scene, he snarled out in a reedy Texas twang, "My name is Bad News Burkett. I'm a robber. And I'm here to rob you, pilgrim."

Hobie nodded at his words; he was well acquainted with men who gave themselves self-imposing nicknames. In the Russells' bunkhouse, he met innumerable men who called themselves "Cyclone," or "Rough House," or "Jaw Jacker." More times than not, their sobriquets rarely matched reality. After someone knocked the hell out of one of those pretend tough guys, they went slowly back to being called their original names: Gerald or Lester or whatever.

He continued his leisurely pace of drinking his coffee. "Bad News, is it?"

The outlaw's eyebrows shot up, as he could not believe the total lack of fear. And he could not believe how this hayseed had repeated his name in such an offhanded and inconsequential manner.

Bad News bared his yellow, crooked teeth. "Now, you can keep on swiggin' on that coffee instead of haulin' out some dinero, but if you continue to go in that direction, I'm just liable to blow a hole through your liver about the size of a rain barrel."

Hobie looked up at the blond features of the flushed outlaw and retorted coolly, "Now, now, Bad News, it's all obvious you've been drinkin'. Why don't you forget all that robbin' stuff before you get hurt?"

Confused by Hobie's attitude, Bad News wiped his face with a gloved hand and shook his head, as if to reset his mental gyroscope. He clicked back the hammer on his Walker Colt and growled, "Do I have your attention now, boy?"

The cowhand replied calmly, "Oh, you've got my attention all right." He nodded as he spoke, but it was not a fearful nod; it was more like a courteous gesture.

The confused outlaw canted his head to the side and asked Hobie, "You ain't touched in the head, are you?"

Hobie sighed, placed his cup on the ground, and gave a clipped, "Nope." He looked up and continued, "You see, Bad News, this ain't a good place to rob." Hobie took a deep breath and pointed out into the darkness, as though it were a black curtain and behind it lay so many promising avenues leading to so many more appealing campsites over in the yonder. "Of all the places you could've robbed, you picked the absolute worst one, Bad News. If I was you, I would holster that pistol, drink some coffee, and gently go on your way. If not, you're goin' to get the bad hurt put on you—and I mean real bad."

Bad News let a sarcastic laugh erupt. "I think it's goin' to be a real pleasure to plug a hole in you, you smart-talkin' fool."

Hobie raised an index finger as though he wanted to get a word in. "Bad News, you rode in with two others ... right?"

Bad News's suspicious eyes narrowed. "Keep talkin', you fool."

Hobie picked up his tin cup and sipped thoughtfully. "Why don't you call 'em in so I can see 'em?" He paused, rolled his eyes, and added, "Or better still, so maybe you can see 'em."

Bad News looked over toward where his men were concealed and back at the calm cowhand, who looked like he had no troubles in the world. Bad News's head began to move side to side, as though he were seriously spooked.

Hobie looked up at Bad News's slitted-blue eyes crazily appraising him. "Bad News, if I'm right ..." Hobie paused as he took a considerable gulp of coffee. "And I know I'm right." He sighed as if he were content with the heavy swallow of coffee. "I'm reckonin' about now, your two compadres are probably all tied up and layin' on the ground, and your hosses are now the property of one John Lee Johnson."

Bad News started moving his head once more side to side, trying to clear his self-doubt. That head shaking was accompanied by a self-conscious, hollow laughter, which lacked confidence. He turned his head and shouted out into the darkness, "Rowdy!" He waited and received no answer.

His next call sounded like a desperate, inquiring question, "Ferlin?" Still no answer.

Hobie sighed as he continued to drink his coffee. "You want some more advice, Bad News?"

Bad News withheld responding, thinking he was in some sort of weird surrealistic dream.

Hobie continued, "You ought to uncock that Walker Colt and just slither back into the night." He offered an afterthought, making a silent snap of his fingers. "But it might be too late." He added, "You should've taken the coffee."

Bad News looked around furtively and began to retrace his steps backwards.

After Bad News disappeared into the darkness, Hobie heard an explosive, fleshy whack. He allowed himself a grin, grabbed John's tin cup, and poured coffee into it.

The next morning, Hobie was up early and collected the bedrolls and breakfast utensils. He thought he heard someone sneeze to his left. As he turned his head, he could see three men in the shallow darkness just beyond the campsite, bundled up in all their ropes. They were all wadded up, lying on the ground in a cluster like a careless stack of firewood.

Curious, Hobie put aside the coffee pot and ambled over to the three men. They looked like they were caught in a spider's web. He could tell they were uncomfortable, trying to shift their bodies around to accommodate each other and also jockeying for as much comfort for themselves.

They stopped jostling and moving as Hobie approached, more from embarrassment than anything. He looked down at them but did not make any chiding remarks. He could see that the man who called himself Bad News was trying to avoid his eyes, but he had no intentions of further humiliating him. He had faced so many humbling experiences in life, himself, which he did not want to rip off the bark and rub the salt in.

His curiosity satisfied, Hobie turned to go back to the campsite when he heard the one he thought might be Ferlin ask the other, calling him "Simon," if he could try and move his elbow. Hobie nodded to himself that Simon was indeed Bad News. Hobie did allow himself a glance downward once more at the shamed face of Simon, who was trying to avert his eyes, knowing Hobie had heard his real name.

Hobie nodded as he thought to himself that it was just as he had supposed: pugnacious nickname, pansy real name. He started moving once more to return to his chores. It was then he heard the voice of the one he thought was Ferlin calling to him. He turned and leaned down to make out what he said.

"Young man, I know you're goin' to take our hosses. And I understand." He paused, and as he continued, his voice quavered. "That black three-year-old mare tied over there was hand-raised by me; she's a gentle one." Voice choking with emotion, he asked, "Will you sell her to someone who'll take good care of her ... please?"

Hobie was moved by the older bandit's plaintive words; he wordlessly continued his chores, which included taking two of the outlaw's horses and putting them on a tether line. He led the third horse, the black mare, to the stream, tying one rein to a willow tree and letting the other dangle, giving the filly access to water.

After doing this, he made an about-face and made his way back to the three men rolled up in ropes. He leaned in so Ferlin could see his face and hear his voice. "I tied your hoss off on a tree over yonder ... left your saddle too."

He caught the sight of Ferlin's gratefully tearful face. Figuring there was no more to be said, Hobie made his way to Big John, who was waiting by his horse.

John's posture was more of understanding than impatience. He had heard bits and pieces of Hobie's conversation with the older outlaw. When Hobie walked up to John, he suddenly worried he might have taken things too much into his own hands.

"I hope you're not sore at me for doin' that, boss," he said sheepishly. "I just had to leave him his hoss."

John gave him a thoughtful smile. He looked into the young man's meek eyes and said, "Hobie, I don't know if it was the smart thing to do, but it was probably the right thing to do." He paused and then added, "I think you're turnin' into a man, and showin' heart is sometimes a strength and not a weakness."

Then he finished off that understanding moment by becoming soberly practical. He thought of Memphis Mayford and Utah Jimmy Pruett heading to Gandy and said, "Now, let's get the hell outta here. We've got a lot of miles to eat up."

Three weeks later to the day, the hefty Shotgun Stevens, highly trusted by Tim Slater, was sent to meet Memphis Mayford and Utah Jimmy Pruett before they reached the undersized hamlet of Gandy. It took some doing, but he found them encamped where Slater suggested they might be.

Stevens had fresh information that he thought was relevant to the situation going on in Gandy. He laid out a description of the town and gave his opinion on how to kill Timms and then make their getaway. He informed the two killers that the local minister had balked on using the church for Big Ruby's wedding, since she had owned a notorious saloon.

He informed them that the wedding was scheduled for noon on Saturday, which was two days away. It would be held in Big Ruby's saloon, with a garden pergola placed in front of the bar, where the two would stand and exchange their vows. Stevens remarked the pergola would make a perfect place to plug the esteemed gunman. He indifferently shrugged as he suggested that they might as well get two for one by knocking off his wife-to-be and maybe curry some favor with the big boss, Sheriff Lee.

Shotgun squatted on his heels and began laying out the plan Tim Slater had given him for the two gunfighters. He recommended they enter at the last moment, to avoid attracting any suspicion. He suggested that they cut loose on the feared Homer Timms just before he said, "I do."

Shotgun drew a diagram in the sand with his gloved finger, showing the layout of the saloon, and pointedly made Xs where each man should stand and to use the backdoor exit to make their escape. Shotgun concluded his remarks by stating he would serve as their rearguard. He would be situated in front of the Baptist church at the end of the street. He assured them he would discourage any wannabe vengeful citizens with his shotgun.

He suggested in their escape that they ride past him and head due west but after a mile make a hard left and make their way to the Pipton Ranch, which was thirty miles away. There they would meet up with Slater and the boys, who were itching to get at John Lee Johnson next and make some real money.

They collectively decided to ride into the town on Friday but in intervals, to lessen unwanted attention. They wanted to get a better feel for the place and set themselves up for success.

Shotgun bid the two gunmen farewell at their campsite and decided he would immediately ride into the small town of Gandy and check into the cheap hotel. He rode away, feeling confident that things were working out as planned.

The following morning, Memphis Mayford rode into Gandy. He made his way to the livery stable, like he and Utah Jimmy Pruett had decided upon. He met the stableman and paid him four bits to have his horse watered, fed, and curry-combed and for himself to sleep in the loft.

Memphis Mayford realized that his appearance: dressed in all black with highly decorative gun belts and two ivory-gripped .44s would not fool too many townsmen. They would know that he was a gunman. He knew he had to keep a low profile and avoid the temptation of visiting the saloon. Therefore, he spent the remaining morning sitting on a small stool in the corner of the dark barn, chawing and scratching.

Utah Jimmy Pruett rode into Gandy about an hour later. He noticed the white painted church directly at the end of the town's main drag that Stevens had pointed out. There were eight buildings of different sizes that comprised the town: four on his left and another four on his right. The first building on his left was an open-doored livery stable. He gave a satisfied smile to himself, knowing that Memphis Mayford was stationed inside and perhaps was even watching him.

Next he spotted up ahead on his left a saloon sign extending from the last building of the row of four. The sign proclaimed in cardinal-red curlicue letters "Big Ruby's Saloon." Adjacent to the saloon but nearer to him was a boxy looking hotel with a short shelf roof. Crude, uneven boardwalks lined the places of businesses on both sides of the street. Fronting the boardwalks were a series of hitch racks that had several horses tied to them here and there. He observed two empty chairs in front of the hotel, one of which would serve him well. Upon arriving in front of the hotel, he slowly dismounted, allowing himself once more to peruse the dreary town. Seeing nothing of particular interest, he tied his horse off and took a seat, barely shaded by the miniature roof overhang.

Meanwhile, Shotgun Stevens, who had whiled away the morning hours inside the confines of Big Ruby's Saloon, was well into his third beer when he decided to cut himself off, knowing he had to be alert. He checked his pocket watch and reasoned that both Utah Jimmy Pruett and Memphis Mayford were already in town.

The rinky-dink piano was belting out a maudlin Irish song as Stevens pushed his schooner aside and cuffed the beer foam from his mouth. He nodded a goodbye at the bartender, who had a horseshoe haircut, and made his way to the batwings that were silhouetted by the bright sunshine from outside. As he pushed the right batwing aside, he immediately was reminded of what a dump Gandy was. The whole colorless town was bathed in yellowish sunlight. He inhaled the air and had the feeling that in Gandy, time comfortably stood still and was a companion and not a threat. Out of the corner of his eye, he caught sight of Utah Jimmy Pruett sitting to his right at the hotel. Jimmy seemed intent as he whittled a stick with a small pocketknife. He knew Jimmy had seen him but, as directed, had ignored him.

Shotgun sat with folded arms on the two-man bench in front of the saloon. He was at least a hundred feet from Jimmy but did not look his way. He looked up and down the dirt way, but seeing nothing of consequence, closed his eyes for a few minutes. After napping for five or ten minutes, he opened his eyes and caught sight of a man to his far right, entering town on a beautiful paint horse, pulling a packhorse. Shotgun kept the horseman in view until he was about a hundred feet shy of the livery stable. He considered the new arrival for a few seconds but then placed him in the back of his mind. He sighed sleepily and stretched his arms out and up, averting his eyes to nothing in particular.

With his arms still in the air, he suddenly dropped them, spurred by a quick nettling thought. He turned attention once more to the rider on the paint horse. Then he focused in on the oversized saddle pommel as the young man rode closer to the stable. It was an exotic Mexican saddle not often seen this far north of the border. It dawned on him that he had seen that horse and saddle before. He tried not to stare, but the wheels in his head kept spinning, trying to remember the horse and saddle, then his eyes widened in a flash of discovery. He suddenly realized that paint horse and the unusual saddle in particular had brought about the strange nickname of a gunfighter named Saddle Roy. Stevens could not fathom that this scraggly young man riding seemingly out of nowhere was frankly man enough to kill Saddle Roy or take his horse.

Thinking about this irregular puzzle, Shotgun stroked his chin. An uncanny fear coursed through the gunman. The only men in central Texas who could bring down Saddle Roy were Homer Timms, who was currently in Gandy, or ... John Lee Johnson. Since Homer Timms had been in Gandy for a spell, the latter choice caused a fire alarm to go off in his brain. Deciding he had been watching the young man long enough, he whistled silently with his lips and stared out at nothing in particular. But his heart was beating faster as he suddenly realized that killing Homer Timms might not be that simple.

Out of the corner of Stevens's eye, he caught sight of Hobie halting his progress in front of the livery stable. Stevens tried to be discreet, but seeing the young man enter the big, unpainted barn not only piqued his interest but gave him a sense of anxiety as well. It was quickly obvious to him that the young man was surreptitiously looking for Memphis Mayford. Stevens watched with growing angst as the young man completed his short stay in the barn and exited too energetically for a simple sojourner merely asking pedestrian questions. He had an idea that the young man would eventually lollygag down the street, looking for Utah Jimmy Pruett. Stevens immediately stood and started walking toward the livery stable. He passed Utah Jimmy without any acknowledgment. He darted down the alley and hunkered down behind a rain barrel. He observed Hobie riding by and could see that the young man was perusing the street.

Across the way, gazing out the window of a mercantile store was a chunky, older cowhand who stood thoughtfully while eating an apple. He was intently observing the same street scene. He saw Hobie enter town pulling a packhorse and watched him stop at the livery and eventually mount up again. He gave himself a satisfied smile. He had been correct that this was the place where he would meet up with Hobie. Suddenly, by chance, he caught sight of Shotgun Stevens sitting directly across from him. He noticed that Shotgun Stevens was spending an inordinate amount of time scrutinizing Hobie. He watched as Stevens stood and walked down the boardwalk toward Hobie but quickly dashed into an alley to avoid being seen. This action struck the voyeur as odd. Presently, he saw Hobie ride by. He could see that Hobie was taking a long gander at a slender hombre sitting in front of the hotel. He watched Hobie turn his horse and packhorse at the saloon, the last building on the left, then disappear from sight because of the bulk of the saloon.

The older wrangler started to make his way to the doorway, still invisible to the street because of the hidden shadows of the store's interior. But something caused him to pause his exit and return his vision to the street scene. He still had the privilege of having a full view from the storefront window. He watched with interest when Stevens came out of hiding from the alley. He could see that Stevens seemed both curious and disturbed to see that Hobie had made the turn and was out of sight. The older gent watched Stevens walk rapidly to his horse. He watched him quickly untie and mount up his horse, gigging his horse into a determined canter, obviously to catch up with Hobie.

Hobie was making tracks as he picked up speed on his paint, pulling the willing packhorse. He had not counted on being followed and did not spend a lot of time looking backwards or covering his tracks. He was four miles from his intended campsite. He knew John would not be there. The big fellow presently was meeting Homer Timms and others at an abandoned ranch house. The fact that John was gone did not bother Hobie. But he knew when he met the boss later that night, he would be interested in knowing that two men who fit the descriptions of Memphis Mayford and Utah Jimmy Pruett were in town.

Meanwhile, Shotgun Stevens was on his claybank and was moving in and out of the scrub trees and greasewood growing beside the trail. He felt positive that Hobie had not seen him and felt optimistic that he'd find the truth about Saddle Roy's horse and discover why the young man was in Gandy, or he would just kill him and leave it a mystery forever. He had Hobie in view and had an idea he was headed to a commonly known campsite along a narrow stream of water about an hour ahead.

What Shotgun did not know was that he was being followed too. Loping behind him and doing the same dodge-and-hide trick was the wily wrangler who was wise the ways of subterfuge.

About an hour and a half later, Hobie had established the campsite with easy access to both shade and water. His second chore was stringing a picket line near the creek. After tying off his paint to the taut rope, he saw out of the corner of his eye a powdery cloud of dust above the scrub tree line. That yellowish fog was accompanied by the sound of oncoming, thudding horse hooves. Hobie, concerned, turned his attention to greet his yet unseen visitor.

Seconds later, the burly Shotgun Stevens brazenly broke the camp perimeter and pulled up his horse violently, sending a cloud of billowing dust across the way.

Hobie could tell the man, who looked like a bullfrog, was in an ill mood.

He gathered by the man's expression that he was displeased for some odd reason.

Hobie froze as he watched the dumpy man dismount, pointing his silvery .44 in his direction.

Stevens didn't mince words. He pointed his gun at the paint tethered to the picket line and demanded, "Where'd you get that hoss?" When he spotted the gun belt around Hobie's waist, he added, "And that damn holster and pistol?"

Hobie realized in an instant that this gunman must have known Saddle Roy. He also knew that if he came clean and confessed the truth about the death of Saddle Roy, it could endanger John Lee Johnson.

While Hobie had been on the trail, he gathered enough information that John was on a perilous mission in Gandy. He had an idea that this surly intruder was a dangerous adversary who could very well upset the positive outcome.

Hobie also quickly determined that Stevens was not a bloviating windbag like Bad News Burkett. This man was for real, and Hobie had a good idea it was the end of the trail for himself. Hobie had garnered a new self-respect while riding with John Lee Johnson. He determined he was not going to throw away that feeling of self-worth, even in the face of danger.

Hobie decided even if it meant his own death, he would not betray the trust John had in him. He straightened up and bravely patted the side of what used to be Saddle Roy's holster. He jutted out his chin and lied like a dog, "I killed Saddle Roy, just shot that bastard dead."

Shotgun tilted his head thoughtfully as he processed Hobie's words, contrasting them with the young whelp standing before him. "There ain't no way in hell you could've killed Saddle Roy."

Hobie figured since he had gone this far, he might as well go for broke. "I shot 'im just because he was ugly."

Stevens snorted in disbelief and shook his head. "Oh, he was ugly all right, but I think a man named John Lee Johnson killed him, and you're tryin' to cover his ass."

Hobie tilted his head as in mock thought, as though the mentioned name meant nothing. "I don't know no John Lee Johnson." He paused as he trenchantly nodded toward Shotgun Stevens. "I've shot tall, short, fat, slim men all over the state." Hobie paused, knowing he was seconds from death. "I was comin' after you too."

Shotgun continued to shake his head in disbelief. "Hell, kid, you don't even know my name."

"Don't matter; you're ugly, and that's good enough reason for me."

Shotgun gave a twisted grin and said, "I've killed a lot of men too, kid. Now they didn't have your sense of humor, but it won't be a problem for me to send you all laughin' and smilin' like … all the way to the Promise Land."

Hobie shrugged his shoulders and broke into a courageous grin. He accepted his fate and replied nonchalantly, "Have at it, you tub of lard." But he had the satisfaction of knowing that his demise would not go unavenged. He figured he had the honorable privilege of displaying his newfound self-image all the way to his death. "I damn guarantee you'll remember this day."

Stevens cocked his silvery Army .44. But before he pulled the trigger, he offered, "If you tell me where this John Lee Johnson character is, I might just let you go."

Hobie answered, "I was born the bastard son of a saloon girl. I was raised dirt poor and never had nothin,' but some overweight bastard like you can't take away what pride I have."

As Stevens lifted his cocked revolver above his right shoulder, making ready to level it to shoot Hobie, a shot boomed out from a distance. The loud concussion of the pistol shot and the trailing reverberation caused Hobie momentarily to take his eyes off Stevens. As soon as that stunning effect quickly passed, Hobie returned his vision to Stevens, who was now staggering in pain. Stevens desperately tried to hang on to his pistol, but it fell to the sand as he attempted to stay upright.

Hobie did not wait another second; he pulled out Saddle Roy's .44, aimed it at Stevens, and pulled the trigger. With the additional pistol ball hitting his pelvic bone, Stevens fell to the earth on all fours. He was bleeding at the nose and wheezing. He was noisily huffing as if willing the wounds to go away, but even he knew they were mortal wounds.

While Hobie watched Stevens die, he saw a form emerging from the scrub trees, stepping around the splayed greasewood shrubs that seemed to be everywhere. He knew the stranger had saved his life. He thought he looked familiar but could not as yet determine where he had seen him. As the man walked closer, he said, "Shore thought you was a goner, Hobie."

Hobie recognized the voice and now the face. His features were no longer covered in the reticular ropes. The stunned Hobie could hardly speak. "Ferlin?" he asked.

"Yep."

Hobie, stunned by the series of events and the unexpected help of Ferlin, was speechless. He wanted to ask Ferlin a series of questions on how he escaped the ropes and why he had followed him, but he desisted. He held those thoughts as he turned his vision to Shotgun Stevens, who had now collapsed on his stomach in a prone position but was still breathing painful, husky breaths.

They both walked toward the dying gunman. Stevens managed to roll over on his back. He had a rivulet of blood streaming out of the corner of his mouth. His pain-filled eyes looked up at the two men peering down at him. His eyes slowly focused in on Hobie. "Will you bury me?"

Hobie paused, pushed up the dented derby with his forefinger, and replied, "Would you have buried me?"

Stevens sighed and slowly shook his head in the negative. "You know I wouldn't, but I was hopin' you were a better man than me."

Hobie reluctantly nodded and then said, "I'll bury you." He leaned down to hear Stevens's last words more clearly. It was obvious the old gunman only had a few minutes left. "What's your name?"

"Leonard Stevens."

Ferlin looked at Hobie first and then down at Stevens. "Are you the one they call Shotgun?

Stevens weakly nodded. He croaked out the words, "I got one more request if you are a-mind to do it."

Not waiting for an answer, he painfully eked out, "I was engaged to a dance hall girl named Terry Jo." Incipient tears appeared in the corner of his eyes. "She works in Teco. Please tell her that I died, so she won't feel I stood her up." He swallowed, and his last words were, "She's a sweet girl. She ain't ever had nothin'." Stevens gave a final death rattle and then died.

Hobie sighed and looked up at the sky in mild frustration. He looked over at Ferlin and shrugged his shoulders. "I'll bury him, Ferlin, but I can't go to Teco."

After rubbing his chin in thought, Ferlin said, "After we bury him, I'll go to Teco." He sighed as he finished his thought, "What the hell? It's not like I have a lot goin' on."

Hobie turned his attention to the problem at hand. "You got a shovel?"

Ferlin shook his head but said, "No, but I got me an oversized iron skillet."

Hobie nodded at the good suggestion. "We can both dig, I suppose." But his curiosity about Ferlin's unexpected appearance surfaced and he asked, "Ferlin, how did you get out of all them damn ropes?"

Ferlin reluctantly confessed, "Well, durin' the night while we was all tied up, I could overhear you and the big fellow talkin'. That's how I learned your name and where you might be headin'. Later, about an hour after you left, one of hands came along and found us."

Hobie pursed his lips and asked, "Hands?"

Ferlin filled him in on how he and the others worked for a cattle spread that had been raided by Comancheros. He mentioned that he and Rowdy and Simon had not been paid for three months and decided to try robbery for the first time. He concluded his summation by stating, "It shore in hell didn't pan out too well, I can tell you."

Hobie allowed himself a chuckle at Ferlin's expense. Then he asked in a lower voice, allowing for possible discretion, "It sounds to me that you came all the way here to thank me for leavin' your mare for you."

Ferlin ran a gloved hand over his face, trying to restrain his emotion, and said, "I was against the robbery attempt from the get-go, but Simon was headstrong for it. And Rowdy did anything that Simon said." He paused as he dropped his eyes. "That don't give me no excuse."

With his eyes still downward, Ferlin continued, "That big man you ride with, he knocked the hell outta both me and Rowdy and later Simon, or Bad News. When I woke up, we was all rolled up together, tied by our own ropes. I don't reckon I felt more ashamed." Ferlin lifted his eyes and looked directly at Hobie. "But when you left me my beautiful mare, which was such an act of mercy I could not forget." His voice quavered as he continued, "I found my saddle and what money I had hid in it and told Rowdy and Simon goodbye and left followin' your trail. I ain't much, but I shore know how to say thank you."

Hobie knew for damn sure he knew how to say thank you. Ferlin in fact had saved his life. But Hobie didn't want to continue that emotional line of talk. He looked down at the dearly departed Leonard Stevens and told Ferlin, "You go through his pockets; anything you find, you can have." He nodded his head with strong conviction. "You shore in hell deserve it."

Ferlin didn't argue the point. He bent down and began briskly searching. In ten seconds, he discovered a money pouch that contained over nine hundred dollars in greenbacks and Mexican gold coins. Ferlin, still stooped over, looked up at Hobie and said, "Are you shore you don't want to split this, Hobie?"

Hobie gave a warm grin, all the while shaking his head in the negative. Seeing the grateful look of wonder in Ferlin's face was worth the loss of half the money. "I'll bet, Ferlin, that's the most money you ever had in your life." It was a statement and not a question.

Ferlin grimly nodded. "It's sad to say, Hobie, I'm forty-three, and this is the richest I've ever been." He straightened and look heavenward as if seeking confirmation. "The most I ever held till now was thirty dollars."

Hobie, moved not only by Ferlin's words but by his thankful expression, meditated briefly on the strange providence that had brought them together. However, the stark reality of the moment sobered those emotions as he once more looked down at Stevens. "Help me drag his body out of the campsite, and let's bury this bastard."

After digging with the skillet for about an hour, they made a sizeable pit to bury the dead outlaw. Ferlin grabbed Stevens's boots while Hobie took his arms and laid him as respectfully as they could in the crude grave. They filled it in and rounded it off with the excess loose sand and dirt.

Hobie, feeling like he should say something over the dead but not knowing what was proper, glanced over at Ferlin. "Ferlin, you got any words to say over …" He paused as he nodded downward to the grave. "You know … Stevens?"

Ferlin looked in mild surprise at Hobie and said, "You mean over this sumbitch?" He inhaled and exhaled the words, "Hell no. I reckon his momma might be sad if she was still alive, but I shore in the hell ain't."

Hobie, not sure of the proper burial protocol, shrugged and nodded at Ferlin's words. He said sarcastically, "Well-spoken, Ferlin; you might've been a preacher if you had a-mind to."

Not having any response for that faint praise, Ferlin shifted his eyesight to Steven's claybank gelding and fancy tack. "Hobie, would it be all right if I took Stevens's horse and gear?"

Hobie shrugged, as if the request didn't matter. "If you're really goin' to Teco, you might need another horse. His shotgun and saddle ought to bring in some extra money."

Ferlin dwelt on that thought, but another matter entered his mind. "Do you think your boss, you know, the big guy, would take me on after I get back from Teco? After all, I'm sort of lookin' for work."

Hobie shrugged his shoulders. "I can't say for sure, but I can talk to him."

Ferlin nodded and said, "Well, that's all I can ask for." He shook off that line of talk and looked over his shoulder to the west. "I reckon I better make tracks; best I remember, Teco is about fifteen miles from here." He sent a gloved hand to the side of his face as he cogitated on the time and distance. "I could make it in four hours, if I get started."

Hobie walked with him to gather in Stevens's horse and then later to his hiding place, where the beautiful black mare was tethered. Hobie told him he didn't know exactly what the plans were, but whatever it was, it would most likely take place in Gandy.

Ferlin inferred from those words that when he finished notifying the poor saloon girl about her late fiancé's death that he was to return to Gandy. He figured he could find both the big man and Hobie without too much problem since Gandy was a dinky hole in the road.

Hobie made a crude rope line for Ferlin to pull Stevens's horse. They gave each other a cordial but wordless nod as Ferlin mounted up. Hobie watched his new friend disappear from sight amongst the stunted trees and myriad greasewood shrubs.

At sundown, John Lee Johnson rode toward the camp that he had directed Hobie to claim. He saw smoke curling above the stubby tree line and knew there was coffee ahead, but out of the periphery of his eyes, he spotted what looked like a freshly dug grave. He reined up and studied on the mound of dirt and the scuffed ground surrounding it. He dismounted and tied off his horse. He felt relieved when he recognized Hobie's worn boot tracks among the two sets of prints. He went back to his horse but curiously studied on the gravesite. Apparently, there was a joker in the deck he had not accounted for. He untied his mount and swung up into his saddle. He knew a story awaited him when he reached Hobie.

When he rode into the camp, he nodded his approval at the site as he dismounted and tied off his big stallion. He walked to the orange flame enclosed by rocks and accepted Hobie's proffered tin coffee cup.

After they sat down, Hobie waited until he had John's full attention and began his story in chronological order. He stated that he had seen two men who fit the description of Memphis Mayford and Utah Jimmy Pruett in Gandy. When he tendered this information, he could tell his boss already knew about this. That did not surprise Hobie; the big man always knew more than he let on.

But Hobie was certain he had further information that John was unaware of. When he began to relate how he was followed out of Gandy by a man who had recognized Saddle Roy's horse that brought interest to John's eyes. When he mentioned the man's name, Stevens, he could see he had John's attention. He continued giving full details of how Stevens rode into camp and braced him, asking questions about the horse and about a man named John Lee Johnson.

He continued his story without embellishment how Stevens held him at gunpoint. Hobie remained silent about his own personal valor because since he started riding with the big man, he had learned a new code of honor with humility. He mentioned that Stevens was seconds away from killing him when the outlaw's life was cut short by lifesaving shot from a friend.

When he informed John about who saved him and about Ferlin's unexpected arrival and help, he noticed a surprised twinkle in John's eyes. But when he asked about the possibility of taking on Ferlin for the remainder of the trip, he was met with a singular silence. John ignored that request. It was obvious to Hobie by looking at John's expression that he had other matters on his mind.

As he sipped his coffee, his eyes took on a faraway look. "Hobie, I'm goin' to send you on a mission really early tomorrow." John thoughtfully swirled the coffee in his tin cup and added, "I know you can do it, and we can wrap this thing up in Gandy."

Hobie didn't reply. He smiled to himself. He felt important. He just met those unusual gray eyes perusing him and nodded wordlessly, sending the message that he would be ready.

The next morning, Memphis Mayford was sleeping fitfully in the hayloft of the Gandy Livery and Blacksmith Shop. He was scrunched up in a knot, lying on his saddle blanket. He was covered only by a thin, worn quilt. The loft itself was dark, and the hay bales he was lying on were stacked unevenly; no matter how he tried, he could never find a comfortable position.

Memphis Mayford, thinking that he heard faint noises, opened his eyes and lifted the ragged quilt. He looked around, but not hearing anything further, he smacked his thin lips and shut his eyes once more. His head slid back into the cover much like a turtle disappearing into its shell.

An hour later, he heard the clarion call of a nearby rooster. That noise groused him, but what annoyed him even more was the twangy voice of Van Edwards, the billy-goat-bearded livery owner, talking in a conversational tone that was much too loud for the time of the morning. He also heard a second bothersome, unrecognizable voice that rankled him even further.

Memphis Mayford, irritated by the early morning chatter and determining to quieten this conversation, stretched his thin fingers out to reach for one of his two Colt .44s. Those pistols were his security blanket. When his fingers could not locate this particular .44, which he had purposely laid nearby at bedtime, his sleepy eyes grew anxious. Suddenly besieged by an emerging panic, he sat up and looked around in the softening darkness. After determining that his holsters were missing, he looked down into the open area of the barn. To his astonishment, his twin gun belts were hanging on large roof pole situated on the far side of the barn.

Memphis Mayford hissed through his small yellow teeth. He now reached out to put on his pants and find the answer to this mystery of personal affrontery. Trouble was ... there were no pants, no shirt, only boots. His small eyes were darting here and there as a frisson of fear replaced his formerly indignant attitude.

Keeping his attention on his pistols on the far side of the barn, Memphis Mayford, dressed only in his hat, red union suit, and now boots, began to scurry through the hay to the ladder that would lead him down into the mall of the barn. He knew he had to have those pistols as his equalizers. As he positioned himself at the top of the ladder and began to descend, he felt large hands grab him, leaving him helplessly kicking his thin legs as he was lifted and toted as though he weighed nothing.

As he swiveled his thin neck, he was able to ascertain he was being carried by a large human being. When he was dropped and pushed up against a stall stanchion, he saw John Lee Johnson fully for the first time. Memphis Mayford reacted as though he had been captured by Lucifer himself. His mouth dropped open, and he turned ghostly white. He did not resist as John Lee Johnson tied him to the round support pole … only a few feet from the wooden pillar where his pistols hang tantalizingly close by.

The hoary-bearded stableman, Van Edwards, nodded approvingly at the rope-tying skills of John Lee Johnson. Seeing the killer was tightly secured, Van Edwards grabbed his sawed-off greener from behind him and gave an unspoken message with his eyes that he was intent on keeping Memphis Mayford in deadly safekeeping.

Hobie, who had been the one to plunder Memphis Mayford's clothes and weapons, stood with Saddle Roy's gleaming Army .44 pointed at the nervous outlaw. Before John made his turn to take care of the second problem, Hobie informed him about the five hundred dollars he had found in Mayford's money pouch.

Memphis Mayford, seeing he was caught in such a humiliating way and also that his stash had been discovered, kept his eyes on the ground all the while shaking his head in frustration. He did manage to meekly ask Van Edwards if he could have a chaw of tobacco.

The older man looked at John for approval. Upon receiving it, Van Edwards reached into his shirt pocket and lifted the thick tobacco twist up to Mayford's mouth. He took a healthy chomp. The tobacco seemed to mollify him some as he resigned himself to the abject opprobrium he found himself in.

Both Hobie and Edwards watched the big man exit the barn. They knew where he was headed. After he disappeared from sight, they turned their vigilance once more to the tobacco-chewing killer.

Utah Jimmy Pruett was on the second floor of the seediest hotel this side of Mars. He was in his beige drawers beneath a moth-eaten blanket. His eyes were half-open. He watched as two mice scurried along the bottom of the swayed wall. He sighed restlessly. Those varmints had made scratchy rackets all night long, keeping him from getting his needed sleep. He felt like drawing his pistol and killing the rodents and then giving a bill to the owner of this rattrap for pest extermination. He was about to swing his feet from the worst bed he had ever tried to sleep in, when he heard a low-level knock.

Thinking it was Shotgun Stevens, he tiredly stood, put on his boots, and walked in his long drawers to the door. He was ticked at Shotgun for standing him up at their decided meeting place the day before. He opened the door, but it wasn't Shotgun Stevens. Jimmy didn't need a swami to tell him who it was. His eyes, which had been directed downward, quickly scaled upwards. Seeing the overpowering bronzed figure standing before him, Jimmy swallowed and moved quickly to slam the door, but a thick boot blocked that effort.

A powerful fist slammed onto Jimmy's temple like an oversized mallet, causing him to collapse like a worn-out accordion. John stepped over the prone Pruett, and immediately catching his attention were Jimmy's cheap britches piled by the crude bed. John found the blood money in a leather bag concealed in Jimmy's hat, near his pants.

The next thing Utah Jimmy Pruett remembered was being carried over John Lee Johnson's shoulder down the boardwalk toward the livery stable. He was too woozy to protest, but he was hoping his back flap was still up.

Jimmy was more or less conscious when he found himself tied back-to-back with Memphis Mayford, with only the thick pole separating them. He looked with dismay up at the rafter beams and asked to anyone listening, "Where's Stevens?"

Hobie, overhearing his question, said matter-of-factly, "He's dead."

Utah Jimmy Pruett let his eyes remain on the underside of the roof. His voice took on a sarcastic tone as he said, "I always get caught up with idiots."

Memphis Mayford, hearing his comment, spat tobacco juice to one side and answered, "You ain't exactly no genius yourself."

Utah Jimmy Pruett smacked his lips in defeat and shrugged his shoulders; all the while shaking his head in disgust. He saw no need to reply.

Both outlaws could see that John Lee Johnson had left. They had no way of escape and knew that he had their money. But his absence was a blessing. He scared the hell out of both of them. For the most part, they ignored Van Edwards and Hobie. They feared neither of them, but the ropes were tight, and those weapons the two guards had were real and loaded. Memphis Mayford and Utah Jimmy Pruett did not speak, but they had a premonition that Big John had further plans for them.

About an hour later, a well-maintained buggy pulled by a large dray horse halted in front of the stable. Inside the buggy were two people: a man wearing a derby and ill-fitting coat, and a very pretty lady wearing a crinoline hat festooned with pheasant feathers, jutting backwards as though in flight.

Hobie, thinking he recognized the man, excused himself from guard duty and walked to the maw of the large barn. He immediately realized that it was Ferlin in his surprisingly new digs.

The attractive woman sitting next to Ferlin was oblivious of any spectators; she leaned toward Ferlin, wrapped her arms around his neck, and gave him an affectionate kiss on the cheek.

Ferlin had caught sight of Hobie approaching but ignored him momentarily as he disembarked and walked around the buggy to help the woman down.

The woman started walking toward the saloon.

Hobie, now in the sunlight just beyond the barn entrance, watched the very attractive lady as she navigated the uneven boardwalk toward the growing number of people situated in the street, queueing up to enter the saloon before the impending wedding.

Hobie gazed longer than he intended to at her lithe figure as she walked along. He watched her stop, open up her parasol, and continue on her way.

Hobie glanced at Ferlin standing on the opposite side of the buggy and then returned his gaze to the woman. At that time, he did not know who she was; it was just that this striking young lady did not fit with a forty-year-old cowhand like Ferlin. It was not like Ferlin was ugly; he was not. He was just plain or average.

Curious about this strange, incongruous relationship, Hobie made his way around to where Ferlin was. Ferlin met Hobie's inquiring eyes with a proud look, accompanied with a satisfied smile. He nodded a greeting toward Hobie as he approached.

Ferlin, seeing that Hobie was interested in the woman he was with, ignored his friend's bemused expression. He closed the distance and extended his hand for a shake.

Hobie shook his hand, all the while taking in Ferlin's derby and jacket, which was a size too small for his frame.

Hobie, still confused about the beautiful lady, took another gander at her back view. He pulled his attention from the woman and looked once more at the beaming face of his new friend.

Hobie cleared his throat as he collected his thoughts. Rocking back and forth on his worn bootheels, Hobie asked Ferlin a question he knew the answer to: "I reckon you ain't still interested in joining the boss and me?"

Ferlin gave a soft smile. "No, Hobie, I've made other plans."

With his eyes on Ferlin, Hobie nodded toward the woman and asked, "Your change of plans wouldn't have anything to do with her, would it?" Receiving no answer, Hobie abruptly asked, "Who in tarnation is that, Ferlin?"

"That's Terry Jo."

A startled Hobie wiped his mouth with the back of his hand and responded, "You mean that's the dance hall gal who never had a chance in life?" Not giving Ferlin a chance to reply, he continued, "The one who was engaged to Shotgun Stevens?"

Ferlin stepped in closer, as if he did not want anyone listening, even though there was no one within a hundred feet. It was though he were psychologically protecting the innocence and reputation of Terry Jo.

"It seems that Leonard Stevens had his details a little messed up, Hobie." Ferlin squinted his eyes as he looked upward as to get the facts straight before continuing. "She was not engaged to Shotgun Stevens. She hardly knew the man. She told me that he might've been in the saloon two or three times. That he would get drunk and start cryin' about his life and usually passed out. She said he did propose to her, but he also proposed to the widow lady who ran the mercantile store and the preacher's wife, who was doin' some shoppin'."

Hobie tilted his head as he processed this information. He nodded in Terry Jo's direction and said, "She ain't a dance hall girl?"

"Nope."

Hobie, realizing that he was dealing with a complicated matter, said, "Ferlin, I just got to ask you … no offense, but why is she with you?"

Ferlin looked down at his new boots and dawdled his head around as if jump-starting his response. "Hobie, the night I got to Teco, they was havin' a funeral. You heard me mention the widow lady who ran the mercantile store? The one Stevens proposed to?

"Yeah."

"Well, she died, and there was a ceremony at a small graveyard. I stopped to show my respects and maybe satisfy my curiosity some. While I was there, the widow's son was askin' if anyone wanted to buy the general store, cause he was done livin' behind a counter. To make a long story longer, I bought the store, and while I was at it, I bought Terry Jo's saloon." He paused and added, "She ain't no dance hall gal; she owned the saloon and the feed and seed store next to it."

"Don't tell me, you bought the feed and seed store too?"

Ferlin shrugged modestly and said, "I bought the whole town, with the exception of the livery stable." A smile ran across his face as though saving the best morsel to last. "Me and Terry Jo hit it off, and we got married yesterday."

"The hell you say."

"The hell I do say."

"With the money you found on Shotgun Stevens?"

Ferlin lifted his eyebrows comically and said, "Sold his horse and gear and shotgun to a rancher for a hundred dollars and got some money left over."

Hobie shook his head slowly in wonderment. "Ferlin, before long, you will be the mayor of Teco."

Ferlin let a modest smile move across his flushed face. "When I bought the store, I was made mayor by default."

Hobie, already overloaded by these stunning details, stood speechless, marveling at the quirky vicissitudes of life. Finally, after taking a deep breath, he asked, "Why're you and Terry Jo here for Homer's weddin'?"

"Terry Jo is Big Ruby's niece." He paused and then added proudly, "She's goin' to be the maid of honor."

Hobie was flabbergasted; silenced by the shocking turn of events, and having nothing else to say, he nodded his farewell to his friend and reentered once more into the bowels of the barn to share guard duty.

John Lee Johnson stood to the right of the large wicker pergola in front of the bar. Standing next to him and in the middle of the arched structure was the groom, Homer Timms. The two handsome men were smiling at the beaming audience. It was also obvious to the assembled that both Timms and Johnson were armed to the teeth. They understood why. After all, in central Texas, it was important to be prepared for trouble.

The people in the crowd were hardworking ranchers, their wives, and cowhands. They wore simple but clean clothing. It was obvious by their expressions they revered Homer Timms. They knew that John Lee Johnson was equally famous in his part of Texas, but seeing the two renowned men together was a treat and would stay in their memory forever.

John Lee Johnson's gray eyes slowly perused the crowded room. Although he knew few of the people, he was seeking someone who didn't belong, an anomaly. Suddenly, his eyes picked up on a thin man with a dipped hat brim, wearing a dusty coat and sitting near the batwings. He looked like someone who had ridden hard and fast and taken the time to tidy himself up as best as possible but had done a poor job doing it.

John could see the man's eyes sliding side to side beneath his sloped brim, as though searching for someone. John had a good idea that he was looking for Memphis Mayford and Utah Jimmy Pruett. The thin man's eyes suddenly looked forward and caught John's gray eyes scrutinizing him. His thin lips suddenly opened in surprise that he had been ferreted out. He broke off that visual connection with the big man and slowly edged to the batwings, where he slithered through, hoping to remain anonymous.

John could not act. He wanted to run through the crowd and grab the interloper before he could report to Tim Slater. He inhaled a large frustrated breath and tried to figure out what his options would be after the ceremony. He realized the man would make a beeline to Slater, reporting that matters in Gandy had gone haywire. John understood that now Slater had the opportunity to make adjustments before John intended him to.

While these things were coursing through his mind, Wagner's *Wedding March* suddenly broke loose to his left. He turned toward the far wall and caught sight of the piano player, a portly man with a derby. He was wearing sleeve garters on each arm of his barber pole red-and-white shirt. He expertly stroked the saloon piano, bringing out sounds few could. He had not played a minute when suddenly both batwings flipped open, revealing the Junoesque Big Ruby in a black dress.

John had heard of Big Ruby for some time but had never laid eyes on her. He was not surprised she was attractive, but he had no idea she was that pretty. She was beautiful: tall, chunky, and curvy, with a sweet face, kind smile, twinkling eyes, and a look of resolute love toward Homer Timms.

Following Big Ruby was Terry Jo: short in stature, a Godey's Ladies Book face, beatific expression, dark hair, hazel eyes, even white teeth. She was dressed to the nines and seemed at ease with all those eyes following her.

After the big entrance, both Big Ruby and Terry Jo moved slowly toward the arched pergola. As they passed the midway point, Stan Johnson, a seedy-looking circuit rider minister (not the local pastor), positioned himself to the side of the flowery archway and waited for the bride and bridesmaid to approach the pergola. Soon Big Ruby, now under the pergola with her face beaming, positioned herself beside the legendary Homer Timms. They gave lingering looks of devotion to each other, but then turned their attention to the preacher.

With practiced fingers, the minister turned to the book of Ruth and read the traditional vow Ruth made to Naomi. He then gave a terse lesson about two people sharing their love and life with each other.

They said their vows before the silent crowd; at the appropriate time, John Lee Johnson fished the ring from his coat pocket and handed it to Homer. After the ring ceremony, the newlyweds chastely kissed, and Stan turned and announced before God and man and the state of Texas that the two were now man and wife.

The crowded room exploded in loud cheers; John Lee Johnson, receiving an understanding look from Homer, made his way to the back door that led him to a small room, where he tossed his borrowed coat, lent to him by the local undertaker, on the cot where the barkeep slept. He exited the back door and walked over to the livery.

At the rear of the livery barn, standing in the overhang shadows near a stack of worn-out leather gear and feed sacks, was a swarthy-looking young man. His face changed from nervous to relieved when he saw the big man walking toward him. The young man was an undercover agent for the US military on loan from a cavalry post in the Nations. He had been involved in the Sabbath Sam-John Lee Johnson war over a year back. He could never forget seeing John Lee Johnson for the first time. It was a jolt to his system seeing such a powerful-looking man; he remembered thinking he was glad he was on their side. But now seeing his approaching, he felt in awe once more.

When John caught sight of him, he felt he had seen him before but could not put a name to the face. But he had a good idea he was working with his friend, Lieutenant Bragg, by his military-like bearing and erect posture.

The man looked anxious; he knew if he were caught talking to John Lee Johnson, it was the same as suicide.

He introduced himself but did not bother to shake hands. He said his name was Lieutenant Hubert Hicks and explained that he was pretending to be a member of Slater's gang stationed at Pipton Ranch. He added that he was not the only one who had penetrated the gang. His associate, Benny Leonard, and he were keeping tabs on Slater's illegal activities, which hopefully would lead to the forceful removal of the corrupt Sheriff Lang.

He explained that he wanted to inform John that Lieutenant Bragg was very much aware of Slater and the Pipton Ranch gang and the threat they posed to him. Hicks added that he would try and alert him if the Slater gang suddenly became aggressive and tried to seek him out.

When John heard that, he replied, "Don't bother. Just take care of yourself."

Hubert stood marveling at the powerful-looking man who stood before him. He said those words without arrogance, just with the self-assuredness of a confident man.

Hubert said he would try and take care of himself, but at the present time, he was in good standing with both Slater and the gang; Slater had entrusted him to watch the backtrail of one of Slater's agents, who was presently in town. He went on to explain that the man he supposedly was protecting was trying to make contact with Utah Jimmy Pruett, Memphis Mayford, and Shotgun Stevens.

John knew he must be referring to the ugly-looking cuss he had just seen in the saloon.

It was obvious by Hicks's furtive looks and ill-at-ease deportment that he was on limited time; as he delivered his message, he was sweating bullets that he would not be seen.

He told John that Slater planned to entice Big John to the ranch in hopes of ambushing him. He went on to relate that it would be wise for John and his men to avoid heading in that direction since there was nothing of consequence there, except five buildings and two freight wagons.

John listened to Hicks's advice but had no intention of following it; his planned trip to the Valley of the Sun in Mexico required him to head through the Pipton Ranch. But when Hicks had mentioned "two wagons," those two words cinched the deal for John. He wanted those wagons. He would head to the Pipton Ranch as soon as he could. He was not worried about Slater and his gang. He wanted them to think they were the aggressors, but in actuality, he'd be pursuing them.

John didn't mention any of this to Hicks; he simply replied, "I want those wagons. I'll be headed your way soon."

Hicks could hardly believe his ears; incredulous, he stammered, "But—but—but there are thirty men there."

The tall man responded tersely, "Just take care of those wagons … and yourself."

Hubert Hicks, seeing that John was adamant and was the type not to be deterred, merely nodded his head. He realized he had to work within that framework.

Having stayed longer than he intended, Hicks knew he needed to leave and get back to his hiding place, where he was his comrade's rearguard sentinel.

With his eyes moving left and right, accompanied by fidgeting leg and arm movements, he nodded farewell to John, abruptly turned, and darted past the pile of worn-out leather tack. He mounted his horse and, without looking backward, galloped quickly southward.

John entered the livery barn from the rear entrance, briskly making his way toward the two guards and the two men tied to the post. Memphis Mayford, who was facing him, blanched when he saw him and spat a nervous shot of tobacco juice to one side. One by one, the others, with the exception of Utah Jimmy Pruett, who was facing the opposite direction, picked up on his presence and turned to face him.

John nodded his head to the two guards, and Van Edwards and Hobie began untying the two scoundrels. After being untied, both Utah Jimmy Pruett and Memphis Mayford gave uncomfortable looks to each other but remained silent as John indicated for them to put their boots and hats on.

Having done so, they looked ludicrous wearing their regular garb, minus weapons and standing in their drawers.

Before Utah Jimmy could complain about this indignity, he caught sight of the stern gray eyes of the big man. It suddenly dawned on him that protesting this humiliating arrangement was certainly not worth getting his ass kicked through his discolored drawers. He found himself consciously nodding in assent, even though it scorched his liver.

John handed Memphis Mayford and Utah Jimmy their requisitioned five hundred dollars and told them to follow him. Hobie and Van Edwards, still brandishing weapons, followed the two disgraced gunmen as they traipsed behind the big Texan out of the barn and toward the direction of the saloon.

There were only a few townsmen who did not attend the wedding, but the onlookers took their time in gawking at the two men walking down the boardwalk in their drawers. Utah Jimmy Pruett kept his eyes upward, as though he was preserving some sort of dignity. Memphis Mayford, on the other hand, disdainfully swiveled his head, meeting the opened-eye stares of the curious citizens. When he caught sight of a certain woman covering her thin-lipped mouth with her hand, he derisively cut loose a heavy stream of tobacco juice in her general direction.

John Lee Johnson and his entourage continued down the uneven boardwalk, with more and more eyes catching this most unusual sight. Reaching the saloon, John pulled back the right batwing and nodded for Utah Jimmy and Memphis Mayford to enter. After they went inside, John led them to the receiving line.

The milling crowd moved aside quickly, their eyes first taking in the intimidating giant and then the two men dressed in their union suits. John led both men, followed closely by Van Edwards and Hobie, into the receiving line that was giving wedding gifts to the newly married couple.

Memphis Mayford, upon passing a table with a bowl of green apples on it, spat his tobacco cud out on the floor and grabbed two apples. He nestled one close to his body, keeping it in reserve, and began eating the other one like a starving man. He stood audibly munching away in the receiving line as though it was socially de rigueur. The queue moved slowly forward until John found himself standing directly in front of Big Ruby. She recognized him as Homer's best man.

She nodded affably, but before she could make his proper acquaintance, her dark eyes quickly bypassed him, taking in the two men following him. To her surprise, they were dressed in hats, boots, and underwear.

She looked back at John, who interjected with a touch of sarcasm, "These two men wanted to give you a weddin' gift so bad they didn't take the time to get dressed."

She nodded cautiously, as though she was taking in the information, but it was a nod that showed reservation as well. She took in Memphis Mayford, who was still eating his apple and seemed oblivious to wedding protocol.

Memphis Mayford, receiving that look from John, moved forward and handed Big Ruby his five hundred dollars.

Big Ruby raised her skeptical eyebrows again. Nevertheless, she unrolled the greenbacks, counted them, and shrugged her hefty shoulders in surprise at the amount. She muttered, "Nice gift."

She gave Memphis Mayford a critical onceover and stated drolly, "Nice drawers."

Her sarcasm went over Memphis Mayford's head. Still munching on his apple, he naively responded, "I paid fifty cents for them in San Antone."

Big Ruby glanced at John, as if this was a practical joke. Seeing John was dead serious, she looked back at Memphis Mayford and said, "You probably paid fifty cents too much."

Before Memphis Mayford could reply, he caught the head movement of John Lee Johnson that signified that he had better move on. Memphis Mayford now found himself standing in front of the seated Homer Timms. Homer, who had seen Memphis Mayford hand over the money to his new wife, smiled and said, "Appreciate your gift, Memphis Mayford." He paused and sarcastically added, "I agree with my wife; you probably paid fifty cents too much for your drawers."

Memphis Mayford, now catching on that he was being made fun of, started to respond, but before he could vent, he was grabbed by the scruff of his underwear and moved quickly forward.

He looked like a spoiled child that had just been reprimanded for the first time and gave John a hate-filled look.

John cinched the cloth tighter and whispered, "You don't go around tellin' how much you paid for your drawers." He paused and added, "Especially to a lady."

He released his hold on Memphis Mayford's underwear and gave him a rough shove to the side, accompanied with a stern, admonishing look that meant to be quiet and not wander off.

John's attention moved to Utah Jimmy Pruett, who was slow to hand over his five hundred dollars to Big Ruby. John shot him a menacing look, and the outlaw placed five one hundred dollar bills in her pink hand.

Big Ruby, delighted by the quick upturn in financial resources, flashed a smile up at Utah Jimmy, who gave noncommittal look back. Big Ruby turned aside to her husband and waved the five conspicuous one hundred dollar greenbacks.

Homer nodded as he glanced at the outlaw, telling him, "Many thanks, Utah Jimmy."

Utah Jimmy never wanted to tell someone to go to hell more than Homer Timms. But he had a good idea that the satisfaction he would receive in saying those words would result in losing his teeth and having his ass kicked all over creation, much less witnessed by a room full of people. Utah Jimmy took a deep breath, holding on to iron restraint until his face turned red; he walked stiffly forward and joined his glum compadre, Memphis Mayford.

They watched their intimidating captor lean down and whisper something in Homer Timms's ear. Homer listened and then nodded, without looking at Utah Jimmy and Memphis Mayford. Homer also whispered something inaudible to John that seemed to please the big man. Both Utah Jimmy and Memphis Mayford supposed the whispers were about them, but neither Homer nor John gave them the satisfaction of confirming that fact. Homer merely gave Big John a satisfactory smile, indicating his approval of some shared plan, and then he reached over and gave Big Ruby's shoulder an affectionate pat.

John canted his head for Hobie and Van Edwards to come forward; they led Memphis Mayford and Utah Jimmy through the curious onlookers and finally out the batwings and down the same uneven boardwalk back to the stable.

Both Utah Jimmy and Memphis Mayford knew without looking that John Lee Johnson, himself, was following behind. The crowd in the street began to snicker at first at the two killers in their underwear, but those giggles soon became mocking belly laughs as they marched toward the livery barn. Utah Jimmy again tried to keep his vision up toward the cerulean sky to preserve some sort of aplomb, but his ears did not cooperate. He heard the catcalls and sarcastic laughter, and it burned his innards.

Once inside the barn, both Memphis Mayford and Utah Jimmy Pruett gave apprehensive looks toward the big Texan. They knew something ominous was up. Although neither man expressed his thoughts, they both were on the same page mentally. They figured since he had publicly humiliated them, the only thing left for him to do was to kill them.

John gave a wordless message to Van Edwards with his eyes. The older hostler departed into one of the stalls and led out both gunmen's saddled horses. He tied both mounts to a nearby stall slat. He was closely followed by Hobie, who had the packhorse and the regular horses ready for immediate travel.

Memphis Mayford's nervous eyes took in the horses outfitted in their full gear. Expecting to be shot immediately, the sight of the horses gave him some hope, but he figured it was false hope. He shot a confused look toward Utah Jimmy Pruett and received the same look back.

Memphis Mayford's alarmed curiosity got the best of him. Gathering courage, he meekly asked, "What gives?"

John nodded at the horses. "Let's just say we're goin' for a ride."

Memphis Mayford's beady eyes narrowed in thought. "If you're goin' to kill us, just do it now. I don't want to be shot out on the prairie."

Utah Jimmy Pruett, upset at his partner's temerity and even more so by his rash rush to judgment, quickly interjected, "Shut up, Memphis Mayford."

Jimmy extended his hands toward John in a plaintive manner. He moved his fingers like he was playing an imaginary piano smiled nervously at Big John.

His conciliatory voice trembled as he added, "What he's sayin' is that we would really like to go on a ride." Jimmy's head nodded up and down rapidly, as though trying to play down his associate's words. "Ain't that right, Memphis Mayford?"

The other outlaw, seeing that he might have been too direct, and catching Jimmy's stern but importuning look, acquiesced. He nodded and pulled out his extra apple, taking a prodigious clacking bite. He asked John if he could eat his apple before they went riding. His question was met by a disdainful look from the big man and a painful silence.

John gave a meaningful nod to Hobie, who brought the big man's big black stallion forward. John lithely swung into the saddle and watched as Hobie made a tether line, hooking both Memphis Mayford and Utah Jimmy's mounts onto it. Hobie then mounted, holding the tether rope.

Lastly, Van Edwards mounted his sorrel gelding, with his hand on the lead rope attached to a dun packhorse.

All that was left were the two gunmen. John authoritatively nodded his head toward them and then let his eyes travel to their horses. "Mount up," he ordered.

Memphis Mayford and Utah Jimmy begrudgingly climbed onto their tethered horses.

John nodded to himself and rode out of the barn, followed by Hobie, who held the rope that pulled the two assassins, clutching to the saddle horn of their saddles. They were followed by Van Edwards, pulling the packhorse. The outlaws took note that Van Edwards had a .10 gauge greener jutting from his rifle scabbard.

They left town around one o'clock and headed due east. They rode steadily for four hours. The ride was as quiet as a dirge. At first, Memphis Mayford and Utah Jimmy Pruett would glance at each other, hoping against hope that the other had some plan of escape. But that was just wishful thinking. John seemed like a man who was on a gruesome mission.

Feeling their time was limited, Jimmy and Memphis Mayford took in the never-ending mesquite and greasewood landscape. In the past, they took this scene for granted, but now in their estimation, it was as though it were the borders of heaven. They now took in every shade of green and yellow with a longing appreciation.

Occasionally, they would turn their heads over their shoulders to check on the possible vulnerability of old Van Edwards. Each time they sneaked a peek, they saw only the older lawman's unyielding and suspicious eyes. His expression was baleful and equally obvious that he was reading correctly their intentions. Each furtive backward gaze was met by the old man menacingly patting the thick walnut stock of his greener, conspicuously placed in his rifle scabbard. Finding any avenue of escape nonexistent, they took deep, fatalistic breaths and morbidly accepted their lot.

At one point, John Lee Johnson reined up and stopped in the middle of nowhere. About a half-mile away was another road that led to the Pipton Ranch. Johnson dismounted and tied off his gigantic horse to a thorny mesquite tree bordering the side of the wagon path. From his vantage point, he could see the two anxious gunmen looking at him with owl eyes. He gave a quick sideward motion with his head that was interpreted correctly as "Dismount."

Memphis Mayford knew what that motion meant but chose to ignore it, trying to milk each second of existence he could. But when he saw Utah Jimmy moving his body to dismount, his heart dropped, and he knew the jig was up. He reluctantly followed suit.

As Memphis Mayford and Jimmy Pruett moved forward, they felt the devil's breath on their hackles. They took shallow breaths and avoided visual contact with the big man, as though hoping he would disappear.

They were secretly praying to the god of stagnant waters or any other pagan deity that might be presently looking on for some sort of relief.

Once they arrived a few feet from John Lee Johnson, they meekly stood ready to meet their fate, but they sure in hell didn't like it. Their downward eyes were now cast on the sand, dreading each succeeding second of time.

John nodded at Hobie, who brought a new lassoing rope of considerable length. Utah Jimmy lifted his head with his wide-open eyes fixated on the rope, but then his vision took in the nearby stunted trees. Trees that were too short for hanging. He discarded that danger momentarily, but another gruesome possibility entered his mind: the thought of being dragged entered his brain, and his fear level surged.

That notion also dissipated when John grabbed both Memphis Mayford and Utah Jimmy by their arms. Their stiff resistance was countered by a force of almost preternatural strength. He slammed them back to back as though they were rag dolls. He took the rope handed to him by Hobie and began tying them with their arms pinned downward by their sides. Tied back-to-back, the two gunmen soon found themselves securely locked together.

Utah Jimmy Pruett shook his head and looked at the sun on the horizon, all the while wishing he had never left Salt Lake City. He chanced a question toward the indomitable John Lee Johnson. "What're you gonna do?" he asked, glancing down at the manila-colored rope holding him glued to Memphis Mayford and then quickly back up at the big Texan.

John remained painfully silent for a few seconds that seemed like forever to the two gunmen. The big man finally sighed and responded, "I ain't goin' to kill you."

The two outlaws simultaneously exhaled big sighs of relief.

John added, "The reason that I ain't goin' to kill you is because you both are incompetent fools. If you were worth a damn, you'd already be dead. Sides, it might sour Homer's honeymoon." Big John turned his massive neck toward the east and ordered, "You two are goin' walkin'."

Utah Jimmy moved his head around, trying to grasp what he said. "Walkin'?" He cogitated on John's words and with a puzzled expression asked, "How do we do that?"

John shook his head as though it were an imposition to answer, but he pointed at the two men's feet and said, "Well, it's like this, Utah Jimmy: You will extend your left leg, and Memphis Mayford will extend his right leg, and you will shuffle to the east. Fifteen miles from here is a little town called Punkin' Center. I figure if you two birds work together, you can make it in a week." He added, "If you make it there, some church people will give you some clothes, and you can shovel horse dung to make eatin' money until you can find some fool who'll give you a wagon ride to Austin."

It was then that John, Hobie, and Van Edwards took note of Memphis Mayford's face. He had an unhealthy pale look that couldn't be faked. Van Edwards asked, "What's wrong with you, Memphis Mayford?"

Memphis Mayford shook his head in obvious misery. "Them green apples I ate are workin' on me."

Upon hearing Memphis Mayford's ominous declaration, Utah Jimmy, facing the opposite direction, agitatedly shook his head and looked up at the darkening sky. "Oh, hell, sweet Jesus, tell me—no." Jimmy tried to crane his neck around to address Memphis Mayford directly, but the tight pinions prevented that. Therefore, his eyes moved heavenward again. "I don't deserve this. Hell, I've been crooked and have done some thangs wrong, but I shore in hell don't deserve this kind of punishment."

Memphis Mayford began to groan. He ignored Utah Jimmy's words because he had a bellyache from hell. He gave a pleading look to both Hobie and Van Edwards. "Can one of you undo my flap? I don't want to soil my drawers."

Utah Jimmy cut loose again. "What about me? You damn idjit!" Utah Jimmy looked at John with distress and pleaded, "Just hang us." He shook his head rapidly and prayed, "Sweet Jesus, have mercy on me." He looked pointedly at John again and repeated, "Just hang the hell outta us."

Memphis Mayford's sad eyes moved from Hobie to Van Edwards. He pleaded, "Just undo my flap is all I'm askin'."

Hobie looked at old Van Edwards and said, "I ain't ever touched another man's drawers." He shrugged his shoulders. "Makes me feel uneasy."

Van Edwards shrugged also and said, "Well, I don't like touchin' another man's drawers, either, but at least they look like expensive ones."

Hobie guilelessly added, "Cost him fifty cents."

Van Edwards ignored that comment and reached between the two trussed-up men and unbuttoned Memphis Mayford's flap.

John, seeing that was done, nodded his head sternly for Utah Jimmy to get shuffling. Jimmy stuck his left leg out and waited on Memphis Mayford to cooperate. They slowly began moving toward the east.

After watching the two men slog along for a few minutes, John and his two men saddled up, making ready to head due south, leaving the two would-be killers alone. But before they turned their horses to begin their trek to the Pipton Ranch, they heard Memphis Mayford emit a sound that sounded curiously like a mixture between a groan and grunt. That noise was followed by a flatulent blast corresponding to the key of F on a tuba. That particular weird sound was quickly followed by Utah Jimmy Pruett delivering a stentorian dog cussing to his fellow gunman.

CHAPTER 4

About seven miles inside the Guadalupe Mountains lay the headquarters of the notorious Comancheros. This nefarious group of outlaws specialized in selling rifles, ammunition, and liquor to the marauding bands of Comanche and Kiowas, who still had not knuckled under to the federal government.

But they also had bands of specialist who majored in various criminal activities: rustling (both cattle and horses), bank robberies, and white slavery (captured white men were sold to Mexican silver mines to work underground until their death; women of all races and ages were sold to Mexicans to work in the bordellos until they died of heartbreak or disease). They would burn down defiant towns who resisted the wholesale looting. These expert arsonists were accompanied by hired killers who took on any local law officials and eradicated any vestige of resistance.

The Comancheros originally had been a Mexican organization, but funded by the money and the sheer numbers of former soldiers loyal to former Brigadier General Frank McGrew, the original group had been ousted and reduced to working for new leadership in secondary roles. Fueled by military discipline and strong leadership and the fact that they were being ignored by Texas's Reconstruction government, they were flourishing financially, making unheard amounts of money.

This small hamlet of thieves had no name but was run by strict rules. Any Comanchero who killed another comrade without proper cause forfeited his own life. If a Comanchero cheated his brethren at cards, he was immediately executed. There were exceptions, one of which was if a Comanchero was called out by one his mates and one was killed in the altercation, the ruling cadre would call this fair and overlook the matter. There was not a lot of sentiment about the deceased; they were no longer necessary and were unceremoniously fed to the pigs, perhaps mourned briefly and forgotten forever.

The small village included a bank, hotel, saloon, medical clinic, livery barn, and cattle pens where purloined livestock were kept until they could get their price from eager buyers from New Mexico Territory.

The buildings were all on one side of a caramel-colored road. It was designed this way for security reasons. They did not want to contend with snooping lawmen using another line of buildings as a blind.

Upon arriving, approved visitors first saw one large warehouse as they entered the small town and one equally imposing warehouse as he exited. One of these repositories contained weapons and ammunition (including Gatlin guns); the other housed a whiskey still and brewery, with boxes of bottled liquor in storage.

This lawless setup was ignored by the state government because the top echelon of the corrupt government were receiving monetary benefits from the Comancheros. Sheriff Lee and the acting governor were receiving one thousand dollars each month in secret but secure bank accounts.

The newspapers were emphasizing the wrongs committed by the former Confederates who had led Texas astray; they went out of their way to ignore the Comancheros, with little or no mention of how this deadly organization raped and pillaged West Texas.

Most Texas citizens were cognizant of the hypocrisy and double standard of justice but couldn't act on their righteous anger. Sheriff Lee was fast to squelch any discontent in the general public. His punitive actions were always lauded by the state-approved newspapers, who continued to hammer home the theme that those still in rebellion were no better than those who pushed for secession in the early 1860s.

By using the shield of righteousness of cleansing the state of former secessionists, the government in Austin had managed to ignore the gorilla in the room in dealing with the Comancheros.

The Comancheros tried to stay apart from the wheeling and dealings of Sheriff Lee, but unfortunately, the corrupt sheriff and his Austin mob sometimes sought help in some irritating matter that was beyond the sheriff's control. One of the latest demands asked them to help get rid of

John Lee Johnson. The Austin crowd insisted that the Comancheros assist them in the matter of John Lee Johnson's death, and that command came from the number one source, former Brigadier General Frank McGrew.

The leader of the Comancheros was a large man named Pugh Larrimore. His florid face was covered in heavy acne scars. His green eyes were an unusual tint but those strange inquiring eyes were usually shaded by the severe, black, dipped hat-brim he sported. Pugh was the second leader of the new Comancheros. He had succeeded Colonel Walter Stafford, who had been an aggressive leader but given to angry impulses, which resulted in unwise decisions. His lack of self-control resulted in his capture by local marshals, and he was executed in Fort Smith, Arkansas.

Pugh was much craftier than his predecessor; unlike the impulsive colonel, he knew how to play the system. He knew when to act and when to play dumb. When those messages came from the Austin bunch, asking for help against John Lee Johnson, he usually found an excuse to ignore them. He reasoned that it would end in Johnson's favor, and he would lose time and money in the process. Those previous run-ins with John Lee Johnson had always resulted in a disaster for him and his men. Larrimore thought if he never saw John Lee Johnson again, he would be a happier man; he chose to let the powerful rancher enjoy domesticity far from him and his south Texas marauders.

Much to his chagrin, however, this particular John Lee Johnson matter had been squarely placed in his lap, with no escape or ignoring. The Austin crowd had informed him that he was to accommodate the California gunman, Mike Jones. Larrimore knew why he was there—to help the most famous gunfighter from Mexico kill John Lee Johnson.

Pugh, who had met Mike Jones and even respected the handsome gunfighter, still resented his being there. He was polite to Jones, but it was a cold politeness. He didn't like any strategy that brought the death-dealing John Lee Johnson near his lair.

At the present time, Pugh was sitting in his office, talking to a disgruntled Robert "Guerrero" Moniehan.

Pugh looked across his desk at the greasy Moniehan, who sat scowling back. Even though Moniehan was not Mexican, he dressed like he was. Moniehan had explained his guise before. Upon leaving the Comancheros, the law would be seeking a Mexican, whereupon he could assume his Anglo name and be able to hide more effectively.

Moniehan wore a dirty sombrero that shadowed his angry yellowish eyes. He inhaled a frustrated suck of wind. He exhaled in the same exasperation.

Larrimore knew why he was there. Nothing of consequence happened in their community without his knowing it. Pugh knew Moniehan resented Mike Jones, the clean-cut California gunman. He knew that Moniehan begrudged the fact that he was working long hours and was involved in a lot of dangerous, dirty work that required traveling long distances, enduring extreme weather conditions. These jeopardizing adventures were usually fraught with many dangerous escapades of being shot at, followed up by narrow escapes.

Pugh understood all too well why some of his men might take umbrage after undergoing unending perils, accompanied with inclement weather and long rides to arrive and find a man enjoying the fruits of their work without turning a tap.

Pugh reasoned that Guerrero could not help but enter the saloon to see the well-dressed Jones, drinking free drinks, eating free food, and playing poker and living a quiet, danger-free life. Pugh had never told the rank-and-file Comancheros why Jones was there. He figured all the waves made by the Californian would dissipate soon when he departed to the Valley of the Sun.

Guerrero leaned forward and said, "I want your permission to kill Mike Jones."

Larrimore did not immediately respond but instead steepled his hands in thought. Before he answered, he let several factors enter his mind. He knew Jones was cleaning house, so to speak, playing poker against the other Comancheros. He knew he was not cheating; he was just good. But he understood Guerrero's position. Here was this impeccably dressed stranger, taking the roughshod outlaws for a ride. He was winning time after time, and it was legitimate. He pocketed their money that had required arduous effort, but that same hard-earned money slid effortlessly into Jones's coat pocket. Larrimore had surreptitiously steered Guerrero's thinking in that direction since he had heard the Comanchero wrangler had a bone to pick. But he had to act as if he were merely a disinterested party.

Pugh also kept in mind that if Guerrero did kill Jones, he would be off the hook to send someone to help Marco Cio. He could use Jones's death as an excuse to stay clear of John Lee Johnson. Of all the men on the planet, he feared John Lee Johnson the most.

Pugh's eyes had been slanted upwards while various scenarios played through his brain; he now lowered his vision so that his eyes locked with the waspish-looking stare coming back at him. "Guerrero, you do know he is the number one gunman from California, don't you?"

Guerrero let a sarcastic smile slide across his oleaginous features. "California," he uttered sarcastically, as though he were talking about a county in Rhode Island. Then he released his pent-up venom. "I work my ass off; he comes in and takes my money." He shrugged indifferently and added, "He never says nothing; it's just that look that he's too good for us, above us." Guerrero let loose a broad, nicotine-stained smile. "I beg you, Pugh, let me have a chance at his fancy ass."

Pugh knew Guerrero was damn good with a hogleg. In fact, he was considered the number one gunman currently working for him. He figured that even if Jones nailed Guerrero, Jones would never suspect that the head of the Comancheros had any hand in the matter. He knew it was damned necessary that nothing negative was passed on to General McGrew. And if Guerrero won, Pugh could excuse himself and his men by saying that Jones was overrated to the Austin crowd. That would leave Marco Cio, the Basque gunfighter, going at it alone against Johnson, granting Larrimore and his men a reprieve from dealing with that big devil from Baileysboro.

Mike Jones, all six feet two of him, was seated at table near the bar. At thirty-eight, he still had a handsome, clean-shaven face. He had hazel eyes, tawny-colored hair, and a quick dimple when he smiled. He was dressed as usual, wearing a brown suitcoat, replete with a short-brimmed California-style hat. He had situated himself facing the batwings of the boxy saloon.

Around three o'clock that morning, he heard from his hotel room the rumbling of a stolen cattle herd moving down the drag. He figured Guerrero had been in the bunch that had driven the purloined herd to the cattle pen outside of town. He knew the prickly bastard eventually would be looking for him, and he was ready for him. Jones had heard of Guerrero's intentions weeks ago and knew he'd come calling today.

Jones never enjoyed killing anyone, but on the other hand, he did not spend a lot of time worrying about it when he did shoot some piece of garbage.

Jones had tried like hell to get along and not ruffle any feathers in his courtesy stay in the outlaw community. He never initiated a conversation with any of these men and always answered someone's comments with civility. He was polite and never tried to act superior to them, even though they were the scum of the earth.

The run-of-the-mill ilk of the Comancheros were not only dirty and covered in grime; they all had serious character issues. Most were misfits and sociopaths, but regardless of their social or mental profile, the rank and file shared one universal characteristic: dog cussing.

This trait set them apart as much as their filthy appearance. They enjoyed spewing out the vilest profanity the human mind was capable of imagining. When two or more gathered, it seemed as it were a contest who could out-cuss the other with the most vitriolic and vile words that only a conscience-free man could speak. Nothing was sacred, whether it be God Almighty or someone's mother. In his short stay at the Comanchero headquarters, Jones had heard some of the most debasing verbal sewage he had ever heard. He was well acquainted with the wharf hands back in San Francisco, but they were amateurs compared to these subhumans he saw on a regular basis.

Jones took note that besides the senseless cussing, these cretins possessed another noteworthy peculiarity: their warped sense of humor. They rarely laughed, but when they did show any levity, it was due to either telling or listening to some debasing story of killing, torture, or rape and mimicking the expressions on the faces of the defiled victims; those stories usually were followed by deep, gravelly, animalistic laughter.

Jones knew that if Darwin, the English naturalist, were present, after scientifically observing these vermin for just a brief period of time, he'd have filled tomes with lengthy documentation, fortified by unending examples. Jones figured Darwin would have changed his thesis; his new conclusion would have been that apes evolved from humans.

It was not only their incessant cussing and animalistic sense of humor that set them apart. Mike had met some pretty rough characters in his time, but they had the good sense to take a bath. The Comancheros not only were dirty and oily in appearance but seemingly took pride in it. Jones knew without a doubt that he was in the epicenter of body odor, gas, and halitosis. He thought to himself if he ever doubted the reality of hell, he was wrong. It was here in the Guadalupe Mountains.

Jones glanced up at Paulie, the short fat man behind the bar, serving as the bartender. He had a horseshoe hairstyle with oily perspiration moving down his forehead. It was obvious that even he knew Guerrero was on the prod. He kept pulling out his watch and nervously checking the time.

Jones also had more than a strong suspicion that Pugh Larrimore knew more about Guerrero's unreasonable hatred toward him than he let on.

From what Pugh said in the short conversations they had, Jones was not optimistic about the impending gunfight in the Valley of the Sun. He felt the outlaw chieftain had subtly encouraged Guerrero to brace him but all the while making it as though it were Guerrero's idea. That way, according to Mike's line of thinking, Larrimore would be free and clear, regardless of the results. If he won, it would validate to these animals that Jones was legit, and they would quit acting as he were sponging off them. On the other hand, if Guerrero won, the Comancheros would celebrate not having to support what they considered a freeloader. Jones reasoned that Larrimore would come out smelling like a rose either way.

As Jones mulled over this and other troubling factors that were plaguing him, the batwings opened slowly. Larrimore entered, his green eyes zeroing in on the California gunfighter. He walked to his table and, without asking, noisily pulled back a chair and sat down. His eyes went to the side profile of Jones, whose focus was on the batwings.

There was an interminable silent pause before Pugh spoke. With an edge to his voice, he said, "You seem like you're waitin' on someone."

Jones shot him a sideways look. He had no time for annoying word games. He ignored the question as he sipped on a beer.

Pugh could see he would have to redirect the conversation. Knowing that Jones knew that Guerrero was on his way, he shrugged and said, "I tried to talk him outta it."

Jones gave the Comanchero leader a blank look that conveyed that he didn't want to engage in senseless conversation. But at last Jones spoke, saying, "I didn't ask to come here." Turning his full vision back to the batwings, he continued, "I was told to come here."

Pugh nodded at his words and asked Paulie for a beer. Waiting on the beer, Pugh replied, "He's good; that is, Guerrero's good. Just wanted you to know."

Jones gave a slight nod that he had heard. "I ain't too bad, either."

Even though Pugh could see that Jones wasn't interested in talking, he accepted his beer from the seedy bartender and continued, "I have another piece of information that I came by last night."

Jones turned again to give a partial look of inquiry.

Pugh took a heavy swig of brew from his schooner. "Macro Cio sent word for you not to show up."

Jones gave a tight smile. "To hell with Macro Cio. I was paid to do a job." He continued to gaze at the batwings. "I'll be there."

Pugh dropped his head in thought. He figured that if Jones did not want to play verbal games, neither did he. He candidly stated, "Johnson will kill both of you."

Jones gave a nod; it was not a nod of agreement but merely that he had heard the words.

Pugh continued, even though it had become more of a one-sided conversation, "I've had dealin's with John Lee Johnson, first in Arkansas and later in Tennessee—and lately here in Texas." He gulped as he emptied his beer schooner. "They ain't a man alive, here, there, Russia that can top him." Pugh belched and concluded, "You may or may not kill Guerrero, but if you come out on top, if I was you, I'd leave this damn place and get as far away as you can from John Lee Johnson."

Jones, shrugged avoiding a response, knowing that his real enemy was Macro Cio.

Jones saw a shadow elongating on the uneven boardwalk beneath the batwings. He knew it was Guerrero. Mike instinctively stood and pushed back the lapel of his coat. Pugh Larrimore, seeing this action, got out of his chair and moved to his left, deeper into the shadows of the saloon.

The grungy bandit slowly opened both of the dual batwings. He let them swing idly behind him and stepped dramatically into the room. His eyes moved side to side, expecting more people to witness his bravado. There was no audience except Paulie and Pugh.

His eyes then settled on Mike Jones. When their eyes met, Guerrero let a cocksure smile move across his greasy features. Seeing that Jones was standing and ready for him, Guerrero extended a warning finger toward the Californian and said, "I aim to send your candy ass to hell, pretty boy." He paused to grace the small audience with a yellow-toothed smile. "Now if you decide you want to live, just pull out three hundred dollars of my money and place it on the table next to you, then I just might consider lettin' you live."

Getting no response from the poker-faced gunfighter, Guerrero asked, "Cat got your tongue, fancy man? Any last words?"

Jones disinterestedly responded, "No, I don't speak chimpanzee."

Guerrero's eyebrows beetled as he thought on Jones's words. He didn't know the meaning of the statement but knew it was pejorative in nature.

Guerrero went for his gun with the best draw of his thirty-year life, but Jones had a liquid-smooth pull that was light-years ahead of the Comanchero. Guerrero took the shot in his chest and went stumbling rearwards. He tumbled backwards through the batwings, with his body falling supine on the crooked boardwalk and his head lolling on the ground of the street in a grotesque death scene. His upside-down sombrero lay to the side of his head.

Pugh, who had witnessed this electric-fast draw, knew for a fact that Jones was the real deal. Before he could reach Jones to congratulate him, four alarmed Comancheros rushed into the saloon. They looked down at the dead Guerrero. Through the open batwings, the Comancheros took turns glancing down and then up and over toward Jones, who was still holding his .44. Instead of being upset or angry at the loss of their comrade, they sent toothy, admiring smiles toward Jones.

The four men, now ignoring Jones, Pugh, and Paulie, bent over and began searching through Guerrero's pockets and pulling at his clothes like a pack of jackals. It was not long before the dead Comanchero was down to his heavily stained drawers. One of the nondescript men asked another if he wanted Guerrero's underwear; the one asked responded, "No, I got a pair just like 'em."

After they fleeced the body of money, weapons, boots, and clothing, one of the men asked Pugh what he wanted done with the body. Pugh gave a toss of his head, indicating that they carry the corpse to the hog lot and feed him to the pigs. They quickly did as they were told and departed with the dangling body.

Jones, still standing, was not at all surprised at the calloused attitude. If anything, he was surprised they did not take his drawers.

Pugh shrugged as though Guerrero's death was of no consequence, and Paulie, who was eating a sausage and biscuit sandwich, laid it aside after realizing where Guerrero would end up.

Pugh walked up to Jones, who had holstered his weapon, and said, "You earned some respect today." When Jones did not respond, Pugh added, "You will see a change in attitude from the men from now on."

With other things on his mind, Pugh then abruptly left the saloon and headed to his office in the bank.

For the next thirty minutes, Jones sat in the saloon, dwelling on his condition. The problem was not the matter of killing Guerrero; it was his heart. He had known for over a year that he had an irregular heartbeat. His personal physician in San Francisco had given him a concoction made from the Greek *aspirini* plant. He had assumed that a doctor-patient consultation was confidential but later he found out, much to his chagrin, that was not the case. It seemed that his secret was not just his secret.

Regardless, he had a two-year's supply in his possession, the bulk of it hidden in his hotel room, the rest in his coat; he obsessively checked on his hidden supply daily to make sure some snoopy Comanchero did not think it was opium and steal it by mistake. Those small tablets were his only chance to hang onto life. If he had a bad spell, his irregular heartbeat could cause a stroke. He knew his fate would be very similar to Guerrero's if he were helpless and left to the mercy of this pack of wolves.

He had been warned not to ride horseback or drink excessively. He had been escorted to the Comanchero camp in a luxurious buggy, along with a retinue of Jim Pemberton's men guarding him and making sure he made it safely. After Pemberton had a brief powwow with Pugh Larrimore and was convinced he would be given good treatment, he bid farewell to Jones and departed to find Johnson, hoping to kill him ahead of time, thus saving a hundred thousand dollars in the process. At least that was the story he hoped the Comancheros bought. Pemberton and his group departed north, hoping to find Johnson and inform him that his life was in danger.

As Jones nursed his beer, he narrowed his eyes and began a slow kaleidoscopic memory walk of his life. He drifted back into time. He was eighteen years old when he first faced a man who was a known killer.

His father owned a large ranchero near San Diego. He was having trouble with another old-time rancher, Don Vega. The crooked Vega, using an outdated Spanish grant document already ruled as spurious by a local judge, was claiming the vital water rights to the Jones's property.

This rancher ignored the judge's ruling and sealed off the stream before it reached Jones's property. In a matter of weeks, Jones's father could not water his cattle and was beginning to suffer financially. Even if the law was on his side, the local officials were intimidated by Vega and were dragging out legal action as long as possible.

Vega had a gunman named Palencio. Palencio was always well-dressed, as though he were rich himself. He frequently rode with the Vega vaqueros as they formed a line, preventing the Jones cowhands from utilizing their own creek.

Palencio had a reputation fueled by the fact that he had killed ten men. He would scowl at the Jones cowhands as they rode close. He would belligerently ride through his gathered comrades and confront the Jones crew, challenging them to take him on.

Mike Jones was known as a prodigy with a pistol, but his father had continually held him back from confronting Palencio. After Mike heard the latest affront to his father's men, he surreptitiously gathered the men and told them to follow him back to the creek.

Palencio watched with his usual sneer as the young Jones rode up, heading a small group. He had heard the cub had some teeth and could fight, but Palencio did not buy it. He smiled to himself and thought it would be good for his reputation to kill this young pup (or at least humiliate him).

In the past, when the two groups had a confrontation, the Jones group would normally stay a hundred feet away from the Vega faction, and they would jaw some back and forth, with the Jones ranch hands eventually retreating. This time, however, they did not.

Mike Jones rode up within ten feet of Palencio and dismounted quickly. He had both anger and adrenaline flowing through him.

Palencio, hoping to make a show for Vega's vaqueros, dismounted slowly, dramatically, as though he were acting in a play. He gave the reins of his horse to a nearby hand and pushed back the tails of his long coat, exposing his ornate gun belt, with a shiny Colt ensconced in his holster.

He gave young Jones a patronizing look and told him he could still turn tail and save his skin.

Young Mike replied that he was there for business and Palencio could save his own skin by backing down.

Palencio, angered by this insolence, immediately went for his revolver, but he was too slow. Jones shot him not once but three times before he hit the ground.

The shocked Vega group, now cowered by this unexpected action, slowly retreated; the rapid draw and quick, violent disposal of Palencio was devastating to their spirit. That slow retreat became a faster one as they deserted the scene, leaving the creek back in Jones's hands.

A week later, the local court again ruled in Jones Sr.'s favor, and Vega not only stopped trespassing on the contested property, he sold his holdings to Jones Sr. Vega took his money, relocated to Mexico, and was not heard of again.

Jones's second gunfight was a year later. He had been content to be his father's foreman, working five or six days a week on the ranchero. But killing the feared Palencio changed those dynamics. Word of the killing spread rapidly, and Jones became a man of note. Within a month, he realized his life had changed forever. He received all sorts of messages and letters from people asking for his gunfighting favors. He spurned them all, but then three sheriffs from Northern California arrived at his father's house.

They explained that a businessman named Solomon was using a man known as Dugger to intimidate a large mining area around Sacramento. Solomon was in fact legally claim-jumping, and the law was basically helpless in the matter.

Solomon worked the same technique over and over: He would make an offer on a claim, and if it was rejected, suddenly bad things began to happen to the miner: fires and unexplained accidents and mysterious disappearances of faithful allies or employees. When the offended man realized he was being strong-armed and had no recourse except violence, it was then the gunfighter Dugger would appear.

Dugger would approach the angry miner and exacerbate the situation with cleverly chosen words that would force him to choose between fighting or cowardice. Dugger would then kill the miner, leaving the estate up for grabs. Solomon, with oily words and legal wiles, would eventually take over the claim and then move on to the next victim, utilizing the same scheme.

However, his latest target owned only half of the mine; the San Francisco Bank and Trust owned the other half. Unbeknownst to the oily Solomon, the bank, now fully cognizant of this scam, reached out to the sheriffs of three counties. The sheriffs had been investigating Solomon for a while but had found no legal reason to arrest him. Since the law was officially handcuffed from taking action, one of the sheriffs recommended that the bank hire a man named Mike Jones to play the intimidator role Dugger had been performing. In plain parlance, to fight fire with fire.

The three sheriffs arrived at his father's ranch, explained the situation, and offered Jones five thousand dollars up-front to rid the earth of Dugger. Jones weighed the situation and decided it was the right moral decision. He accepted the offer and within a week departed for the mining camp near Sacramento.

On an early foggy morning, he rode into the settlement. Dugger had been alerted by all sorts of verbal leaks about Mike Jones but did not take him seriously, nor was he expecting him this soon.

Dugger was a large, ruddy-looking man. He had a flushed face and protruding belly, barely covered by his button shirt. Misshapen or not, he was known far and wide for his gun skills. That particular day, he stood in the shade on the porch of the mining town's saloon, sleepily shaking off his debauchery from the previous night.

Jones scouted around the small town before making his entrance; he didn't want to be surprised by a hidden gunman. Seeing nothing to warrant that concern, he rode deeper into the hamlet and dismounted a hundred feet from the saloon. After catching sight of the man who had been described to him, he tied off his chestnut mare and began walking purposely toward the gunman.

Dugger, who had not expected Jones to arrive this early, was not looking in his direction, but when he glanced toward the approaching tall Jones, did a double-take. He knew immediately that he was about to be challenged. Dugger turned toward the oncoming Jones, pointed a finger of warning toward him, and said, "Just ride outta here and no harm done."

Jones did not reply; he did not want to waste his breath responding to an inane comment with an inane comment. When he was close enough, he pushed his coat tails behind his back, exposing his gun belt and ivory-gripped pistol butts.

Dugger went for his weapon with more speed than Palencio. But Jones was on another level; he killed Dugger with two quick shots that thudded into his stomach, catching his cheap vest on fire. Dugger fell from the porch face-first in the street. Jones did not hang around. He saddled up and headed toward San Francisco.

Solomon's hold on the miners was broken. He realized he could not hire anyone to match the Southern Californian's speed, and he also had caught wind that the San Francisco Bank was backing this play. Discouraged by this turn of events, Solomon sold out his interests and moved quickly eastward before the law came calling.

A few days later in San Francisco, Jones collected the rest of his fee. While he was there, he met James Boykin, the bank president. After an extended conversation, it became obvious to the stolid bank president that Jones had proclivities for banking, and he offered him a job.

The next year, after Jones's father died, Mike, newly married, sold the ranchero and moved to San Francisco. He bought a moderately sized ranch and invested the money from the sale of his father's ranch into bank stock. Another year passed, and he was made a member of the board of the burgeoning San Francisco Bank. With this quick start, he began concentrating on a career that was not based on violence.

But the next year, a situation occurred that thrust him into an unwanted limelight. When it was over with, he had to forget just being a man of finance. He would reach a level of unwanted notoriety that only a few could attain, even if they desired to.

The docks of San Francisco were a rough place in the first place, made worse by Sydney Ducks, immigrants from Australia who were ousted by the Commonwealth police. They soon found easy pickings in San Francisco's shipping yard. They worked the area and soon began utilizing the same sabotage routine they had back in Australia. Although they were ostensibly stevedores and routine dockworkers, they actually were a tight-knit criminal organization. After firmly establishing themselves along the extended wharf front, they soon exposed their true colors. They would destroy a ship's cargo, claiming it was thieves doing it. They demanded the ship owners to pay them a 10 percent surcharge, and they would see to it that the fictitious thieves would be driven away with no more damage to the cargo.

The owners, seeing they were being bilked but not accustomed to this large-scale graft, were initially flummoxed. They could not utilize the police because the crimes were so well planned and in every instance evidence free. Thus, they hired private detectives who tried to blend in with these so-called Sydney Ducks and find the ringleaders. Almost without exception, each undercover man would invariably be found dead, with his throat cut.

Moreover, the Ducks hired a gunfighter named Nicholas "the Greek" Karabatsos to patrol the wooden quay twice a day to intimidate any hired gunman or snoopy lawman threatening their gravy train. The Greek would meet some private detective or police official on the wharf and would eventually kill him, with the Ducks and their cohorts vowing the victim initiated the conflict. The shipowners and the San Francisco police determined that the Greek had to go but did not have a ready plan. Since some of the shippers were facing financial ruin, they felt they had no further recourse; they appealed to their creditors.

After a meeting with the local bank presidents and the police officials, the ship owners asked for the services of Mike Jones. With the backing of the San Francisco police department and some financial guarantees from the San Francisco Trust Bank, Jones agreed to rid the harbor from the looming presence of the Greek.

Jones was twenty-eight at the time. Although working regularly at the bank in the loan department, he continued to hone his shootist skills. Jones, assured that he had the blessings of the law, met with the police chief and county sheriff and together made plans to rid the harbor of the Sydney Ducks.

On a bright June day in 1856, Jones rode his chestnut to the harbor area; he handed his horse to a plainclothes detective and began walking down the expansive harbor walkway to where Nicholas Karabatsos was reportedly located.

Only a trained psychologist could explain how the harbor workers knew trouble was in the air. But when they saw Jones casually walking down the way, they knew he was dangerous. Immediately, there was a buzz of lifted voices.

The Greek was situated at the far end of the lengthy wharf; he sensed almost immediately that he had a challenger. But it was more than just a feeling. There were external factors as well; the word-of-mouth moved quickly down the length of the dock. These warning words were accompanied by alarmed shouts of the alerted dockworkers that caught the Greek's ears. It was obvious to the Greek that some ominous stranger was in their midst. Narrowing his eyes, and in mid-bite of a steak and biscuit, he got up and left the small seaside café. He began walking briskly toward where he felt he would meet his antagonist.

The two men moved inexorably toward each other. When Karabatsos saw the tall Jones in the distance, he knew he had to kill him. He could just sense he was different from the others he had confronted. Jones exuded an aura of dangerous confidence.

Jones, too, knew even before he saw the Greek that the Sydney Duck gunfighter was on another skill level compared to Palencio and Dugger. Now that he could see Karabatsos in the distance, he realized he would have to be at his best. The Greek was young and lean, and he had an eager, predatory mien. He had the overly confident look of someone who never imagined he could lose.

As they got closer, their strides quickened. Neither showed signs of fear or second thoughts. Both knew this deadly showdown would result in death. When within fifty feet, they both instinctively knew this was the needed distance to settle matters.

They simultaneously pulled their guns and fired. Karabatsos's pistol was not yet horizontal when Jones shot caught him in the upper chest. The Greek, appearing stunned that he had been bested, stumbled backwards, reflexively firing his Colt and sending an orange flame tangentially to the side.

The Greek collapsed on his side, losing his hat in the process. Karabatsos's feet pedaled as though he imagined he was walking in his final moments, his brain or ego not accepting his deadly loss.

Jones, seeing his service was completed, holstered and turned away, but not before he saw hundreds of plainclothes police and county deputies rush out from hidden places. Over the next several days, the ringleaders of the Sydney Ducks were arrested and arraigned.

This particular gunfight resulted in Jones receiving even more unwanted fame. The major newspapers along the West Coast lionized his bravery and skill. He became a California celebrity. Although he did not bask in this attention, he did not withdraw into seclusion, either.

For the next few years, his fortunes increased, as he solidified his position on the bank board and was considered a rising financier in the San Francisco area.

But as charmed as his life had been, when he was thirty-seven, his ideal world collapsed into misery, much like Job in the Bible. His wife died of cholera in the spring. Her death broke his heart and knocked him figuratively to his knees. His severe grief was a major catalyst to his arrhythmic heart condition.

That was the first misfortune, followed closely by other severe tests of character. He had purchased a neighboring ranch, emptying his savings and mortgaging his own ranch as collateral. The ranch was well stocked with very expensive English Hereford cattle. If things had gone as planned, he would have tripled his investment, but they didn't. The worst case of hoof-and-mouth disease to ever plague California wiped out the complete herd. Mike was left with an insurmountable debt.

To make things worse, his son's law school tuition was due in a few weeks. But the real problem was that his balloon note, the loan to buy the ranch, was due at the bank. The feeling of being in arrears from all fronts caused his health condition to deteriorate even further.

Mike sighed as he remembered the day he had gone to his office in the bank. He was completely insolvent, finding himself in the nadir of his seemingly charmed life. He had just enough money for a week's rent on a hotel room and limited food, but that was all. He had let himself into the bank early to avoid any awkward meeting with Boykin.

He emptied his desk drawers of all his important papers. He recalled rising from his desk to make his getaway, hoping to avoid any embarrassing interaction with his professional friends. As he reached for a few extraneous items to place into his leather valise, he was caught short when Boykin entered his office.

Mike cringed in embarrassment seeing the staid, by-the-book head man. But to his surprise, Boykin was in a good mood. The bank president overlooked the obvious desk-cleaning process that was taking place. Boykin reached over the expanse and shook Mike's hand, giving a sincere smile and saying, "Congratulations, Mike, you have been reelected to the board for this coming year."

Stunned by this turn of events, Mike did not have an appropriate answer; meanwhile, he kept pumping the energetic banker's hand, wondering what in the hell was going on. He did catch a glimpse of a shorter man standing directly behind the tall, angular president.

When the jovial Boykin left his office, Mike more fully took in the distinguished man who apparently had followed Boykin to his office.

Jim Pemberton introduced himself and then asked if he could sit a spell and talk. Mike, still extremely puzzled by the turn of events, nodded his assent and settled back into his own chair, still trying to piece together what had just taken place.

He instinctively knew that Pemberton held the key to the morning's serendipity. His eyes locked with Pemberton's, but it was more amicable than adversarial. Pemberton slowly sat back in the leather visitor's chair. He reached downwards to grab his own valise and pulled out a dossier of legal papers.

Jones watched him curiously, still trying to piece together what the hell was happening.

Pemberton casually placed one document at a time on Mike's desk. After the important documents and papers were arranged in a neat pile on Jones's desk, Pemberton spoke in a calm but businesslike voice. "Your own ranch and the ranch you purchased have all been paid for." He let a soft smile crease his face and added, "Here are the deeds in your name."

Pemberton pulled a cigar from his coat and offered one to Jones, who quickly nixed it with a negative motion of his index finger.

Pemberton took his time lighting his long-nine cigar. After taking a few puffs, he continued, "Your son's tuition is taken care of until his graduation ... plus living expenses for a year afterwards."

Mike's eyes narrowed, not so much in suspicion as still trying to solve this conundrum of unexpected good fortune.

Pemberton added almost nonchalantly, "You now have thirty thousand dollars in your bank account ... more than enough to keep you on the board."

Still Mike remained silent. He realized that a lot of his problems were now solved, but he knew there had to be a quid pro quo that was currently unspoken but was definitely understood.

Pemberton went on to inform Jones that his heart doctor had been paid a year in advance and his boss had a two-year supply of heart medicine waiting for him at her office.

Although he felt irked at the breach of doctor-patient confidentiality, Jones let it pass, considering all the gifts that were fortuitously stacked on his desk.

Pemberton folded his arms and then remained silent for a few seconds. He intended for Jones to digest all that had just transpired. A faint smile began forming on Pemberton's face as he anticipated Jones's questions.

Receiving a blank look on Jones's face but reading the young man's mind, Pemberton continued, "You're asking yourself if there's a catch to this." The short man's smile broadened as he answered, "Of course there is a catch."

Jones's eyes narrowed as leaned forward. It was becoming clearer. "You want to hire my gun?" The tone of the question was not accusatory but on the order of a sudden realization.

Pemberton did not respond to the question. He knocked the ashes off his long-nine cigar and canted his head in the direction of the bank entrance. "There is a hansom outside to take you to the boss."

Jones tilted his head. He recalled hearing the pronoun "her" earlier. He echoed, "The boss?"

Pemberton gave a small nod. "Marilla Urmacher."

Jones sat transfixed. He had heard of the reclusive, beautiful millionaire for two years. He knew she was the second-highest stockholder in the Central Pacific Railroad. He was aware that she owned a shipping line and a chain of hotels and banks that ran from California to Oregon Territory.

Mike knew that Marilla was the subject of many murmured conversations in saloons and fashionable bistros. Those secretive whispers were filled with tales of her mysterious beauty and her riches.

Remembering Pemberton's mention of the hansom, Jones rose, placed his no-longer-needed valise on his desk, and sent a positive nod of thanks toward Pemberton. With his head held high but in an anxious mood, he left Marilla's agent and his office behind.

After exiting the bank, he found a slick, well-upholstered hansom waiting for him. It was pulled by a horse bedecked with an ornate, expensive harness. Behind the cab, the driver was dressed in English-style clothing, wearing Wellington boots. The driver, standing ramrod straight behind the cab, looked down at Jones and gave a courteous nod, indicating that it was time to depart. Jones returned an acknowledging nod and climbed in. With a slight lurch, they departed.

Mike remembered the ride. The twenty-minute excursion took him through the richest part of town. The hansom stopped in front of a large, granite stone wall divided only by an expansive metal gate. From his vantage point, he could see only the roofline of a gigantic house that loomed above the trees, beyond the walled fence.

The gates creaked open with the sound of groaning metal. The young gunman could see two men from the picturesque guard house off to his right, working the levers. As the hansom made a quick right into the cobblestone driveway, the hidden house began to materialize. The architecture was English gothic style.

When the cab came to a halt, Jones took it on his own to disembark. He stood looking up at the mansion's three stories until two men wearing similar uniforms as the driver appeared in the large doorway of the mansion; they walked out to the top of the broad sandstone steps.

The two men cordially called him by name and beckoned him to walk up toward them.

After Jones completed the short walk upwards, they led him through the double-door entrance into a foyer that would have made royalty proud.

Jones realized the owner of this habitat had more money than Croesus. He removed his hat and looked around at the elegant Queen Anne furniture and dark teakwood paneling on the walls. As he turned to comment to the two men who had escorted him in, he found they had mysteriously disappeared. Jones swiveled his head, trying to locate where they gone, but in doing so had seen out of the corner of his eye an attractive young woman in a flowing yellow dress appear from seemingly nowhere. She had a coppery complexion with pulled-back black hair that ran down her back.

At first, he thought it might be Marilla Urmacher herself, but upon seeing that she was carrying a notepad, he deduced she was a secretary of sorts. She gave him a soft smile and asked in an accented voice if he would follow her. But before she took a step, she introduced herself as Yellow Bird.

He returned his name and watched as she swirled as if in a hurry and just started walking.

With his hat in his hand, he followed her through one door after another; they walked through room after room lavishly furnished and fastidiously clean.

Still on the first floor, Yellow Bird led Mike Jones to a large, imposing door that obviously led to the headquarters of this opulent house. She rapped three times on the dark wood exterior and paused for a few seconds, giving the person inside time to compose herself. She then opened the door and stood aside, using her free hand to bade him enter.

Jones, with his head still turned to look at Yellow Bird, walked into the spacious room. He did not at first catch sight of the woman behind the heavy teakwood desk. But when he did, he caught his breath. He realized that he was looking at Marilla Urmacher. His throat tightened. Sitting just ten feet from where he was standing was the most beautiful woman he had ever seen.

Jones, who took pride in knowing public etiquette, realized that staring was definitely inappropriate. But he found he could not draw his eyes away from this Homerically beautiful woman. He could see she had an ineffable elegance that was beyond anything he could possibly imagine.

She looked like the personification of some Mediterranean pagan goddess. Oceans of raven-black hair with different shades of ebony framed her flawless face. Her olive skin was like delicate china. But it was her eyes that mesmerized him. Her iris and pupil seemed as one entity. He noticed those beautifully shaped orbs did not flicker or flitter, as most people's eyes. Her eyes eased slowly from side to side, much like a pearl floating in olive oil.

Her red lips were pouty and heart shaped. Her teeth were almost unnaturally white. Jones just knew people who looked like her should never grow old or die. They were God's gift to humankind.

He tried to gauge her height by observing how regally she sat in her leatherback chair. Not only did she look tall, she looked athletic and shapely. The flowing black-satin outfit could not disguise her accentuated figure.

Jones knew she was one magnificent human being, and seeing her in person surpassed any aesthetic experience he had ever had. He just hoped to keep his wits and not make a fool of himself.

Although she did not meet his eyes, she motioned with her elegant hand for him to sit.

He nodded, embarrassed, realizing that he should have sat earlier. He took a deep breath and sat down, with his eyes looking downward at his boots. He knew he had to regain some equilibrium. He held his hat in his hand to the side, all the while making a promise to himself not to stare at her. But when he looked up, he knew that promise quickly went out the window. He could not take his eyes off this ninth wonder of the world.

Her voice was warmly modulated, hypnotic. She did not waste time by greeting him. There were no formal introductions. She began the conversation in a businesslike manner.

She laid out who was who in her story, from John Lee Johnson to the venal Brigadier General Frank McGrew. The gist of the message was that John Lee Johnson, a former enemy, was now very important to her and must be protected from Macro Cio at all costs.

Jones assumed correctly that he was the "at all costs." He also concluded that she was in love with the Texas rancher; she did not expressly say that, but what emotion she did show was telling. When she said his name, her eyes would suddenly take on an inner glow.

In the final minutes of their conversation, she never asked him if he would accept the job. It was assumed from the beginning it was a fait accompli.

She suddenly stood up and asked Jones to remove his coat. She informed him that it would be returned to him in the morning, but that the jacket would have to have some alterations to accommodate some of his heart medicine that would be placed inside an inner pocket. Before he removed his coat, she held up an envelope that had the name "John Lee Johnson" written in an elegant script.

"After you kill Macro Cio, your last duty is to give this letter to this man," she said, adding that the letter would be inside his jacket. She pointed at a small box at the edge of her desk. "That is the rest of your medicine for you to take with you now."

She paused, and her mesmerizing eyes slowly moved left and right. Her voice and the message stayed with Jones for months as she said, "You must not fail me. You will not fail me; you are California's finest." Following that trenchant statement, she lowered her voice and added, "Now go and be ready to leave tomorrow at 6:30."

CHAPTER 5

It was a hot midday sun that sat high in the Texas sky. Beneath those orange rays, three men rode inexorably south. John Lee Johnson led the way. He was in no hurry. Both Hobie and Van Edwards knew there had to be a reason he was taking his time. Usually, the big man went at breakneck speed, but not for the last few days. The two followers wanted to inquire about the dallying pace but didn't have the temerity to ask.

They trotted and walked their horses until sundown and made camp near a gulch. Pitching camp out in the open with the campfire beaming out into the night seemed carelessly, uncharacteristic of the big man. But he did just that, and no one asked why. They just assumed that, like always, he knew what he was doing.

Hobie's view of John Lee Johnson was colored by hero worship, but he knew he was a practical man. He did things logically and with a lot of forethought. He rarely if ever expressed why he was doing certain things, but whether explained or not, they usually turned out the way he planned.

Hobie had heard a lot of men—men he considered wise—say, "All things happen for a reason." It seemed no one ever questioned that remark. People usually said that after some unexplained calamity or inexplicable disaster to give the speaker and listener the idea that it was part of an unknown but divine providence that was beyond what mortals could comprehend.

But since being with John Lee Johnson, Hobie concluded that Johnson did not subscribe to this idea. After a careful and thoughtful analysis of the strange man came to the conclusion that Johnson believed there was a reason why things happened. He was also likely to hold the view that accidents don't just happen; they are caused.

Around one o'clock in the morning, Hobie heard the sound of approaching horses. He grasped his newly acquired seven-shot Spencer, taken from Utah Jimmy, lying beside him. As he threw back his canvas cover to meet the intruder, out of the darkness, he heard Johnson's voice, calmly admonishing him to put away his rifle and just wait.

Five minutes later, Homer Timms arrived on his big sorrel, pulling a packhorse laden with supplies. Homer's weary nod of greeting could be seen by the dying campfire rays as he dismounted and looked over the three gathered men. The realization of why they had been lax in their travel speed now became obvious.

Van Edwards questioned the gunman about leaving the honeymoon bed.

Homer gave a tired smile and answered, "We've been honeymooning now for five years. I reckon I can take a break."

His comment was met with a few knowing smiles but ended in a weary silence. All three men unloaded the packhorse, and Hobie watered and fed the mounts. Hobie and Van Edwards gave a knowing smile to each other as they made ready to go to their bedrolls. They went to their sleep sacks, thinking the pace to the Pipton Ranch would be considerably faster on the morrow. They were wrong. Once again, Johnson kept the same leisurely speed. Only he and Homer knew why.

The Pipton Ranch, located twenty miles due south of the Johnson campsite, was filled with men, a lot of armed men. Henry Haggard and his band of wily outlaws were holding a joint drinking party with Tim Slater and his own ignoble crew. The outlier outlaw gang had been invited to entice them into attacking John Lee Johnson's advancing party.

Slater was deeply shaken a few days earlier when his spy, Cut Worm Weaver, told him that both Memphis Mayford and Utah Jimmy Pruett had been captured.

Cut Worm Weaver, Slater's weasel-looking spy, had been spotted by John Lee Johnson during the beginning stages of Homer Timms's wedding. Cut Worm, realizing he was caught in the spotlight of John Lee Johnson's vision, quickly departed the saloon but later found refuge in an alley. Not a half-hour later, still hiding in the narrow space between two buildings, Cut

Worm peeked his beady eyes around the edge of a building and caught the incredible sight of Memphis Mayford and Utah Jimmy, in their underwear, walking down the warped boardwalk toward the saloon.

Deeply troubled by this turn of events, Cut Worm stayed hidden in the shadows of the alley for another hour or so. He knew it was too early to leave town. Later, when he saw John Lee Johnson depart with his two prisoners in tow, guarded by the big Texan's two armed cohorts, Cut Worm's brain was spinning. Although the big Texan's numbers were few, his traveling party was too well armed and made more ominous by pulling a heavily laden packhorse. It was obvious John Lee Johnson was not going out on a jaunt. Cut Worm concluded with a certainty that this dangerous party would be headed eventually to the Pipton Ranch.

Augmenting his fears, Cut Worm saw Homer Timms exiting the saloon as he was mounting up to leave town. Cut Worm, at that moment, had an epiphany. He caught Homer, though freshly married, looking longingly in the direction his friend had departed earlier. To Cut Worm, this proved that Homer Timms would soon join up with the big death dealer to make a formidable threat to the motley collection at the ranch.

Cut Worm, motivated by fear and adrenaline, knew he had to deliver this information at once to Tim Slater. He yanked his roan's neck around and departed town immediately. As he rushed desperately to Pipton Ranch, it suddenly occurred to him that Shotgun Stevens had been conspicuously absent. Shotgun should have been on the scene but was nowhere to be found. It made logical sense that Shotgun had been killed. When he reached Slater and told him this catastrophic news, it would have to be in confidence or it would frighten the hell out of the remaining gang members.

When Cut Worm arrived at the Pipton Ranch, he ignored his own fatigue and quickly sought out Slater. He pulled Slater aside and revealed privately what he had seen and what he thought would happen. It was as Cut Worm thought; when Slater had been given the information about the capture of his gunmen and the shocking news of Shotgun Stevens's disappearance, the leader tensed tighter than a heavily starched shirt. But to disguise his own fear, Slater brusquely dismissed Cut Worm for the time being. He wanted the harbinger of bad news as far away from himself as possible in order to recoup.

Cut Worm trudged tiredly to his bunk. He was willing to give Slater the benefit of twenty-four hours to come up with a good plan; otherwise, he was going to bail and ride out to God knows where. He wanted no part of that giant he saw in Gandy.

After receiving the disastrous news, Slater took several shallow breaths, trying gather his wits and ignoring his own doubts. For some time, he continued staring into space, his frozen body trying to rein in his fears. He realized he had to counter these negative setbacks. It was as though for the last few days, he had been dealt nothing but deuces and treys. He knew if he did not adjust quickly, it was over for him and his career, not to mention his life. It was at that time he conceived the idea of utilizing the local bandit king, Henry Haggard, and his gang and give himself enough time to plot the death of John Lee Johnson.

The Pipton Ranch itself was a misnomer. It wasn't a working ranch and had never been one. It had large abandoned buildings left over from Confederate General Henry Sibley's march into New Mexico Territory during the late war. And now they were utilized from time to time by buffalo hunters or moving bands of outlaws.

There was a nearby creek that supplied water, but the soil surrounding the creek was too dry and sandy to sustain cattle or sheep. There were no towns or settlements around for miles, and far as anyone knew, the so-called ranch lay on unclaimed ground.

There were five buildings left standing, with doorless doorways and vacant windows. It was a given that the new occupants had to go on a scorpion and rattlesnake hunt before utilizing the buildings as shelters. At the present time, it was the headquarters of Tim Slater and his band of thirty men.

One day later, after the private confab with Cut Worm Weaver, there was a party going on, with fiddle music in the background accompanied by the shouts of drunken men, Tim Slater and Henry Haggard were having a private conference at the edge of the compound.

Henry Haggard was a tall, slender man with a long face with lots of lumps and bumps covering his countenance. A wide brim of a dirty hat shadowed his suspicious, fifty-year-old eyes. Haggard, the local outlaw-gang leader, had the run of three counties. Although given a free pass by Sheriff Lang and receiving some legal leeway in the courts, Haggard still feared the autocratic Texas sheriff. Lang's benign spirit shielded him but could easily change. He also feared the Comancheros, who were stretching further and further into his area of influence.

Haggard tried his dead-level best to stay clear of both powerful entities. Under normal circumstances, he would have ignored Slater's entreaties, but since he knew Slater had the sheriff's ear, he showed up with his whole gang. He knew he was going to be asked to perform a service, and he also knew he probably would not like the assigned job. But he knew he and his gang would receive some money, money he needed badly. That fact alone made the yet-unknown service more palatable.

Slater, who had been making small talk, finally got down to the subject at hand. "Henry, I got three, maybe four men dogging me and headed this way. I would like you to take care of that problem for me."

Henry, at first, did not speak. He gave Slater an inquisitive look that suggested he wanted to hear more. Haggard knew that Slater had enough men to do the job himself. Henry thoughtfully scratched his jaw and did not immediately respond.

Slater, seeing he had to sell this job, continued, "It is worth a thousand dollars to you ... up front." He saw Haggard's eyes light up with that comment, and he continued, "When you dispose of the problem, I will give you another thousand dollars."

Slater, seeing that Henry seemed more amenable to the task now, continued with a lie he hoped Haggard bought: "Henry, the reason I'm farming this out to you is because I got bigger fish to fry."

Seeing he was on a roll and noting Haggard's agreeable look, Slater continued laying it on thickly: "Since you're in the neighborhood and on good terms with Sheriff Lang, I decided to turn over this problem to you."

Slater sighed as he looked out over the yellow, barren horizon.

As though an incidental fact had just come to him, he admitted, "Now one thing, Henry: Homer Timms, the gunman, is one of them coming after me." For the time being, he left John Lee Johnson's name out of the mix. He had an idea that Haggard had never heard of the deadly West Texas gunman in the first place, and secondly, it would be counterproductive to explain who the big man was.

Henry Haggard rubbed his chin. "Are we talkin' about the famous shootist, Homer Timms?"

Slater knew by the way Haggard asked the question that it was a critical moment. Slater knew better than try and downplay such a famous person. He knew it would come out phony and lacking sincerity if he attached little importance to such a man.

Taking another tack, he said, "Homer has two or three other men … but it is only three other men at the most." Slater extended his hand to the sky as a visual aid to his selling job. He decided to appeal to Henry Haggard's ego. "To some people, Homer Timms is a big deal, but hey, you ain't no slouch yourself." Slater paused and came to what he considered an almost irresistible conclusion: "You're the famous Henry Haggard."

Henry ignored the compliment and got to the point: "Where are them birds now, and where will they likely camp?"

Slater squatted down and found a stick to draw things in the sand. Henry Haggard joined him shortly, with his eyes intent on Slater's words and geographical markings.

"Based on the information I got, they should make this dry creek arroyo about midnight tonight." He paused and added that it was less than twelve miles away.

Henry nodded to himself and then suddenly stood. He knew that gulch well and had utilized it himself in times past. He suddenly liked the deal and starkly shot his hand out to receive his thousand dollars. Henry was paid quickly, and as he turned and started walking toward his men, he said over his shoulder, "We got to make them twelve or so miles. See you tomorrow about the rest." He and his men quickly saddled and were off.

After the Haggard gang left, Slater sighed with relief. He figured that even if Haggard was defeated, he and his gang would do enough damage that it would be a simple matter of mopping up for him and his men. Henry Haggard had fifteen men. Fifteen against four seemed good odds to Slater. He wanted a victory over John Lee Johnson, and this was the hand he was playing. He walked toward the music makers in the distance, smiling genuinely for the first time in weeks.

After going at a careful and watchful pace and considering Homer Timms's likely path to the arroyo, Henry Haggard caught sight of what he thought was Homer Timms's campfire on the horizon just a few minutes past one in the morning. In the bright moonlight, Henry threw up his hand to halt his gang following him. He figured if he went any closer, the sound of his horses could be heard.

He looked over his shoulder and motioned for Pee Wee Tucker, his segundo, and Sage Jensen, his top scout, to ride up next to him. He told them to find the horses of the Timms's outfit and steal them, leaving the three or four men grounded.

Henry had prior knowledge of this gulch and went into great detail about the wash that separated his gang from Homer's men; he also knew where there were places along the arroyo that could be easily scaled. He told Pee Wee that Homer had probably tied his horses in the gulch itself that was close to the campfire now visible in the distance. He suggested Pee Wee choose three men to go with him and use the Timms's campfire as a beacon; they should just stay stooped over as they walked down the gully, shielded by the natural dirt wall, until they found the horses.

A short time later, Pee and his crew returned with gleeful expressions, pulling the unsaddled horses of John Lee Johnson's men.

Henry Haggard emitted a low-level chuckle when he saw his men leading the six horses toward him in the moonlight. He felt like a prophet now that he had correctly called the tune. Still unaware he was opposing not only Homer Timms but John Lee Johnson, he gathered his men in close for a quick parley.

"Boys, this is goin' to be like shooting target practice." He flashed a ragged smile and added, "Homer Timms is goin' to go down faster than chitlins on a poor man's plate."

He assigned the guard duty of not only the recently purloined horses but his own horses as well to a dour-looking man named Jasper. Jasper gave a short nod that things were in good hands.

Haggard divided his men into two main groups. He assigned Sage a band of eight men and told his group to walk down the edge of the gully until he was a hundred feet past the campfire, which was clearly visible on the other side of the arroyo. He next told Sage to descend into the gully where there was a shallow decline. Once in the wash, he was to seek another gentle incline, and he and his men would walk up it to the other side with drawn weapons to join him and his bunch, who would be a short distance down from his position.

He then concluded his short talk by saying, "Show them no damn mercy."

He then turned to Pee Wee and told him to get his shotgun and cross the ravine and come in on Homer Timms's campsite from the opposite side.

"Me and my men will go into the ravine with you, but you'll climb out and up at once. I plan on walkin' toward Sage and climb out about fifty feet from Sage's position. With our spacin' we'll have them boxed in. We can cut down on those fools, and none of 'em will escape."

Pee Wee gave a confident nod. He already had his shotgun and was ready to act on Haggard's plan.

Henry's small group entered the ravine began traipsing toward Sage's position. Things were going like clockwork. As Henry led his group by the blue moonlight, he could see in the distance what he thought were shapes of Sage's men now in the ravine. Hoping to coordinate the prior plan with Sage, Henry's men found an easy slope, climbed up, and now stood at the periphery of the campsite. By the dying embers of the campfire and the blue shadows of the moon, they could see four separate blanket-covered shapes.

Haggard was ticked when Sage's group did not immediately join him. He wordlessly cussed beneath his breath. He waited a couple more minutes and decided he could not wait any longer. He gave his men a curt nod that meant to shoot. His men pulled out their revolvers and fired at the blanket-covered mounds before them. Loud booms reverberated and orange pistol jets looked even more vividly orange in the veiled darkness. They fired until their pistols were empty.

Henry Haggard's eyes suspiciously narrowed as he observed the blanket-covered shapes. He was not the only one who noted that there were no jerking of limbs or cries of anguish. Henry slowly holstered his weapon and cocked his head, trying to figure out what in the hell just happened. He gingerly walked to the nearest body and pulled away the pistol ball-riddled blanket, only to find sand.

His bloodshot eyes quickly moved side to side in their sockets. He knew something was out of kilter but he had not yet realized he had been tricked. He heard someone climbing up the dirt grade behind him; as he was whirling around, he drew out his Army .44 and leveled it at the source of the foreign noise.

He saw a hatless Pee Wee, who was supposed to be facing him on the other side of the encamped men with a shotgun; instead, he was standing forlorn and looking shell-shocked. As Haggard scrutinized him, he noticed Pee Wee had no shotgun. In fact, he was weaponless; moreover, he was without his boots as well as his gun belt. His beaten face looked as though it had been thrust into a wasp nest. The only thing Henry Haggard could think of to say was, "What in the hell?"

Pee Wee shrugged sheepishly and began, "Boss, you remember the hosses we stole?"

Haggard nodded in the affirmative.

"Well, they got 'em back."

Before Henry Haggard could respond, Pee Wee continued, "And besides that, they done stole our own hosses."

Henry's mouth flew open in shock.

Pee Wee continued, "Jasper's either dead or missing."

Haggard's breath caught, but again, before he could respond, Pee Wee continued, "That was not Sage's men you saw earlier." He paused and audibly sighed. "When I first climbed up that dirt embankment with the shotgun, I got caught up by a man like I ain't never seen before. He beat the hell outta me. He dragged me back down the side of that gully and beat on me some more.

"He told me by the time you climbed up here at the campsite, your other men would be gone, meanin' Sage's men. I remember hearin' in the distance where we had the hosses hidden, a sound like Jasper cryin' or somethin' and then the sound of the hosses being taken away." Pee Wee shook his swollen head and sighed again. He bent over at the hips, trying to catch his breath. "I was told by that awful-lookin' giant that your other men would be gone, and you and a few others would be all that's left."

Upon hearing this news, Henry Haggard's thin lips formed a shape that expressed both fear and disbelief. He cupped his hands over his mouth to amplify his voice and shouted, "Sage" as loud as he could. That imploration was met by complete silence.

Henry Haggard's eyes were now as big as saucers. He dropped his hands at his side as his eyes walled around crazily, trying to catch up with his brain. Then his eyes went from wide open to thoughtful slits. He remembered Pee Wee saying the word "giant."

Haggard looked across the expanse into Pee Wee's swollen eyes. "What giant are you talkin' about?" He paused and added, "Homer Timms is big, but he ain't no giant."

Pee Wee again bent at the waist as though still trying to catch his breath and at the same time forget about the nightmarish episode he had just experienced. "It weren't no Homer Timms." Pee Wee paused and then said, "It has to be a man named John Lee Johnson that some of the Slater bunch mentioned back at the fiddle party."

Haggard's eyebrows furrowed. "Who did you say?"

"John Lee Johnson."

Haggard had never heard of him, but it was obvious that knowledge of this man had been hidden from him. It was equally obvious to him that he had been suckered by the Slater gang. Haggard walked to the edge of the wash and shouted out into the darkness in a stentorian voice to his unseen nemesis, "Okay, what's your terms?"

A stronger voice came seemingly out of nowhere: "Drop your guns and put the money you got to kill us on the ground in front of you, and just start walkin'."

"And if I don't?"

"Hell, you'll die where you are."

Haggard knew the strong voice meant what it said. He did not play games. He undid his gun belt, pulled the thousand dollars from his pocket, and placed the roll on the ground alongside his belt and holster. His men, seeing him voluntary disarm, followed suit.

Haggard then shouted out, "Now what?"

"Start walkin', and you'll live to see another day; if you want to argue, I'll kill you now and stop a bad conversation."

Henry and his men began walking along the lip of the arroyo. After a few minutes, they came upon a coat stretched over a greasewood plant stretching over the gully. Leaning up against that greasewood bush was an empty shotgun. Down in the wash, Sage and his disarmed men were hunkered down, cowering. For the last fifteen minutes, Sage and his men, after being waylaid by Homer Timms and the rest of John's men, had assumed by the blue-violet moonlight that the silhouette of the plant with the coat draped over it was an armed guard.

Henry Haggard did not cuss or engage in any verbal recrimination about the embarrassing plight Sage found himself in. After all, he had been fooled himself. Strangely, he did not resent John Lee Johnson as much as the thought of being maneuvered into this awkward situation by Tim Slater. He reached for the leaning shotgun and pulled some shells from his pocket. At least he had a weapon. With a disgusted voice, he ordered Sage and his men out of the gully. He fatalistically motioned for his remaining men to follow him as they started trudging westward.

In the predawn light, Cut Worm Weaver lay belly down on a nearby ridge and watched through his handheld telescope as Henry Haggard's dejected gang plodded across the prairie. Cut Worm shook his head in disappointment, knowing Haggard's gang was not a collection of schoolboys. They were credible foes. He knew the big Texan had won another singular battle and that he and his legendary friend, Homer Timms, soon would be setting their sights on the current inhabitants of the Pipton Ranch.

He then swung his telescope over to his far left to view the John Lee Johnson party. He saw the big man and Homer leisurely mount up. Through his circular lens, he watched them have a conversation from horseback and then take off side by side, undoubtedly headed to the Pipton Ranch. The other two men of his party gathered up the large remuda of horses, making a network of tethers. They were probably headed to a nearby town called Brumfeld to sell the newly acquired mounts.

Cut Worm slammed his scope together and then scurried to his hidden horse and mounted up. He intended to do his duty and deliver this mortifying news to Tim Slater, just to watch his reaction. He knew the supercilious Slater was now backed into a corner and decided that if he had no answer, he would desert the ranch and head somewhere far away from that devil John Lee Johnson.

Cut Worm trotted his horse for a while and then began to gallop. It nettled him that John Lee Johnson didn't give a tinker's damn about the opposition at the Pipton Ranch. It was as though an inexorable force was on its way—even if it was two against thirty. Few ordinary men would accept those odds, but these two men were far from ordinary. This sort of irresistible confidence scared the hell out of Cut Worm.

When Cut Worm came close to the ranch compound, he saw two mounted sentinels watching for him, spaced about a half-mile apart; he waved his arm in the air to signal them. He watched them leave the high ground and ride at an angle toward him. Soon they joined him and they arrived together to be met by a large greeting party shaped in a semi-circle of twenty-seven men, plus Slater himself.

Slater and all his assembled men's eyes were locked on Cut Worm's face. Slater, looking for any prescient message, ignored the two worthless riders positioned on each side of Cut Worm. Cut Worm, catching Slater's inquiring look, dejectedly shook his head in the negative. The message was clear. The Haggard gang had failed. There was a collective gasp among the onlookers.

Slater maintained his poise. Although he was crestfallen, he masked that sinking feeling by expressing a defiant look. With that same face, he turned around to address his men. In his best military posture and authoritarian tone, he lifted his hands and called the twenty-seven men to gather in closer.

His determined eyes panned the assembly of men now before him. His neck tendons bulged when he shouted out, "To hell with John Lee Johnson and Homer Timms."

He expected some positive reaction on his fervid words, but there was none. As Slater panned the faces, he noticed twitches, nervous side-to-side glances, or outright looks of fright.

Slater shouted again, "We have them bastards just where we want them."

Again he noticed the twenty-seven-man assembly looked at him as though he had lost his mind.

Slater threw his arms into the air. "We got thirty men. It's just John Lee Johnson and Homer Timms and some other losers helping him." Slater thought he might have made some headway with his men with those words, so he continued, "They have to come here, gentlemen." He paused and shot up an index finger, orator style, to make his point. "Here, I repeat, here."

If anything, reminding his men that the big Texan would soon be at their door seemed to increase their nervous anxiety.

Slater decided on a different strategy. "Look, each one of you were handpicked by me and Deputy Commissioner Braxton Gray. Each one of you has skills. If we work together, we'll bring down that big bastard, once and for all."

The assemblage gave edge-of-the-eye looks toward the next man standing close by. They didn't remember being handpicked. They recalled answering a newspaper ad about men being needed for guard duty or security: "horse and gun required." Most of the men there were aware that the majority of their group was ex-military but they had no real gunfighting skills.

Slater overlooked their dubious expressions as he continued, "If I was a mind to, I could go down the line talking about your expertise in fighting or gunplay." He paused long enough to single out a pear-shaped man named Cecil. He pointed to the sweaty-looking man and said, "Two weeks ago in a saloon over in Brumfeld, as you know, Ol' Cecil got into a fight and cleaned house."

Most of Cecil's friends looked nervously at each other. They remembered Cecil having a fight, all right, but they didn't remember his cleaning house. They recalled that he and a saloon girl named Ida Redd got into it over a dollar. Ida Redd knocked the holy hell out of Cecil and was winning the fight until she slipped on a puddle of beer on the floor and fell, hitting her forehead on the edge of the table and knocking herself out.

Slater paused long enough to get a read on his audience. Thinking he was making headway, he pointed out another man named Fud Benfield. "See, Fud there, he can knock walnuts off a fence railing with his .44, like dominos falling across a table."

Fud knew he never shot a walnut off a fence rail, and so did his friends standing close by. They thought he had shot tomatoes. Fud swallowed and barely acknowledged the false praise. He knew it was gourds he shot at, and he missed half the time. He did not want to reveal that part after receiving the boss's fictional praise.

Slater's voice dropped a register, and he looked calmer. "If you boys do like I tell you, we can get John Lee Johnson in a crossfire and end this matter today." He inhaled a heavy lung of air and decided to check on the mindset of his band of men. "We can be known as the men who killed John Lee Johnson and Homer Timms."

After a dramatic pause, an emboldened Slater asked, "Now how many of you are willing to make history today?"

His eyes panned his men again; Slater was well aware of how average his gang was. He saw mediocrity everywhere. These so-called tough guys had been living on the gravy train, but when it came down to real danger, they didn't have the ability or the heart.

He asked for a show of hands of those who wanted to stay and fight.

Absolutely no one raised a hand. Slater took in an audible breath looked thoughtfully up into the hot, blue Texas sky. His eyes slowly lowered as he took in all the nervous and scared men once more. "You know what?"

Fud, standing close by, tentatively asked, "What?"

Slater dropped his arms to his side, looked longingly eastward toward Austin, and said, "Let's get the hell outta here."

The dispersal time of the gang might have set a record if they had been properly timed. As soon as Slater finished, they immediately took off as though Judgment Day was at hand. Many shouted in joy at Slater's words, all the while bellowing out various versions of "I heard that" and "I know that's right." They quickly saddled their horses and made ready to leave, with no particular destination in thought.

After watching his men stampede to their horses like their lives depended on it, Slater walked to the shed where he had his horse and packhorse already saddled and loaded. He sincerely believed he could persuade his men to stay and fight; he imagined that he could motivate and inspire them. But he also knew if words did not rally his men, he had a contingency plan to haul ass, with an escape route for himself already thought out.

When he saw Cut Worm, still mounted and looking at him curiously, Slater said, "It's obvious you don't know where you're going like those fools; go load up your own packhorse and head to Austin with me."

Cut Worm nodded agreeably.

Slater muttered to himself more than for Cut Worm's benefit, saying, "John Lee Johnson hadn't seen the last of me."

The morning after Homer Timms's wedding and after spending the night in the Gandy Hotel, Stan Johnson, the circuit rider preacher, stood with a groused, sleepy look while he peered out the open doorway of the dinky hotel lobby. Standing near him was the deacon, Bufford Don Skipper, who looked equally disgruntled. Stan gave a disapproving look at the proprietor of the hotel, who stooped over a counter that looked like it had been rescued from a termite attack.

Stan didn't especially care if he was overheard or not as he told his deacon, "He's got a lot of nerve to charge fifty cents a night here."

Bufford Don ran his hands over his weary face as he nodded in approval. "My room was so small, the cockroaches walked in single file. I think he previously rented out my room to a platoon of cavalry with bad kidneys."

Stan found humor in Bufford Don's comment in spite of the bad night's rest. He added, "My room was so small I saw a stoop-shouldered rat."

Bufford Don gave a quick look at the clerk, who was listening to their comments. The seedy clerk, wearing a green visor, was none too happy with their sense of humor.

Bufford Don, seeing the clerk had their attention, turned to him and said, "Next time we come here, I expect you to give us fifty cents to stay here instead of the other way around."

The clerk became angrier and turned away, tired of their comments.

After leaving the hotel, they went to the H&R Livery, where they retrieved their horse and buggy. They quickly departed for Punkin' Center for a scheduled meeting on the morrow.

With Stan handling the reins of the buggy, they rode for most of the morning hours wordlessly. Occasionally, they would refer to the bad hotel and laugh, but they were tired, and talk did not come easily.

Around noon, Bufford Don, sitting in the passenger seat, commented that there was a chill in the air. Stan regarded the remark as just plain silly, as he looked up at the orange ball sitting above them and knew it was getting very warm. But as Stan turned to respond, he noticed the outline of what looked like a bottle in the deacon's coat pocket. Stan took in that form pressing from inside the coat fabric, turned his head, and glanced up at the noon sun again.

He cleared his throat and remarked, "Maybe there's a slight chill in the air, after all." Again he made a throat-clearing throat noise, returning a quick glance at Bufford Don's coat.

Bufford Don, getting his cue, reached inside his coat and pulled out a bottle of 90 proof Kentucky whiskey. He uncorked it and handed it over to Stan.

Stan tilted the bottle up and took a healthy swig. The sharp bite caused him to flinch, and he handed the bottle back to Bufford Don, who took his turn tilting the bottle up and taking in a healthy swallow.

As he corked the bottle, Bufford Don added, "Now we're fortified against the chills."

Stan looked again at the bottle that was in the act of being put away and added, "I might need another swallow to make sure my throat's clear."

Bufford Don uncorked the bottle and handed it back to the pastor. Stan once more took in a heavy swallow. He sighed as he handed the bottle back to Bufford Don, who also decided he needed another drink for chill maintenance.

After putting away the bottle, they rode again in silence for another hour. Stan was not feeling any pain as his head lolled around at the prosaic countryside, but out of his peripheral vision, he caught sight of an unusual thing. He thought he saw two men tied together off to his left, struggling to walk across the sandy prairie. At first, he thought his vision might have been impacted by the cough medicine, but after focusing in on the two men, he could tell that it was not an illusion but a strange fact. He brought the matter to Bufford Don's attention. The deacon leaned forward to look past Stan and confirmed what the pastor was looking at.

Bufford Don clucked his tongue and remarked, "Them poor souls, whoever did that to them must be an unprincipled man."

Stan steered the large dray horse off the road and made an immediate left, trying to avoid the heavy sand mounds as he drove the buggy toward the two struggling men.

Utah Jimmy Pruett was the first to see the rescue buggy coming their way. For the first time since being tied up, he gave a smile of relief. He looked over his shoulder and told the weary Memphis Mayford that help was on the way.

Memphis Mayford, with his short legs and still feeling the aftermath of his bout with the green apples, was laboring. He could only mutter, "Thank God."

Stan could hardly believe his eyes when he drew close. He had never in his life seen two men tied back-to-back in their drawers, apparently struggling to walk sideways. It was made even more bizarre that they had their hats on as well as boots. He took note they looked parched and weary to the point of complete exhaustion.

Stan pulled back on the reins, set the brake, and stepped down in the ankle-deep sand. As he walked toward them, he pulled his Barlow knife from his front pocket, eased the sharp blade out, and asked, "What happened to you fellers?"

Bufford Don, fearing Stan was acting too impulsively, cautiously queried, "Who did this to you?"

Memphis Mayford answered quickly, "It was a big galoot named John Lee Johnson." He paused and added, "He took our horses, clothes, money … everything."

Stan, who had begun to move toward them with his knife, suddenly froze in his tracks. He exchanged an alarmed look with Bufford Don, who took up the conversation, "Are we talkin' about a giant of man who rides a big, black hoss and who is meaner and tougher than hell?"

Jimmy Pruett nodded vigorously and answered, "The one and the same."

Stan pulled his knife hand back and folded the blade back into the handle. He slowly began retreating with his open-mouthed expression still directed to the two men. Memphis Mayford and Jimmy Pruett suddenly realized that their rescuers were no longer rescuers.

Utah Jimmy Pruett, knowing this was the case, exclaimed, "I can tell by the way you're dressed, you're men of the cloth. You can't leave us out here in the middle of nowhere." He paused and added with more emotion, "It ain't godly."

Stan shrugged indecisively at Pruett and said, "We'll give you a shot of water and be on our way."

Memphis Mayford turned his head toward them from his awkward position. "If you by chance have somethin' on you stronger than water, I shore would like it."

Bufford Don pulled his half-empty whiskey bottle from inside his coat. He walked up to Utah Jimmy and placed the bottle opening in his dry cracked lips. Bufford Don quipped as he poured a snootful of whiskey into Jimmy's maw, "Here's to your rescue by someone else besides us."

Jimmy Pruett smacked his lips in appreciation. "You ain't worth a thimble's worth as preacher-men, but that's some damn good whiskey."

Stan ignored his remark, as the deacon next emptied the bottle into Memphis Mayford's mouth. Memphis Mayford sighed with pleasure as he felt the hit of alcohol in his system. "There really is a God in heaven."

Bufford Don insouciantly flipped the empty bottle over his shoulder and started backing up, quickly joining Stan walking toward the buggy.

Utah Jimmy shouted after their retreating backs, "Cain't me and Memphis Mayford at least have a blessin'?"

Stan hollered over his shoulder, "May God have mercy on you two turds, but I shore in hell won't."

Memphis Mayford and Jimmy stood immobile until the buggy returned to the road, hoping against hope they would have a change of mind and return to rescue them, but as the fast-moving buggy becoming a mere dot on the horizon, they began trudging along again.

About an hour later, Les Moffatt and the Hankins brothers were riding from Punkin' Center, headed to south Texas to join up with the Comancheros.

Les Moffatt was a burly man. He rode slightly ahead of the two brothers. With his eyes shadowed by the sloped brim of his dirty hat, he concentrated his vision on the thin path that led through the myriad greasewood shrubs dotting the prairie.

David Hankins, chunky and apple cheeked, was riding to his right. He kept his mount close to Les to take advantage of the narrow trail that lie ahead of them.

Tommy Hankins, thin and leathery, rode to Les's left. He allowed Les to call the shots but always seemed wary of the bearlike man. They quarreled often, but Tommy realized he would rather have Les as an ally than adversary. Tommy and David had been with Les for over a year. They had grown close, and their relationship had grown. Each man depended on the other. They shared one other bond: They all had had run-ins with John Lee Johnson, and all those occurrences had been bad.

When they made a sharp bend in the trail, there were Utah Jimmy and Memphis Mayford, sidestepping in their drawers; Les immediately raised his hand to the Hankins brothers to slow the speed.

The two brothers immediately followed suit, seeing the same strange sight and having the same reaction as Les. They steered their horses in the direction of the two struggling men.

When Utah Jimmy and Memphis Mayford heard the sound of oncoming horses, they stopped walking and stood, wearily and expectantly, hoping this was their chance to be free.

Les and the Hankins brothers reined up side by side, six feet away from them. Les canted his head in various thoughtful poses, trying to ascertain exactly what he was looking at. "What in the hell are you two birds doin' out here in your union suits?"

The weariness of their arduous trek and the devastating effects of being rejected by Stan and Bufford Don caused Jimmy Pruett to respond caustically, "What's the matter, never seen two men in their drawers walkin' across the plains?"

Seeing the negative effect his words had, judging by their collective scowls, Utah Jimmy changed his tone of voice and said apologetically, "Listen, we have been walkin' forever. We've seen day snakes, night snakes, lizards, and varmints I didn't even know existed … all of 'em with five thousand teeth and mean as hell." He sighed and shook his head, nonverbally indicating his need for help. He asked plaintively, "So, if you can see fit?"

Les gave a half-smile in return. "We've all seen snakes and varmints, but I want to know why you're tied up before I haul off and cut you fellas loose. I reckon I'm owed an explanation."

Memphis Mayford, weary and spent, responded, "A man named John Lee Johnson robbed us of everything we got, except for what we got on."

The name Johnson's name had the same electric effect on Les and the Hankins brothers that it had earlier on the religious travelers.

Without any explanation and without hesitation, Les and the Hankins brothers backed their horses off, yanked their mounts around, and made a beeline to the trail they had left.

Utah Jimmy and Memphis Mayford watched the inexplicable behavior with open mouths.

Utah Jimmy sighed and said, "Damn it, Memphis Mayford, cain't you please stop using the name 'John Lee Johnson'?"

The two men continued to trudge forward, buoyed by the fact they knew Punkin' Center was not too distant. At nightfall, on the outskirts of the community, they saw a medium-sized ranch house with some outlying buildings, including a chicken house. Since they could not sit down, they took respite leaning against the exterior wall of the crude chicken hutch and slept a heavy slumber.

About six in the morning, they were awakened by sharply thrown pellets of gravel. Utah Jimmy and Memphis Mayford's eyes opened quickly, feeling the prickly bursts of pain.

Two small, towheaded girls wearing Mother Hubbard dresses, ages eight and nine, were standing with handfuls of gravel and giving them the evil eye. Jimmy and Memphis Mayford, seeing the younger one wind up to deliver another handful of gravel, hunched over, wincing and holding their heads down to allow their hats to catch most of the biting, sprinkling impact.

Now fully awake, the two men began to sidestep it in fast time, moving away from the biting pain. But as they were making some distance, they were halted by a threatening older male's voice.

The two bound men lifted their downward hats to see a man in his fifties, holding a double-barrel .10 gauge shotgun. Those two circular shotgun bores seemed as large as rain barrel openings. The chunky man holding it had a floppy hat on, much like a Tennessee mountain man. He had one gallus holding up his baggy overalls, and his face peering down the two barrels looked like a bulldog.

"Chicken thieves don't live long around here."

Before Utah Jimmy could inform him of their nonthreatening and destitute status, he was roughly overridden by the angry father's loud, threatening voice. "I done sent for the law." The rancher seethed out more diatribes. "Skulking around here in your drawers, scarin' women and children. You two birds need hangin.' You two are indecent vagrants, thieves to boot."

It was just a matter of minutes when the town marshal and his two deputies arrived on horseback. The marshal was almost a carbon copy of the rancher: chubby, angry, unforgiving-looking face. The two deputies looked like poorly dressed refugees from a mental institution.

The town marshal cussed both Memphis Mayford and Utah Jimmy for ten minutes, accusing them of crimes that would have been impossible for them to commit. Not accepting any backtalk from the two indigents, he ordered his deputies to shackle them. For the first time in days, the ropes were taken off, but Jimmy and Memphis Mayford still had to shuffle their feet indignantly down the road to the jailhouse, which was a half-mile away.

By chance, three days later, Tim Slater and Cut Worm Weaver, heading to Austin, passed through the hole-in-the-road town and stopped in Punkin' Center's well-known mercantile store.

Luckily, Cut Worm Weaver, riding behind Slater and pulling the two packhorses, saw Memphis Mayford peering forlornly through the thick bars of the crude jail window. When Cut Worm notified Slater of this fact, the imperious Slater turned a hard left and rode to the town marshal's office. Regardless of the fact the two gunfighters had failed him, he needed them to go with him to Austin as witnesses that he had been compromised in his efforts.

The obstreperous town marshal at first resisted releasing his prisoners, but after Slater introduced himself and produced his bona fides as an agent of Marshal Robert Lang, the blusterous town marshal suddenly morphed into an obsequious servant of the law—even to the point of offering his protective services for their ride to Austin.

CHAPTER 6

IT WAS A HOT AND WINDY MORNING WHEN JOHN LEE JOHNSON RODE into the Pipton Ranch from the north. Cautiously, Homer Timms rode in from the south. Both had an idea the ranch would be abandoned. But if by chance someone other than the men they were looking for was hiding out, they wanted to close the jaws of the trap. Now seeing that probability was unlikely, their eyes were searching through the swishes of dust clouds blowing here and there for Hubert Hicks, one of the two men who had been planted in the Slater gang by Lieutenant Bragg.

Hubert Hicks was in actuality a second lieutenant in the regular army; he had surreptitiously joined Slater's group of thirty. He and his companion, Sergeant Bennie Leonard, had wormed themselves into the group and quickly became known as competent gunmen. But they had lived on the edge the last two weeks because of their frequent forays on horseback, unsuccessfully trying to contact John Lee Johnson in order to warn him.

With tensions increasing daily about the big Texan's unstoppable forward march to the camp, a growing number of apprehensive gang members questioned them about their frequent disappearances. Each time, fortunately, Hubert and Bennie covered each other's asses with satisfactory excuses. But in the last two days before the diaspora, taking no chances, they had halted their scouting missions altogether.

On the day Slater gave in to his men's fear and his own fear, the two army agents joined in with the panic-stricken mob. The two men pretended to be as alarmed as the next guy and soon were just another body running for his horse to escape. They both, as prearranged, had separately ridden a mile in different directions from the ranch before reining up. Both men searched the countryside for any possible incriminating witnesses. Seeing none, but still maintaining a cautionary attitude, they took pains to ride a circuitous route back to the Pipton Ranch. This doubling back was done in order to both communicate with John Lee Johnson and protect the two freight wagons he had requested.

But Hicks was heavily troubled by fact that he had overheard a drunken Slater three days earlier confess to an equally intoxicated Cut Worm that he intended to kill a woman in Austin named Benson for being an informant. This admission alone alarmed Hicks, but when he heard Slater carelessly announce her name, he knew he had to act as fast as he could without blowing his cover.

Before John Lee Johnson's arrival, he took it on himself to send Benny Leonard to see Lieutenant Bragg in Austin as soon as they arrived back at camp, to circumvent any embarrassing or intrusive questions. Hicks knew it was imperative to inform Lieutenant Bragg as fast as possible about this threat against an invaluable ally. Mrs. Benson was their star witness against the corrupt Texas sheriff.

Hicks had reluctantly stayed behind to assist the two legendary gunmen. But when he had completed his mission, he had plans to head to Austin, hot on the heels of Bennie, before it was too late.

When Hicks saw the two feared men moving boldly down the main drag of the dreary compound, he breathed a sigh of relief that he could finally be shed of the place. He walked boldly out into the street and waved a hand of recognition.

Hubert quickly introduced himself again and explained briefly that his associate had been sent to Austin due to an emergency situation. He hoped these terse words about his partner's absence would dismiss the subject and no never-mind would be paid to it, but he could tell immediately he was wrong. Both John Lee and Homer's eyes suddenly took on a look of interest. Hubert knew the subject would be revisited.

But for now, Hubert received a friendly nod from both John Lee Johnson and Homer Timms; he tilted his head for them to follow him. They walked their horses behind him as he went across the dirt way to another empty building, directly across from the one Hubert came out of.

Upon entering through the gaping side entrance, Hubert stood aside as John and Homer dismounted, tied off to a rickety hitch post, and joined Hubert at the large opening. Hubert then extended his hands as if introducing the two large freight wagons that stood intact on the other side of the empty building.

John Lee Johnson nodded his approval. This was the main reason he had chosen to come to the Pipton Ranch and not bypass it. He needed those wagons. He and Homer huddled in conversation for a moment, and then John signaled for Hubert to join them. He reach out to shake Hicks's hand and said with sincerity, "Thanks for your help."

John did not explain why those wagons were necessary. But they were vital to carry water and provisions across the Chihuahua Desert. And if the hundred thousand dollars in gold coins proved to be valid, once he reached the Valley of the Sun, he needed them to transport the heavy cargo back across the desert.

Having the transportation problem solved, John felt he needed to know why Hubert had deemed it necessary to send his compadre to Austin. He felt he had the right to know, since most of his problems emanated from the capital.

John was not blunt or rude, but he conversationally asked the lieutenant why this was done. Hicks at first seemed reticent to answer but finally yielded to the intense gray eyes perusing him. Plus, he reasoned that since his superior, Lieutenant Bragg, had the utmost faith in the big man, he felt he had no other choice but to entrust with him the truth.

"I overheard Slater tell Cut Worm there was a widow woman in Austin, a Mrs. Benson, who's been sleeping with Marshal Lang. This woman, it seems, had been the mistress to Judge Roy before him, but now was very much involved with the sheriff. He went on to say that Lang was enamored of her, and being in love, he told her his every move." He paused and added, "What he said is true, but on her behalf, she has been in bed with the enemy, so to speak, but in order to get information. Which she has passed on to Lieutenant Bragg in some secret manner."

Hicks's eyes knowingly narrowed when he added, "The way I see it is that it's damn hard to keep anything confidential in Austin, but she has managed to do just that." He caught their looks of interest and continued, "One thing I know and Slater doesn't know is that she can hardly stomach

Sheriff Lang. She is just doing her part to bring that cutthroat bastard down."

Seeing the intense look on the two gunfighters, Hicks continued, "But here's Slater's plans: He recollected that Marshal Lang gave her a hope chest—a large one to fit at the end of her bed. Slater plans on secretly killing her at night and stowing her body in that same very hope chest. Later, one of his associates will come along in a wagon, place the coffin-like chest in the wagon bed, and haul it out to Tate's Swamp, which is known for quicksand; they'll dispose of the body there. He figures before long, it will be out of sight and out of mind." Hicks ended his words by adding, "The reason he's so intent on killing her is because Slater blames all his failures on her." Hicks gave a thoughtfully wry smile and added, "That's only partly true; the other reason he has failed is because of you."

John Lee Johnson did not respond to that remark. He remained pensive as he sorted through his mind about the woman in question. He readily remembered that a Colonel Benson, who had been a powerful figure in the secessionist movement and later a vital assistant to the Confederate general, John Bell Hood, had been married to a beautiful woman named Cornelia. He also recollected that after the war, certain Reconstruction advocates saw fit to assassinate the colonel because of his outspoken criticisms of the radical new government.

John wordlessly but correctly figured that this Mrs. Benson was quietly seeking revenge for her dead husband, even by sleeping with the enemy. He admired her courage but knew the stomach-turning pain she must have endured, pretending to care for both the venal Judge Roy and the repulsive Sheriff Lang.

After thinking it through, John gave a chin motion toward a tethered horse he assumed belonged to Hicks. "Get what supplies you can muster and head to Punkin' Center; get a spare horse there, and double-time it to Austin. I just wish I could go with you."

Hicks nodded at the words, tangentially wondering why the big Texan couldn't go with him, but he lacked the temerity to ask.

Hicks, however, did ask, "What now for you?"

"Waitin' for some mules."

Hicks, knowing that would be the only explanation he would receive, extended his hand for a farewell handshake with the two renowned gunmen. He turned briskly and headed to his horse and then toward Austin.

The following day, Fud Benfield, the gunman Slater had claimed could shoot walnuts off a fence railing, was miles away in ridiculously small saloon in a dreary town named Dripping Springs. As he was working on his fifth beer, he began taking on some bottle courage. He was trying to shake off the emotional effect of just galloping away in fear when Slater had dismissed the twenty-seven men. Like most of his associates, Fud had just ridden off, hoping to survive, but his other comrades at least had an idea of where they were going. He had just saddled up and galloped away without a destination in mind because, tragically, he had none.

As he rode through the night, he was plagued by his own character and personal faults: stupidity, cowardice, and loneliness. Continually bothered by his spineless escape and still hoping to think of someplace he could land safely, he, by chance, came upon a small godforsaken community named Dripping Springs. He saw three buildings, one of which was a miniature saloon. Here he thought he could drink away his self-doubting fears and give himself time to heal his self-image.

Much later, lifting his fifth schooner of beer, but still emotionally suffocating on the lack of music and noise, along with the bleak shadows of this cracker-box saloon, he sat slumped over in a blue funk.

Hoping to purge himself into a better frame of mind psychologically, he suddenly began speaking out loud to no one in particular. "Damn Tim Slater." He took another hearty gulp from his schooner and continued, "Damn John Lee Johnson."

The chunky, oily bartender cast a curious glance his way but continued wiping glasses. Fud was not the only patron in his saloon ever to have a one-man conversation. Therefore, the barkeep chose to keep a neutral attitude and simply ignore him and serve him until he could no longer pay.

The only other patron, a well-dressed Mexican standing at the end of the short bar, let his eyes glide to the gringo inquisitively from the dark shadows of his broad sombrero. When he heard Fud mention John Lee Johnson, this half-drunk gringo suddenly had his full attention.

The Mexican did not show any outward signs of attentiveness, but after Fud bellowed out some more drunken slurs directed toward the two unseen men named Slater and Johnson, he stealthily moved toward his table. He didn't ask if he could sit down. He just tossed a small leather bag on the table directly in front of Fud; the bag jingled with coins.

Fud looked at the bulging leather pouch that had landed in front of him. He could tell it contained money. His drunken eyes seemed to take on a refreshing clarity. He raised his vision to see the swarthy man standing across the table. Fud gave a small acquiescing nod, and his visitor sat down with a soft smile beneath his full mustache.

The well-dressed Mexican obviously was not some migrant vaquero. His name was Theo Fierro. He and his brother, along with five others, were camped outside of this small burg.

They had been sent north to Texas to find and then kill John Lee Johnson. They had been given a map of his likely path toward the Chihuahua Desert and even his likely route toward the Valley of the Sun. But after weeks of futilely searching for this elusive man and finding not even a smidgeon of his whereabouts, they had given themselves forty-eight hours more before abandoning the mission.

But now, seated across from his first positive tip, Theo felt rejuvenated. He motioned for Fud to pick up the leather bag. Theo said in unaccented English, "I gather you do not like this Slater and John Lee Johnson."

Fud, knowing he was feeling the alcohol, was guarded at first. He looked across at the seemingly benign man with the calm, impassive face and asked, "Who wants to know?"

Theo shot his hand across the table and gave Fud a firm handshake. He introduced himself and nodded at the money bag, now pulled close to Fud. "That dinero is all yours. Just tell me where this man, John Lee Johnson is." Theo paused and added, "Better yet, I'll pay you more if you take me."

Fud and Theo began talking. Fud would make a statement, and Theo would follow up that statement with a question. They covered the whole gambit, from the disaster in Baileysboro to the concentration of men at the Pipton Ranch. John Lee Johnson's name came up often, like how he had aborted Slater's mission.

The bartender, who was only halfway listening, suddenly tuned in to the whole conversation when he heard the name Homer Timms. To the bartender, Homer Timms was a knight in shining armor. When he heard Fud mention that Homer Timms was riding with John Lee Johnson and that their associates were currently at the Pipton Ranch, he strained to hear each word. As the conversation continued, the barkeep ascertained that the well-dressed Mexican had a crew outside of town that had been commissioned to kill John Lee Johnson before he crossed the Chihuahua Desert. He did not understand all that was being said about the necessity of stopping Johnson before he crossed the Chihuahua Desert, but he knew he had to act.

After Fud and Theo left together, the bartender immediately closed the saloon and walked out the back door of his business and found his chubby brother, Cletus, who was out back, cutting wood. He told his brother what he had overheard. His brother had the same reaction he did. They both were admirers of Homer Timms. Cletus decided to ride to the Pipton Ranch and warn Homer Timms and the man called John Lee Johnson.

Less than an hour later, Theo introduced Fud to his brother, Roberto, and the fellow gang members. They surmised accurately that he knew what he was talking about as far as location of the ranch, but they also quickly sized Fud up as useless and of little value otherwise. Nonetheless, they paid him a little extra than the gold he had already received for him to lead them directly to the old fort, now known as the Pipton Ranch.

They departed immediately and headed northward, galloping at first and then settling into a steady trot. They rode the rest of the day and into the night. They stopped only to water their mounts but kept up the desperate pace. The Fierro brothers were bent on completing their mission and returning to the comforts of Temecula.

Around four o'clock in the morning, they came into view of the five buildings by the glow of the gibbous moon. Although there was enough blue moonlight for them to see the shadow-blackened shapes of the structures, there was not enough light for them to see any discernible sign of life.

Theo reined up roughly and shot his arm out horizontally for the others to slow. Catching his cue, they pulled up, taking in the same view that he was perusing. Satisfied that he had the element of surprise on his side, Theo nodded firmly to his men. They quickly dismounted and handed their reins to Fud.

Fud could see they had relegated him to being the horse-keeper. He immediately began tying off their horses to the crooked mesquite limbs jutting outwards. Theo and Roberto walked to him and told him to stay there and guard the mounts. It was understood that he do it or die, although they did not verbally express that—their body language and lupine eyes did.

Fud gulped. Unlike Slater, these guys were deadly resolute. They did not vacillate. Incompetence meant death. He nodded more vigorously than normal, hoping to allay their fears that he was not up to the task.

The two brothers gave him one more reappraising look, and then they and their men disappeared into the blue-violet shadows with drawn pistols. Fud looked and listened, thinking he might hear an errant noise, but he didn't. It was apparent that the Fierro brothers' stalking abilities were a definite cut above the mediocre Slater gang.

With the horses securely tied off and the Fierro brothers now out of sight, Fud dropped to a sitting position and rested on his haunches. With little to do, he found a match in his pocket and stuck it in his mouth. He felt both bored and useless at the same time. With the lack of noise and suffering from the after-effects of sleep deprivation, along with too much beer, Fud drifted off into sleep.

That sleep was interrupted by the sound of booming pistol shots in the distance. Fud spat the chewed match out and jumped to his feet. As he whirled around to face the ranch, his eyes widened as he saw vivid streaks of yellow and orange gunfire flashing from all parts of the ranch compound. It looked like a Chinese New Year celebration.

He could hear human shrieks of death and pain. The endless colorful show of orange pistol jets continued for another five minutes. This violent outburst of weaponry was followed by a palpable, deadly silence. It was as though it had never happened.

Fud swallowed. He looked down at his .44 as though he might use it, then back up at the blue shrouded horizon before him. He knew there was no way in hell he was going to go investigate, so he returned his gun to his holster.

He was now wide awake. His eyes moving jerkily, hoping to find some sign of whether John Lee Johnson or the Fierro brothers won. He stayed in wary upright position for another two hours before he saw a solitary figure moving toward him in the nascent dawn's light.

The figure moving down the road was huge. As he came closer to Fud, he realized that he backed the wrong men again. When he saw John Lee

Johnson more clearly, Fud began to make frightful noises in his throat. He had never witnessed a human being who looked like him.

John Lee Johnson reined up on the road and looked over to where Fud stood with the horses. The deepest voice Fud had ever heard commanded him to stay there with the horses until a wagon came along. Fud swallowed and nodded. He knew he could not run; he didn't have the strength. He watched the big man move southward, soon disappearing into the trees and shrubs.

A few minutes later, two wagons made their way down the road toward Fud. The first wagon was driven by an older man with a billy-goat beard, the following one by a young man wearing a worn derby. Another man sat on the elevated seat with the young driver. He had seen that passenger in Dripping Springs and correctly assumed he had somehow had prior knowledge of the attack and had ridden to warn the Johnson party.

Fud took his eyes off the informant and shuddered when he saw the tall figure following the wagons. He looked like the grim reaper. Fud knew that had to be Homer Timms. He suddenly realized that he had been facing a foe who was impossible to defeat.

Hobie's wagon came even to Fud's position; he set the brake, disembarked, and walked briskly toward Fud.

At first, Fud was afraid that the young man would just kill him and go on his way, but as he observed Hobie's facial expression and overall demeanor, he realized he was not there to murder him. In fact, he looked friendly enough.

Fud gave a cautious nod and received one in return.

Hobie began, "I will make you a tether for you to tie the horses to. Keep 'em bridled but unsaddled and toss the kaks in the bed of the wagon so I can sort them out later without no trouble."

Fud, who was just glad he was still alive, complied quickly with the order. He saw the rope loops that apparently Hobie had made earlier and tied the mounts off quickly, all the while looking expectantly at Hobie from the corner of his eyes. Finally, after completing his task, he garnered enough courage to ask, "Now, what about me?"

Hobie shrugged indecisively. "I reckon I'll give you two canteens of water and some beef jerky, and let you go."

"Is there any way I can go with you?"

Hobie shook his head and locked eyes with Fud. "You don't fit in. From what one of the dying Mexicans said, you worked for Slater and showed them the way here." He paused and added, "That shore in hell don't sound too promisin.'"

Fud looked at the ground. "I got over a hundred dollars on me. If you take me with you, I'll give it all to you."

Hobie canted his head as he mulled over Fud's words. "Why in hell would you do that? More importantly, why would I do that?"

Fud did not answer for a while. He fiddled his fingers as his eyes misted over. "'Cause I don't have a place to go, and I ain't worth nothin'."

Hobie remained silent for a moment as his mind wandered back to the day when he met John Lee Johnson at the entrance of the Russell brothers' ranch. He scratched his jaw, shuffled his worn boots around, and sighed; then he said, "Keep your money, and get in the wagon."

The Comanchero Lonzo Chamberlain, segundo to Pugh Larrimore, had seen Mike Jones leaving the outlaw community with fifteen of Pemberton's men (minus Pemberton). He witnessed all these men accompanying Jones as he departed in a plush buggy, replete with leather roof and horsehair seats. He knew someone held Jones in the highest regard to accommodate him in such expensive security.

Lonzo had limited information, but he did know that Jones was headed to Temecula, Mexico, and then would go to the Valley of the Sun, where he would assist Macro Cio in bringing down John Lee Johnson. This mass exodus of Jones and companions sent avaricious notions running through Lonzo's imagination.

An hour after Jones and company disappeared from sight, Lonzo, still thinking about the California gunman, sat across from Pugh Larrimore in the big office in the rear of their bank. He watched his boss sign a document with a scratchy ink pen. Not wanting to bother Larrimore, he started to rise to go to his own desk.

Pugh, fully cognizant of Lonzo's persistent presence, cleared his throat and gave a subtle head movement that communicated he wanted Lonzo to stay seated.

"Lonzo, you either got something to say or something to ask; whatever, get it out of your system."

Lonzo made a brief cant of his head in the direction of the newly departed Mike Jones, as though Jones's departure portended something of consequence. "It's been bruited around that four gunmen, Jones being one of 'em, are goin' to fight it out over a hundred thousand dollars in gold in the Valley of the Sun."

Pugh laid his pen aside and leaned back in his chair with a steady gaze at his muscular assistant. "That's somewhat correct." Pugh tilted his head as he continued to fixate on Lonzo. "You got something to say, Lonzo, so just come out and say it, damn it; I got things to do."

Lonzo paused, trying to put together his words. "Why don't you let me gather about twenty good men and let me go into the Valley of the Sun and just take that hundred thousand dollars?" He let a subtle smile ease across his features. "I kinda like the odds of twenty against four."

Pugh had been leaning back in his chair, relaxed; now, he shot his body forward and slammed his clenched fists on the scarred desktop. "What's the matter, Lonzo, are you tired of living? Tired of eating and drinking and living a better-than-decent life with money in our bank to retire on?"

Lonzo was suddenly taken aback by his boss's vehemence.

Pugh continued sternly, "Why don't you just go through the back door, take out your .44, and blow your damned brains out?" Pugh could see he had Lonzo's rapt attention. "Listen, I thought you were an intelligent man, Lonzo, but I can see you ain't smart at all.

"John Lee Johnson ain't human. I suppose he eats and farts and has the sniffles like any other man, but I tell you, the man is not human. If you picked the best checker player in Texas to play him, Johnson would win. If you picked the best bronc buster in the damned state to go against him to tame a wild stallion, Johnson would win. I reckon, you've heard that old expression here in Texas that there ain't a horse that can't be rode and a man who can't be throwed, well, that don't apply to John Lee Johnson. You see, Lonzo, if John Lee Johnson is over there, I want to be over here. I want to be as far from that big bastard as I can. As long as he is somewhere else kicking ass and causing mayhem, that's just fine with me.

"Shore, Macro Cio, or Emancio Godoy, his real name, is damned good. He has erased some damn good shootists in Mexico and wherever else he's been." Pugh, seeing a now-sobered Lonzo, leaned back once more in his seat.

"But he ain't going to beat John Lee Johnson." He let his words hit home and added, "And we can't beat him, either."

Lonzo, seeing that he had been thoroughly upbraided, nodded and said apologetically, "I just hate seein' that hundred thousand dollars just go to other hands."

Pugh, ignoring that remark, which he considered ignorant, leaned forward again, but said with an understanding look, "What you do, Lonzo, is when you have dealings with that big devil, get the hell away from him as fast as possible." Pugh let a smile move across his craggy features. "But you can sure as hell bet on that big bastard. You see, Lonzo, I made a personal wager of a hundred thousand dollars with Pedro Morales, one of the silver miners in Temecula. The terms of the bet are that between John Lee Johnson and Macro Cio, that Johnson would come out alive and Macro Cio would not.

"Nine weeks ago, we both placed our bets in the bank of Temecula when all this was talk of a showdown was coming down, winner take all."

Lonzo nodded pensively as he processed Pugh's words. "What if this Senor Morales decides to send out riders to take out John Lee Johnson and insure his bet?"

Pugh shrugged and replied, "Then Morales will have a whole lot of dead hired guns on his hands." Becoming exasperated with Lonzo's line of questions, he added, "Look, Lonzo, for the last time, Johnson doesn't lose." He paused and pointed at his temple, indicating his brain. "I learned long ago, you don't mess with John Lee Johnson."

Lonzo nodded, satisfied with Pugh's explanation and having a limited but negative experience with John Lee Johnson himself; he was gratified his boss's line of thinking was dead on right. And he felt that Pugh had stopped him from a fatal mistake.

As he was in the act of rising from his seat, Lonzo asked, "Other than John Lee Johnson and Jones, who are the other two men?"

Pugh moved his head around as he put together his thoughts. "One is Homer Timms, who always rides with Johnson. He's deadly; just think how many of our men he's killed in the past. Next is Macro Cio; he probably is the fastest hombre that John Lee Johnson will ever face, and that includes that bastard, Sabbath Sam."

Lonzo raised an index finger in the air, indicating that he had one question remaining. Seeing Pugh's amenable expression, he asked, "What is the story on this Macro Cio? Where does the word 'Macro' come from? What does it mean?"

Pugh's University of Pennsylvania education exposed itself when he answered, "It's from the Greek, meaning 'large or prominent'; he probably gave the title to himself."

Although he was pushed for time, Pugh knew he had to settle this matter. It was important they be on the same page mentally, that Lonzo did not go off with half-cocked information.

He reached down, pulled out a bottom drawer, and brought out a yellowed page with copious notes written on it. Shoving the drawer back with a heavy wooden jar, he placed the paper on the top of his desk and turned it around for Lonzo's perusal. Pugh didn't need to see the upside-down writing. He began reciting the information as though he knew it by rote.

"It says he is a Basque, born in the Pyrenees Mountains, between France and Spain. It goes on to say that he was in Europe when he was recruited by the Austrian Maximillian, who now claims to be the Emperor of Mexico."

Pugh sighed, letting the information soak in before continuing, "Emancio Godoy, also known as Macro Cio, came to Mexico with Maximillian in 1864 and could see the handwriting on the wall pretty damned fast. It didn't take him long to see that Maximillian was on a sinking ship. Last year, he politically deserted to this Indio named Juarez and his political movement and sold his services to the silver miners, especially this Ruiz gent.

"This report goes on to say he is approaching twenty-seven years of age and has killed twenty-eight, one more than the years of his life. It also says he is considered the premier gunslinger in the world."

Pugh suddenly whirled the paper on his desk around so Lonzo could no longer read it. He leaned in closer to Lonzo and spoke sotto voce.

"Let me tell you what's going on in Temecula. The owners of the three biggest silver mines in Mexico all live there in great big haciendas. The richest of the three, a man named Arturo Ruiz, hired Macro Cio to intimidate the other miners. He wanted to be the dominant one, the one to call the shots, so to speak. But things kind of blew up in his face in a way he didn't see coming. In less than a year, Macro Cio took a liking to Ruiz's wife, a real liking. He has been sleeping with her over a year now, and this

Ruiz fellow can't do anything about it. He's scared brainless of Macro Cio and stays away from Temecula; he's hired other gunfighters to kill him, big-money-type gunslingers, but Macro's killed each and every one of them."

Lonzo sighed and said, "All this Ruiz fellow has to do is wait on John Lee Johnson to come along, and his problem will be solved. He can save himself a whole lot of money."

Pugh smiled as he leaned back in his cushioned chair. "Lonzo, you're not so dumb after all. You've done seen the light."

In a lavish suite on the top floor of the most expensive hotel in Temecula (owned by Arturo Ruiz), Macro Cio, the handsome Basque gunman, was in bed with Ruiz's wife, the voluptuous Alicia Ruiz. They lay intertwined in a blissful postcoital glow. From frumpy, individual satin pillows, they stared at each other as though they were the only two people on earth. Alicia's limpid eyes took in her rakish lover, who lay interlaced with her. He had jade green eyes, tousled black hair, and a manicured spade beard; his even white smile was now lovingly directed to her. He was hard bodied. He was dangerous. He was in love with her.

Alicia ran a thoughtful hand down the side of Macro's face. "Arturo's hired another killer." Preoccupied with her beauty, Macro did not respond to her words; she continued, "His name is Cipango Avila."

Macro Cio shrugged as he nuzzled her cheek. It was if she had told him that a cloud was seen somewhere nearby. He finally allowed himself to answer her remark. "Yes, *cara mia,* I know. He's the Japanese-bred gunslinger from over in the Baja."

She sent a concerned look at his calm face. She looked soulfully into his unusual green eyes, all the while stroking his cheek; she wanted to stay young and remain captive in that moment forever. "Where is he, that is Cipango, and when are you going to face him?"

Macro shrugged, as though Cipango were of no importance, "At the cantina, but I will get to him soon enough. I just did not want to ruin our moment because of that dog."

Alicia's eyes narrowed as she slid her body over his and placed her chin on his chest so she could look at him more intimately. "My husband is a toad, such a *bastarde.* He is always causing trouble. This is the third gunfighter he has hired to kill you."

Cio sighed as he gently continued to caress her cheek. "Such a waste of money. Soon, he will get the message after he sinks another five thousand dollars *por nada.*"

Alicia placed a thoughtful palm on his chiseled chest, moving it up and caressing his jawline. After dwelling on his words a moment, she hugged him tightly. She mulled over his words as she continued the diatribe against her husband. "He has been a liar from day one." She inhaled and confessed, "Before we got married, he told me he was a lion, made of a hundred pounds of explosives."

Macro Cio affectionately ran his fingertips through her lush blonde hair and responded, "He probably forgot to tell you he was a hundred pounds of explosives with a one-inch fuse."

Alicia exploded in lascivious laughter. Their faces moved together for a wet kiss. But after a minute, she broke the kiss with a thoughtful look on her face and said, "In the long run, what will you do with my husband, Cio?"

"Here is the plan, my love: Today, I will kill this Cipango and later in July, this John Lee Johnson. I will collect the hundred thousand dollars and attempt to buy your husband out. If he won't sell, I will kill him. If he does sell, I will still kill him, but regardless, I will take over his mine and marry you.

"We will have a big hacienda outside of Temecula. I want you to have it all."

With that said, Macro Cio slid out of bed and walked over to the other side of the room, where his clothes were. On the wall was a lengthy vertical mirror. He bypassed his clothes and stood in front of the mirror, looking hypnotically at his image, running his fingers through his jet-black hair.

As he stood there looking at himself, Alicia, nude as Mother Eve, eased out of bed and came up from behind him, pressing her naked breasts against his back. She laced her arms around him, placing her face in the crook between his neck and shoulder. She joined him at looking at his image.

Alicia said admiringly, "You're beautiful, Cio, so handsome."

Cio nodded at her words. "You know, Alicia, it is so difficult to leave a mirror when you look like this."

She giggled at his words as her own eyes locked with his distinct green orbs in the mirror, taking in his disheveled black hair and muscular body. She found his self-love part of his devilish charm.

"I look good today, Alicia, and tomorrow, I will look even better. And the day after that, I will look even better." He sighed as he took his fingertips and made a sweeping motion up and down his body. "There's no end to my own personal power and beauty."

She loved his boastful humor and emitted a silvery laugh as she continued to enjoy his self-adulation.

Cio sighed as he placed his caressing hands on top of her grasping arms. "Alicia, I get so excited just being me. When I wake up in the morning, I know that I am Macro Cio, and no one else is."

He inhaled, taking another lingering view of himself. "Damn, I'm good." As he continued to stare at himself, unwilling to let go of his image, he turned his head side to side in the mirror and finally asked, "What do you think I should wear?"

Alicia made a thoughtful moue with her mouth. "Are you talking about the gunfight with Cipango in particular?"

He nodded as he continued to stare at his image. "It is hard to dress for a gunfight." He paused as he considered on his words. "If I wear black, it is so obvious that I am trying to appear morbid, so much so that it somehow appears to be pretentious. If I wear brown, which seems understated, it seems as though I am consciously dressing down." He exhaled as he though he were deliberating an exhausting dilemma.

She caught his eyes in the mirror and replied, "Wear the tan suit; it's snug, shows your shape, and also brings out your eyes."

He nodded his approval. His appraising eyes met hers, as though he should have been the one to think of it. "What about the black hat with the silver band to go with it?"

Alicia nodded her head and said, "Yes, wear that particular hat, but Cio, that tan suit also emphasizes your broad shoulders. When you wear that suit, it makes you look so continental and yet so wickedly jaded, my love."

He nodded his approval at her statement. "You have such a way with words, cara mia."

Seeing he was getting dressed, she walked to the foot of the bed and began putting on her pantaloons. She stepped into her underwear and said over her shoulder, "When do you plan on killing Cipango?"

He shrugged, as if it were inconsequential. He briefly took his eyes off the mirror and thoughtfully shot a glance her way. "We got plans?"

She now had her pantaloons on and was reaching for her crumpled dress lying at her feet. "Can you meet me in back dining hall of the bodega in two hours? It should be lunch time, and you know he serves lamb on Tuesdays."

Macro shrugged. "I will kill him within an hour and take his horse to the stable." He made a complete turnaround from the mirror as he took in Alicia's well-shaped backside. "I want his horse. He has an appaloosa with a silver saddle." He turned back to the mirror once more and said flippantly, "Order that same red wine we had a week ago. Red wine with lamb is a must."

The large and fashionable saloon that Macro entered was not your typical Southwest or Mexican cantina. Although the exterior walls were adobe, there no stereotypical cracks on the surface.

The inside was high dollar: expensive, hardwood, round card tables, a long mirror hanging behind a fashionable mahogany bar. The Mexican influence was demonstrated by the lone guitarist strumming from a darkened corner and the abundance of flowers hanging in metal containers affixed to the rafters.

Macro was egocentric, but he was also careful. He eased the left-batwing open and peeked into the interior. His eyes immediately caught sight of a man sitting along the far-left wall, directly in front of him. The man had a wide, ostentatious sombrero and frippery clothing. His fancy clothing was stitched in shiny threads attached with flakes of shimmering metal. But something about him made him appear too obvious. To his extreme right and just in the range of Cio's peripheral vision, he caught sight of a man who had his head craned downward with his sombrero hiding his Asian features. His giveaway to his true identity was an ornate gun belt, only partially covered by the plain gray serape.

Feeling he had been ferreted out, Cipango jumped up from his table, whipped his gray serape aside, and kicked back his chair. He already had his Army Colt in his hand. He fired first but too hurriedly. The pistol ball hit the wall inches from Cio's head, digging out a divot of adobe. Cio did not miss. His shot caught the Japanese-Mexican in the throat.

Cipango's second shot, a glowing orange in the umbra, was reflexive and to the side. He then dropped his pistol and reached with his hands to stanch his bleeding throat. He staggered and fell forward.

The young hombre wearing the ornate clothing was an accomplice of Cipango; he rose with his pistol outstretched in Cio's direction, while all of Cio's attention was on Cipango.

Cio's sixth sense kicked in. He threw himself back-first to the wall that aligned itself with the fancy gunman. A pistol ball whizzed past him and nicked the top of the left batwing.

Cio quickly dropped into a crouch and fired twice. His shots mirrored the killing of Cipango. Both shots caught the second gunman in the throat. Only the man did not grasp his throat in pain, he just fell backwards, crashing into the chairs and upending the table where he had been sitting.

Cio looked back and forth at the two would-be assassins. Seeing no life, he holstered and walked to the bar, where the bartender offered a phony look of gladness to see he had survived another gun battle.

The bartender, Ramon Ruiz, the brother of Arturo Ruiz, had a practiced smile on his face without any real warmth. Overlooking Ramon's cool politeness, Cio's eye darted toward the crumpled Cipango to his right. "There are his two saddlebags. I trust you to take them the bank and deposit the five thousand dollars in my name."

Ramon could not help but wince at the overweening gunman's words. He knew the bank assignment was an insult to him and his brother, but he recovered quickly and nodded.

Cio turned to walk off, but looked back and said, "Oh, Ramon, tell your brother thanks; I was running low on spending money." Cio struck a burlesque thinking pose with one finger under his chin. "One more thing; tell him there is a man for hire in Oxana whose name is El Rapide. Ask him to send him next week." As he turned to leave with a dark smile on his face, Cio said, "Tell your brother hello for me and Alicia."

Ramon's face grew red with anger, but he coldly nodded that he would do as Macro Cio had asked. But he had no intentions of telling his brother those words. Ramon knew his brother's life was in hell. Arturo was telling people that Macro Cio was holding Alicia hostage and forcibly raping her daily.

Ramon knew differently; if anything, it was the other way around. Alicia was the predator, not the gunman. He recognized that his brother had to believe she was an unwilling hostage and suffering physical indignities so he could live with himself. In the past, Ramon had always envied his very rich brother, but now he pitied him, hiding out and quivering at the notion of showing his face in Temecula.

Two hours later, a very serious discussion was taking place in the Temecula bank office. A conversation that had started off as friendly brother-in-law banter about mundane matters had suddenly transitioned into a very heavy-handed discussion about Pedro Morales's bet with the Comanchero, Pugh Larrimore.

Auguste Maduro, the richest banker in western Mexico, sat back in his cushioned leather chair. In his late forties, he had thinning black hair and a Prussian-style mustache. His clothes were expensive. His black linen suit complemented with a short, silk tie made him look like a figure of authority. He was. He had clear skin, lighter in complexion than most.

Pedro Morales was shorter, fatter, and not as well dressed; he sat on the other side of the desk from his commandeering brother-in-law. He was confused by this sudden change of conversational tone. Pedro moved his head slowly side to side, as though evaluating Auguste's sudden dark mood. After hearing Auguste's initial comments about the Macro Cio-John Lee Johnson bet, he could tell that Auguste was disturbed, but Pedro could not fathom why.

Auguste steepled his fingertips and leaned back in his chair. He began talking, and his tone of voice indicated that he was not to be interrupted. "Let's you and I do some recapitulation, Pedro. When Arturo Ruiz first lured Macro Cio away from that fop, Maximillian, you hated that fact because it appeared on the surface that he was using this deadly gunman to intimidate you and the other mine owners, trying to get an edge; is this not true?"

Pedro, seeing it was not his time to talk, gave a guarded nod.

Auguste continued, "You even surreptitiously hired a gunfighter to kill Macro Cio. Is this not correct?"

Pedro nodded again, although he did not especially like where this was going.

"Macro Cio not only kills your gunman but several other gunslingers hired by the other mine owners who held similar views as yourself, correct?"

Pedro grew irritated; no longer in the mood to nod, he just sat there with his eyebrow pinched over his eyes.

Auguste continued, "But as time went on, and as you could see that Macro was becoming more and more involved with Ruiz's wife, you suddenly began to appreciate him more."

Morales gave a begrudging, thin-lipped smile back at those words.

Auguste leaned slowly forward, stopping at a rigid military position. "You became big amigos with the gunfighter after it appeared that Macro Cio had humiliated Arturo Ruiz enough to cause him to leave town in disgrace. You now are good friends with Cio and even admire him; is this not true?"

Pedro started to respond but desisted, seeing Auguste had more to say.

Auguste then leaned back to his original position in his black leather chair. "Which brings us to the matter of the bet."

Pedro, who had been polite, now leaned forward nonplussed by the type of questions and innuendo offered by his brother-in-law. "Auguste, we are family. What is on your mind? I do not like sitting in the witness chair while you grill me. Whatever it is, get it off your chest."

Auguste's placid look was replaced by a red flush to his face as he leaned forward, slamming the side of his fist on his desk like a gavel.

"You, Pedro, have made a foolish bet. Because you have become enamored of this seemingly invincible Macro Cio, you have threatened not only your future but my sister's and my nieces' and nephews'."

Pedro held his palms up and retorted, "How so?"

Auguste, still leaning forward, his voice demonstrating anger, bellowed, "You bet a hundred thousand dollars you don't have. You put up your mine as collateral. If you lose, since I am the one who gave you the loan, I will have to repossess your mine. Since both Maximillian and Juarez's constitutions forbid banks and the Catholic Church from amassing any more wealth, I will have no choice under the law of either of the two constitutions but to sell the mine to the highest bidder." He paused as his voice took on a particular bite. "It won't be you, brother-in-law; you will be broke ... and according to law, I am forbidden to buy it and sell it back to you."

Pedro was stunned; this fact had never occurred to him. He realized he had taken for granted that Macro Cio could not possibly lose.

Auguste, far from easing up, continued, "Pugh Larrimore, the detestable

Comanchero, could end up owning your mine, Pedro. If that happens, he will start charging all of you more for those gringo slaves and keeping the best for himself, all free to work his new mine. Giving himself an advantage.

"But the day you made the bet, many thoughts began to plague me, Pedro. Why would this contemptible man, Pugh Larrimore, bet on John Lee Johnson? Pugh works with us and is considered an ally of sorts, so why would he be so sure that this man will beat Macro Cio?"

Pedro, who had no answer, sat with worried eyes, waiting on Auguste's explanation.

"I checked on this John Lee Johnson and discovered he was the one who beat the famous pit fighter in Sanchez, Mexico." He paused as he collected his thoughts. "I was informed recently that Pugh Larrimore bet on this gringo before the fight. It became obvious that this John Lee Johnson was a character I needed to look into. You would think that a man who handles his fists would not be so adept with his pistols, but I am not so sure now."

Pedro noticed that he was left out of the equation, which made him feel unimportant. But still he didn't respond.

"So a few days after you made the wager with Pugh Larrimore, I sent the Fierro brothers and five of my best security guards to kill John Lee Johnson before the gunfight could take place."

Pedro's spirits rose some as he leaned forward, expecting a positive response.

Auguste emitted a long, frustrated sigh. "They disappeared from the face of the earth."

"The Fierro brothers?"

Auguste set his mouth in a concerned thin line. "Yes, the Fierro brothers, and five others, all gone."

Auguste paused and added, "This Robert Lang, the big power in Texas, notified me a month before I sent the Fierro brothers that he would kill John Lee Johnson from ambush in the Valley of the Sun, from the Mons Rojo, but I do not trust him to do the job, and I still don't. Foolish promises are a waste of time. I cannot trust those I cannot control."

Auguste leaned forward once more, seemingly chaffed about another matter. "It seems that Frank McGrew, a former Union general, has a undying hatred for John Lee Johnson and has lured Johnson into facing Macro Cio. But it could be that you and I have been seeing it all wrong; it appears that John Lee Johnson has turned the tables on the general, and it is he who is doing the beckoning.

"But the wild card that I do not understand is Mike Jones, this gunfighter from California. Someone in California hates John Lee Johnson as much as General McGrew, and they are working in collusion. If that is true, you might have a chance, Pedro, but there are too many loose ends for me to get a clear picture. All I know is that you need to get your ducks in a row and find a way that ensures victory for you."

Pedro raised his eyebrows and asked, "And how am I supposed to do this, Auguste?"

Auguste did not upbraid him for his callow response, since it was his bet; he simply ended their meeting by saying, "I imagine tell Cio to work with Mike Jones."

It was ten days before Jones was to appear in the Valley of the Sun. The Pemberton crew was in a village near Temecula. The small community had few amenities, but cold water was one. It was a good benefit because it was 90 degrees and climbing. The small town seemed bathed in a thick impressionist painting of lurid orange and yellow sun rays.

The Pemberton group was worried. Twice, Mike nearly passed out due to the unrelenting heat. At the moment, he was lying on an outdoors cot beneath the dappled shadows of two Joshua trees.

The crew kept giving him cold water and wet towels. He was taking his medicine, but the heat seemed to counteract all the things his physician told him to do. On top of that, his medicine only gave him moderate relief.

When Tullis, Pemberton's right-hand man, walked over to the cot, he could see that Jones was dangerously weak. Tullis sympathetically knelt down to confer with him. Tullis knew he would face a serious reprimand from Pemberton, but he asked Mike, "You want to call this whole thing off? We could head north where it's cooler."

Mike did not respond, but remembering his loyalty to Marilla, he lay there for another five minutes and suddenly forced himself up. He sat straight up on the edge of the cot. While rolling his neck around, he stated, "Give me a shot of whiskey."

Tullis shook his head and replied, "You know what the doctor said; no hard alcohol."

Jones looked at Tullis at responded, "I'm not going to live much longer anyway. If you want me to kill that bastard Macro Cio, get me a bottle of whiskey."

Tullis turned to his segundo, the angular and tall Joe Carson. "You heard what the man said. Get him some whiskey."

Carson looked at Jones and back at Tullis, hesitating to obey the order.

Mike looked at him and said, "Look, Carson, we aren't going back north. At least I ain't, but if you want this outcome to be like we planned, get me some damn whiskey."

Carson got the damn whiskey. Later, to the surprise of the Pemberton riders, Jones had perked up, but he did not continue to drink. After two belts, he stood up, walked to the nearest cantina, and ate some frijoles. He had made a remarkable recovery.

Three days before the showdown in the Valley of the Sun, two heavy-duty, mule-driven wagons sat at the back entrance of Auguste Maduro's bank. Ten heavily armed men from Sheriff Lang's office sat on horseback, watching the loading proceedings. Nine men from the Pemberton group, also heavily armed, were situated on the periphery, watching the bank employees loading a hundred thousand dollars in gold bullion onto the two thickly made wagons with magnum axles.

The money had been withdrawn from former Brigadier General Frank McGrew's account. Auguste Maduro, along with two auditors, supervised the money being loaded onto the beds of the reinforced wagons.

Maduro did not mind losing the McGrew account. It was not his money in the first place, and he didn't especially like dealing with the high-handed Anglo, but secondly, by sending it in bullion form, it would be highly unlikely if Johnson won that he could transport it back to Texas on mules. Maduro assumed it would wind up back in his bank's vault once more. Therefore, he wanted the count to be fastidiously accurate since he expected to see it again ... soon.

Maduro felt strongly that if Macro Cio won, the gunman intended to deposit the money in his bank and then collude with Pedro Morales to buy Arturo Ruiz's mine. He once thought this was a done deal, which is the joint effort of Pedro Morales and Macro Cio to ruin Arturo Ruiz and drive him out of the country, but the thoughts of John Lee Johnson coming in and upsetting the financial and social applecart was now weighing heavily on his mind. If Johnson won, that would mean Macro was dead. It would break Pedro Morales financially, and Arturo Ruiz would again be the most powerful man in Temecula, a position Maduro coveted.

Maduro was spooked because he simply could not get over the shock of the Fierro brothers, along with five of his top security guards, vanishing from the face of the earth. He could not fathom how John Lee Johnson and a few of his men could have just run roughshod over his best men, as though they were nothing. He knew that had to be the case because the Fierro brothers and the guards he sent with them were well-paid and loyal. It was not in their character to forsake their duty.

But Maduro had accepted the rankling fact that they had died on his orders, orders he vowed he would not repeat. He would let matters run their course and not try and tamper with the outcome again.

But having the Comanchero chieftain betting on the big Texan and betting large, along with the fact that John Lee Johnson seemed unstoppable, caused him sleepless nights. For the first time in over a year, he was worried about Macro Cio and his own future.

CHAPTER 7

It was a late June afternoon when Tim Slater and his remaining crew made it to Austin. Even though dog-tired, they took the time to stable their horses before trudging wearily to the Austin Hotel. Slater was exhausted but still on alert for anyone who might recognize him, especially those in the employee of Lieutenant Bragg. He thought he knew all his agents and snoops, but the success of his mission hinged on his staying out of sight and out of mind.

The desk clerk, Bill Baker, was an older man; he was stocky and wore the traditional green visor and sleeve garters, earmarks of his trade. It just seemed odd that his old friend, Emil, the former desk clerk and old confidant, was nowhere in sight. Ol' Emil had been there for a decade and gave special information and favors to the Sheriff Lee faction.

Lieutenant Bragg had his own network of spies, and they were difficult to spot on the surface; therefore, Slater seemed suspicious of all strangers and new people until they were tested.

Baker seemed somewhat bored when they queued up at his counter, but upon hearing Slater's name as he wrote it on his ledger, he gave a subtle reaction that was picked up by Slater. That dodgy take bothered Slater, and he asked the clerk if he had ever heard of him.

Baker appeared surprised that he would ask him that question and artfully asked one of his own: "Mister, I don't know you from Adam, but should I?"

Slater let the matter go. He felt he might be showing his paranoia, but still, he was not totally convinced that the older clerk was not being devious. Not wanting his name bandied around in the hotel lobby, he let the matter go; he gave a fake smile, accepted his key, and began moving toward the near staircase that would lead him upstairs to his room.

As soon as the Slater party had signed in and paid and departed out of sight, Baker called for his assistant to take over while he took a toilet break. Baker went out the rear door that led to the outhouse, but after exiting, he made a beeline due west from behind the hotel down two blocks and crossed the street, making his way to Lieutenant Bragg's office.

Slater, disregarding sleep and leaving his men behind at the hotel, decided to check on his job status and see if he was still on the payroll; he began hoofing it down the hotel hallway and down the staircase. As he was taking two steps at a time down the landing, he noticed that the older clerk was no longer behind his desk. He told himself he would check on that on his return trip to the hotel.

He felt a necessary pressure to get to the sheriff's office before it closed. He knew he had to make his case before Sheriff Lang castigated him for a slipshod job or fired him. He felt that he had enough support to keep his job, but on the other hand, it was obvious that he had failed miserably.

But upon arrival at the courthouse, he was both surprised and disappointed when Lang's secretary told him that the high sheriff was in south Texas on business.

That business, unknown to both the secretary and Slater, was to oversee the gold shipment that was being brought to the Valley of the Sun to lure John Lee Johnson into what Lang considered the jaws of death.

As Slater turned to go back to the hotel, he saw Deputy Commissioner Braxton Gray out of the corner of his eye, as Lang's colorless second-in-command was leaving an office farther down the hall.

Braxton at first gave him a critical look that soon softened. Slater couldn't tell from Gray's expression whether he was welcomed or not. Braxton simply motioned for Slater to come into his office.

Slater walked toward Gray and went through the office door. He entered the office and took a seat on a leather chair facing Gray's desk.

Gray shut the door and took his time to make it to his desk; Slater had no idea that he would be frozen like this or he might have made other plans.

Without removing his hat, Gray sat down, took a cigar from his pocket, and slowly lit it. He didn't bother offering a cigar to Slater, which he would have done in the past. It was obvious that he had become persona non grata.

Gray lit his smoke, took several drags, and then let his watery blue eyes fall fully on Slater. "Tim, I'm surprised you came back."

Slater studied on his words and decided he had little status to lose; he answered, "Braxton, you know why I failed. At every angle from Baileysboro to the Pipton Ranch, it seems like John Lee Johnson and everyone and his brother had prior knowledge of what my plans were."

Gray nodded as though he agreed with him, but it was a guarded nod. He puffed some more and then became candid. "Be that as it may, the bottom line is ... you failed. It may good for you that Marshal Lang is gone. He's got a head and chest full of steam for you." He exhaled a thin blue line of smoke and added, "A whole lot."

Slater sat silent for a moment. He decided to go for broke since it was obvious that his career with the Texas state government had come to an end. The days of being important were over. The days of being an idle patron of a saloon and working for pittance were ahead. "You understand that Cornelia Benson's getting information from Lang through warm flesh, cool silk, and pillow talk, don't you, Braxton?"

Braxton allowed himself a begrudging smile. 'That's a nice way to put it, Tim."

There was a silent pause before anyone continued. Each man wanted the other to continue the conversation. Neither wanted to say too much.

Slater continued, "Love and lust are powerful intoxicants to some men." He paused and then said dramatically, "It's me that got caught in Lang's love-starved, blind eye this time, Braxton. But what about you? And it may not take long, I'm his whipping boy now, but you may be the next in line."

Braxton did not reply directly to that remark. Being a good politician, he gave tacit approval to Slater's comment and then said, "A few weeks ago, me and some of the boys decided to do a little experiment. We told Lang that we were going to hire some men and hit that new federal bank over in Stevensville. We told him that the robbers would get 20 percent, and we would get the rest.

"He asked us when this would all take place, and we told him in four days." Braxton placed his cigar in the corner of his mouth and leaned back thoughtfully in his chair. "We didn't pull the job off; it was all just an experiment on our part to see where the information would lead, but we did take note that four days later, the town of Stevensville had a dozen men from the cavalry unit here in Austin dressed in civilian clothes, waiting on that robbery that we never intended in the first place."

Slater gave a sarcastic smirk. "Like I said, you could be next, Braxton."

Braxton ignored that remark as he leaned forward with head hovering over halfway of the desk. "Now Tim, your days with us are through. You know it and I know it, but I got a plan for you."

Slater tossed his hands to the side to indicate he was listening.

Braxton leaned back and looked downward to a bottom drawer of his desk. "I got five thousand in greenbacks in my desk. If you kill Cornelia Benson, the money's yours, as long as you do it right and don't get caught."

Slater smiled inwardly; he had planned on doing it for free, so to be paid for it was a bonus. "How long are you giving me?"

"The rest of the week."

Slater nodded and asked, "How about tonight?"

Gray gave a small-lipped smile. "If you do it tonight, come by tomorrow night at nine. Meet me by the back door facing the alley, since my office will be locked. I'll have two saddlebags filled with the money. After you get your money, get the hell outta Austin, and stay the hell away from Lieutenant Bragg and Sheriff Lang."

Slater stood up from his chair and sounded all business as he said, "I got things to do, Braxton."

Gray nodded and replied, "Bet you do at that."

Slater returned to the hotel and caught a glimpse of the bothersome clerk, who was again behind the counter. The fact he had returned somewhat mollified his suspicious mind. However, he kept him in view as he moved to the stair landing. Putting the clerk momentarily aside, he made his way up to the second floor.

Later that afternoon, Cut Worm descended the stairs and made a quick left to go out the hotel's rear entrance. He was headed to the livery stable to rent a buckboard and team.

Baker, the desk attendant, noticed his exit but did not act on it. He was confident that Slater would make his appearance soon.

Sure enough, a half-hour later, Slater also descended the stairs, but as he started toward the back exit, he noticed the troublesome clerk watching him. The clerk's look was brief and appeared innocuous, but it caused

Slater to hold his view on him longer than normal. When he didn't receive a curious look back, he let the matter go and departed out the back door.

Baker, sensing Slater's suspicion, allowed some time to pass before leaving again. He did not want Slater to make a surprise return and catch him gone. Satisfied Slater had left for good, Baker notified his assistant that he had a call of nature again. But this time, he did not go out the back door. He skirted around the counter and headed out the wide front entrance. He was not blatant in his actions, but he did cross the street and enter the military building from the rear.

Baker soon returned and resumed his assigned duties. He offered his curious assistant no explanations as to his digestive troubles. But Corporal Dale Tidwell of company D, posing as Baker, had done his job. He just hoped his comrades did theirs.

The buckboard driven by Cut Worm with Slater as his passenger made its way in the gloaming shadows to the outskirts of Austin. Slater had timed it correctly. He knew it would be dark when they reached the antebellum-style mansion a quarter-mile from the last house in the city.

The night had become pitch-black, aided by a heavy overcast, when they caught sight of the house with only one orange solitary glow coming from a vertical side window. Slater gave himself a satisfied smile. He knew Cornelia Benson was home. Killing her wouldn't totally equal the prestige he had lost in this venture, but it sure in hell would help. He once had it all but now was considered a pariah to his brethren in Austin. Her death would be an equalizer of sorts for him.

The widow of a Confederate leader had been the hapless victim of old Judge Roy, the corrupt, rakish leader before Sheriff Lang. She had no choice in the matter—become his mistress or find herself in penury. She played her role the best she could, without the opprobrium she thought she might face.

But after the judge was killed, she had gone out of her way to seduce Sheriff Lang. She realized this was her ticket to bring down the whole crooked administration. She still loved her late husband, but without traditional weapons to avenge him, she chose the only ammunition in her arsenal: her charm and body.

Lang had been enamored of her for a long time. It seemed the whole city of Austin knew he was blinded by love. In their relationship, he conveniently overlooked anything suspicious because he could not bring himself to believe she did not care for him in the same way. Lang felt their love was so strong that he could tell her anything. He felt he had finally met his soulmate, and to prove his deep love, he'd tell her his deepest secrets and most sensitive plans.

Cornelia loathed Judge Roy and only tolerated Sheriff Lang; she used him mercilessly and regularly passed along his plans to the clever but honest Lieutenant Bragg, the quintessential good citizen, who disliked the so-called Reconstruction government policies. Her safety deposit box in the bank conveniently had two keys: one for her and one for Lieutenant Bragg. This had been their means of communication for almost two years.

Slater and the rest of Lang's whole cadre knew the sheriff was blinded by false love; the lovesick sheriff blamed all his failures on the ones who blindly carried out his orders. And when those plans blew up in their collective faces, the men who carried them out were called fools and incompetent.

Slater remained seated on the wagon seat, submerged in the heavy shadows of the small grove of trees. He let his eyes adjust to the environ. He took in the semicircular driveway that left the main road and cut toward her front lawn and bordered her columned porch.

Feeling the rush of acting on what he had schemed of doing for months, he slid out of the buckboard. As a second thought, he leaned in and whispered to Cut Worm, "When I turn up the lantern in the side window, come in and help me put the body in the hope chest."

Cut Worm did not verbally respond but gave him a two-finger salute that could be seen in the darkness.

With that, Slater, now fully out of the buckboard, disappeared into the darkness.

After Slater had been gone for over ten minutes, Cut Worm began watching the front door, anxious to catch the light break when it opened. Enduring this tense wait, he didn't see anything out of the ordinary; there was no noise except stridulating insects. He had to admire Slater's skulking skills; he had become invisible with the night.

But then two things happened in quick sequence: The front door noiselessly cracked opened, emitting a thick orange sliver of light; secondly, Cut Worm felt the presence of someone close, and then he heard someone else.

His eyes went from the thin line of orange to his immediate surroundings. He saw a darker shape emerge from the surrounding night shadows, climb up into the buckboard, and sit down in the same spot that Slater had exited from earlier.

Cut Worm reached for his sidearm, but the new passenger's shushing voice caused him to hesitate in drawing his pistol. He could now see that the new passenger was Hubert Hicks. Hicks placed a vertical finger over his lips, as he now had the alarmed Cut Worm's attention.

Cut Worm whispered in a confused voice, "What're you doin' here, Hubert?"

"Same as you," Hicks replied calmly. "Helpin' carry the ol' biddy to Tate's quicksand slough."

That answer did not set right with Cut Worm. He had not heard Slater mention that others would be involved. His puzzled face showed his concern, but he said nothing because of the sensitive situation taking place in the house. Suspicious, he continued to keep Hicks's darkened profile in view.

After leaving the buckboard, Slater had skirted the exterior right wall where the big window was emitting its oily rays. He peeked into the window only to see a ladderback chair, slowly rocking back and forth. He could not see Cornelia Benson herself from this particular angle. He looked some more but concluded there was nothing else to see, then he continued to slither along the outside walls. He checked the back porch and two sheds for suspicious signs or possibly additional horses. There was nothing out of the ordinary. He then completed his full circle of the house and crept onto the porch. He glanced to his right at the murky outline of his rented buckboard, and then he pulled his .44 from his holster.

He thought the door would be locked, but it was not. This fact fleetingly troubled him. Turning the knob, he pushed it open slowly, just enough to accommodate his sideways entry. He did not totally close the door behind him to soften any secondary noise. He found himself in a large, dark foyer. The orange light shining through the crack under the door guided his way.

He now was in the edges of the lighted parlor and could see the back of the rocking chair, rhythmically rocking to and fro. He clicked back on the hammer of his .44. This was the climactic moment he had dreamed of.

He didn't hesitate; he pulled the trigger three times, digging out chunks of disseminating wood debris from the back of the chair.

To his surprise, after his third shot, he could see, through the cloud of gunsmoke, the chair still rocking, even with the ladder back supports shot all to hell. Just then, his eyes went to the floor level, where he caught sight of a length of twine attached to the side of one of the rockers—that line was being pulled by someone concealed in the darkness, beyond the pale of the coal oil lamp.

Slater now knew he had walked into a trap; he began to walk backwards toward the entryway. He took two wary steps, and then multiple gunshots opened from all the dark places of the spacious room. He was hit three times as he was knocked to the side of the door opening. He painfully slid down the wall and slumped to the floor.

He was still conscious as he watched, powerless, as all the darkened silhouettes walked over to him. He saw Sergeant Brewer, Lieutenant Bragg's right-hand man. The next man he saw shocked him; it was Guy Morris, the so-called rustler from the Nations who had spurned his offer to rob the bank in Baileysboro. Slater now knew why; he was a damned federal. He was over being shocked when he saw Bennie Leonard, a man he had personally hired. Slater began to cry. All his plans had gone awry. He apparently had been betrayed, and on top of that, he knew he was slowly dying, and he had a good idea of what his doomed destiny would be.

Slater looked up at Sergeant's Brewer's face and said, "I guess I'm going into the hope chest and later tossed into Tate's quicksand."

Brewer nodded as he reloaded his .44. "Just like you intended to do to Mrs. Benson."

Slater nodded his head to indicate his partner, still sitting in the buckboard, and asked, "What about Cut Worm?"

Brewer shrugged and said, "That depends on him. He can't tell anyone he came out here with you. Lang would have him killed in five seconds. So I reckon he'll be the one who dumps your remains." He paused as he holstered his weapon. "So he'll live."

Slater looked up at the darkened ceiling, shook his head at his fate, and gave out a final sob before relaxing in death.

When the shooting began, Cut Worm's head was jerking with each gunshot he heard in the house. The outlaw's look of apprehension was not mirrored in the expression of his passenger. It was obvious that Hubert Hicks did not share his anxiety.

Knowing the answer beforehand, Cut Worm asked, "Was Slater set up?"

Hicks spoke calmly as he answered Cut Worm's question: "He's probably dead now, Cut Worm."

Cut Worm licked his lips and asked, "What's goin' to happen to me?"

Hicks shrugged and said, "Nothin'; me and you will go inside and put him in that whatever-it-is we are supposed to store him in. Then we'll carry him out here, load his sorry carcass up, and go dump him at Tate's swamp or quicksand site, whatever it's called.

"After all this is over, you'll go back to the stables and check in this wagon, and then you'll go to your hotel and never ever mention this night or ever being with Slater, or Lang will have your head."

Cut Worm's eyebrows pinched over his eyes. All of what Hicks said made sense. He asked about Slater's horse, stabled at the H&R Livery barn, saying that if it were still there, it would look suspiciously like Slater had been killed or apprehended.

Hicks informed him that the horse had been taken from his stall hours earlier and was now on its way to the cavalry unit just west of town, making it look as though Slater had taken his leave since he was no longer a viable member of Sheriff Lang's cadre.

Cut Worm nodded at the meticulous planning. "What about Mrs. Benson?"

Hicks gave him a firm but terse retort: "She's safe." It was obvious by his tone that the matter was to be dropped.

Cut Worm looked past Hubert Hicks's darkened profile toward the house and said, "Well, let's go get that bastard's body and get the job done." He sighed deeply and added, "I'm tired as hell."

CHAPTER 8

THE JOHNSON-TIMMS PARTY MOVED ACROSS THE CHIHUAHUA Desert; they had prepared for it well. They carried eight magnum kegs of water for the mules and horses and four casks for themselves. They carried ample fodder for the animals and enough shoes for a small cavalry unit.

They made good time, with enough rest for both humans and animals to replenish their strength. The trip was actually enjoyable, with lots of campfire conversations and time to get to know each other better.

Two things of note took place on the journey: One was an itinerant group of outlaws, a mixture of Mexicans and Anglos, who were moving northwards toward south Texas, with all intent to rob a series of banks; they caught sight of the Johnson-Timms party on the horizon.

Having no idea who they were (and caring even less), they immediately sized up the group as easy pickings and decided to bull-rush them and just take over the wagons and mules. They charged the Johnson-Timms group from two sides. Fifteen minutes later, the whole unit of outlaws was wiped out, with the exception of two severely wounded bandits, who rode back toward Mexico hanging on for dear life, clinging to their saddle horns, with the enormity of their mistake indelibly branded in their minds.

The second thing of note was how the Johnson-Timms group suddenly took to Fud. He worked hard to gain their trust, and he succeeded. He was among the first to rise, having the food and coffee ready. He was so good with the maintenance of both horses and mules that Van Edwards offered him a job at his livery stable in Gandy when the mission was over. His attitude was so positive and his humility so genuine that he soon won over the whole party. After a short period of time, Fud, whose real name was Fred Benfield, suddenly felt like he was one of the boys.

But one night in a conversation, he proved his worth even more, without realizing it. The whole group was gathered around the campfire, talking, with the exception of John Lee Johnson, who was out scouting the countryside, as he usually did.

Homer Timms mentioned to Fud that he was curious about the Mexicans who attacked them while they were encamped at the Pipton compound and what motivated them to travel all that distance.

In the past, Fud would have been too intimidated to talk, but now feeling part of the group, he began to speak freely.

He said the two brothers were named Theo and Roberto Fierro, and they worked for a banker named Auguste Maduro, who was interested in the Johnson-Macro Cio wager made between Pugh Larrimore and a local silver miner named Pedro Morales.

Homer Timms stopped him to ask him how he knew all this, since he didn't speak Spanish.

Fud gave a shy grin and shocked all of them by admitting that he was fluent in Spanish; he didn't want the Fierro brothers and friends to know that. He said he grew up along the small communities that bordered the Chihuahua Desert, living and working daily with Mexicans, and had learned their language; he also picked up on the different dialects.

He made his listeners grin when he confessed he didn't want the Fierro brothers to know that fact, in case he overheard them say they were going to kill him. He told them a lot of facts they already knew, but when he related a campfire discussion he had overheard among the Fierro brothers and their five associates, he had Homer's full attention.

He said the Fierros had stated that Sheriff Robert Lang, the high authority in Texas, was supposedly headed to their area and was going to oversee the transfer of a hundred thousand dollars of gold to the Valley of the Sun. But what really captured Homer's attention was the information that Lang intended on sniping John Lee Johnson from Mons Rojo, a small butte that sat beside the mouth of the valley itself.

Fud went on to state that the Fierro brothers claimed that Lang had been a sharpshooter in the Union army in the late war and was planning to lodge himself with his weapon in this particular butte and kill Johnson from long range. He modified his information by saying that the Fierro brothers could not say for sure that Lang was actually going to do this, so they had been sent northward to cinch the deal.

Homer felt that Lang's dry-gulching plan was legitimate and not mere supposition; he had an idea that since Lang did not have the intellectual qualities of the late Judge Roy, he had to make up for it by being overly zealous. He knew the sheriff had to be a complete toady for McGrew. He would obviously be there for the handling of the gold to entice John Lee Johnson for the Macro Cio gunfight. It was also in character for Sheriff Lang to shoot John Lee Johnson from a cowardly ambush and take full credit for it from the high boss.

By chance, he asked Fud if he had ever been to the Valley of the Sun, and Fud answered in the affirmative. He said that a year ago, he had been part of a gang that tried to rob the bank in Temecula but had failed. He claimed they had made a ragtag retreat through the Valley of the Sun and remembered the geographical area well; it was a dreary place with various hogbacks and high ridges and buttes that surrounded the valley, much like a horseshoe.

Homer handed him a stick he found on the ground and asked him to draw what he remembered.

Fud took the stick and began to etch in the sand the horseshoe shape of the valley, with its opening facing north. He imaged the eastern butte that Lang would probably be in, but his sand sketch also had a smaller rocky hillock across from Lang's location that bordered the opening to the valley.

Homer asked him once more if he felt he had drawn this pretty much in detail. Fud could sense that Homer was going to act on his information, so he felt the pressure of being accurate; after considering a moment, he nodded. "If you're goin' to do what I think you're goin' to do, I want to tell you that I have done the best I could, accordin' to my recollection."

The next morning, Homer took John Lee Johnson aside and told him what Fud had said about the crafty Texas sheriff and his plans of a sharpshooting assassination from one of the rocky hills near the mouth of the valley. He also relayed to John his plan of preventing this, which required his leaving early to the Valley of the Sun.

The big Texan, like everyone else, held Homer in the highest esteem. Therefore, he didn't deter him in this project, since Homer was rarely ever wrong on his analysis of a situation and the action needed to make the outcome favorable. Therefore, he readily nodded his assent at his valuable ally and best friend.

John appreciated Homer's sage grasp of the situation and his willingness to act on it immediately.

John knew that a Sharps .52 could do serious damage even at a half-mile. He also knew he did not need that threat hanging over him when he rode into the valley.

Homer mounted up and rode off without further comment, with the butt of his own Sharps .52 jutting conspicuously from its specially made sheath.

Sheriff Lang, who had not been present at the loading of the two wagons of gold in Temecula, later joined the wagons at the edge of town as they set off for the Valley of the Sun. He eyed Pemberton's California contingent suspiciously but kept his thoughts to himself. But innately, he distrusted them since he had no viable connection with them.

Both groups, riding on different sides of the wagons, slowly advanced to the bleak valley. Although the valley was shaped like a horseshoe, surrounded by smaller mountains and buttes, there was a cut in the backside of it that led to an old Aztec altar and the ruins of a Jesuit mission.

Once there, and confronted with the violent vestiges of a bloody past, they pulled up and soberly sat on their horses for a considerable time, taking in the sight of the stark altar that had been used in human sacrifice in the pre-Columbian age.

One hundred feet from this pagan locus lay the partial rocky outline of an adobe mission, laying forlornly in the sun as a reminder of the horrific waste of human life that was written in its ruins. It once had been a beautiful mission but over a century back had been laid waste and the priests butchered by the local Yaquis, who felt these black-robed men had offended their native gods.

Here in the heart of this desolate valley, the incessant wind and the hot, orange sun created a sterile world that appeared more likely created by the devil and his angels than God. Both parties slowly dismounted and began struggling to place the gold on the offensive Aztec altar.

Once the wagons were unloaded and the gold counted by an accountant who had made the trip, Lang and Pemberton's men headed back to Temecula, hoping to leave behind the memory of this dreadful place.

Sheriff Robert Lang rode at a tangent from the riders heading back in the direction from which they had ridden. The Pemberton group took note of that, but they knew it would be impossible for him to steal the gold. Therefore, they took his departure in stride and did not think much of it, other than it was either idle or foolish.

Lang, who had corresponded months earlier with Auguste Maduro about trying to kill Johnson from long range, rode toward a butte close to the northern entrance. This particular reddish-colored bluff had been chosen by some of his subordinates acquainted with the area months back.

He rode to the backside of it and found it to be ideal for his scheme. After dismounting, he climbed the slight incline of the bluff and found it to offer an excellent view of the entrance. He knew if he were to get a fair shot at the big Texan, this was the ideal location.

Lang knew that once he brought down John Lee Johnson, he would forever be in McGrew's good graces. Lang understood that McGrew's hatred for Johnson knew no boundaries and that if he were successful in this endeavor, he would be given all the power and money he ever imagined.

He confidently smiled to himself. He had been considered one the best sharpshooters in the whole Army of the Potomac. Now he felt he had the upper hand. Johnson would have to come through the entrance and would be an easy target. He had certainly made more difficult shots. He was confident that he would succeed, unlike Slater and the other morons he had employed.

After taking care of his horse and tethering him where he could easily see him from his elevated position, he concentrated on his craft. He unpacked his scoped rifle, which he had concealed from his own men as well the Pembertons. It was a long-barrel Sharps. The blue barrel had been buffed to lose its gloss. Its scope had been calibrated by the best gunsmith in Austin. He carefully cradled the deadly weapon as he leaned forward and moved up the embankment. He decided to make his camp on a level shelf that accommodated his view of the entrance between two sentinel-type citadels of rock.

After making two trips up and down the soft-inclined bluff, he had all the supplies and ammunition he'd need for the next two days. At last, he settled down on the inviting ledge where he would spend the rest of the afternoon and night.

Early the next morning, as the unyielding Mexican sun peered over the horizon, Robert Lang arose from his bedroll and made his way to his chosen shooting location. His scoped Sharps lay in its shooting perch. He scrunched down into position as he raised the rifle and looked through the scope. He panned the area through the circular magnification; upon seeing nothing of note, he lay the rifle aside and slithered back to his original position, where he made a small fire and began making himself some coffee.

He dozed off after drinking two cups; when he awoke, he grabbed some beef jerky and returned to his perch to reestablish that he was in command of the time and situation. By virtue of his own eyesight, he found no sign of anyone or anything. Wanting to make doubly sure, he scoped the entrance of the valley. Again, he saw nothing but the depressingly low mountains and the complete lack of life.

He gave himself a satisfied smile that things were as they should be. He lay his rifle aside. The only problem he could see was adjusting to the direct sunlight and raw heat it brought. He lay on his side and scooted to utilize the shadows of the two jutting rock sentinels that flanked his position.

He ignored the hot temperature as he continued to check and investigate the valley entrance throughout the shank of the day. He kept up this routine throughout the afternoon.

Around four o'clock, he scoped the entrance again; discovering no sign of human life, he turned his circular sight to the surrounding countryside. As he idly panned to the opposite rocky hillock, he thought he saw something, but checking again, determined that it was his imagination. So he moved past the hillock to other locations, but the niggling thought that he might have seen something and overlooked it caused him to swerve his circular vision once more to the rocky tor.

This time, there was no doubt; there in his sight, he saw a man's face, and he was holding a rifle with a scope looking back at him. Lang's head jerked up from the rifle sight, and his eyes filled with alarm. He quickly sent his vision back into his circular rifle scope. As his eye bulged into the scope, at that moment, he caught sight of an orange rifle flash in the round lens, erupting from the opposite hill. That was the last thing he ever saw;

his scope went black. A rifle ball crashed into part of the glass lens of the scope and entered his right eye socket, shattering his features.

Sheriff Robert Lang, the angular, autocratic dictator of Texas, groaned, dropped his rifle, and fell onto his stomach. His body trembled and spasmed. He was dead within five minutes.

An hour later, Homer Timms climbed the backside of the butte, where he found the dead sheriff. He thoroughly cleaned up all evidence that Lang had been there: the burnt campfire remains, skillet, coffee pot, sleeping bag, everything. He claimed all the money in the sheriff's possession and disposed of the sheriff's badge and other identification in a deep crevasse.

He dragged Sheriff Lang's body down from the bluff, feet first, and undressed him down to his drawers. He placed his clothes and boots in an empty provision bag to be picked up later. Next, he saddled and bridled Lang's horse. He tied a rope loop around Lang's ankles and mounted the sheriff's sorrel, he circled the pommel with the rope, and began pulling the dead body face down across the rocky terrain until it was unrecognizable and then dismounted and threw the bloody corpse into an abyss a mile away from their origin. He undid the rope and retied it to the saddle and rode back to the bluff.

There, he conveniently took Lang's rifle sheath and rifle and adjusted it to his saddle. He bundled up Lang's clothes, boots, and hat in a canvas carryall and placed these bagged items over the cantle of the sheriff's horse. Later aboard his own horse and pulling the sheriff's mount, he rode in different directions hiding bits and pieces of his clothing in different rock fissures.

Homer did not want the sheriff's horse returning to Temecula, so he took him with him until he knew the horse would be disoriented enough to go for the smell of water rather than rely on his instinctive need to return to his place of origin.

He pulled him though the valley's entrance and kept pulling him for the rest of the day and up into the night. Homer made a silent camp until dawn and then resumed his journey. Coming to a place where he knew water was nearby, he stopped and removed all the horse's gear. He tried to shush the bewildered horse away. The horse milled for a few minutes but after Homer shot a pistol over its head, the big sorrel broke into a gallop, heading across the bleak horizon. Homer concealed the horse's tack in various locations on this trek to meet up with his friends. As he rode along, he gave silent thanks for the providence of meeting the man named Fud.

Back in Austin, Braxton Gray, the second-most powerful man in Texas, was worried. Tim Slater, who had promised to kill Lang's mistress, had missed his appointment to pick up his money for doing the job. That meant he hadn't done the job. Since he knew that Slater was needing funds, and since he hadn't shown, that he must be either dead or captured. Gray hadn't counted on this unforeseen quandary. He had thought this plan to kill Cornelia Benson was confidential, a two-man deal, but if Slater was dead, that meant Lieutenant Bragg might have had prior knowledge. Why Bragg was involved and how he was implicated he could not fathom, but regardless, he certainly didn't want to tangle with the officious officer. He was well aware of the lieutenant's persistent telegraphing to his Washington cronies and the number of federal agents that were already in Texas in sheep's clothing, sent on Bragg's repeated messages claiming egregious malfeasance in the sheriff's department.

Gray was mulling over these negative matters as he walked from his second-story office down the short hallway to the stairs of the courthouse building. One question that festered in Gray's mind was, who might have been with Slater when he went missing?

When he reached street level, he saw something that startled him: Cornelia Benson was riding by in her buggy. She looked as though she had no worries in the world. She graced Braxton with a cheery smile and an affectionate nod of her head.

Gray stood momentarily flummoxed. She definitely was not dead. He concluded that Slater had not only failed in his mission but was most likely dead, himself.

As far as Cornelia Benson, she had never shown him any notice in the past but now had eye contact and a smile obviously meant for him. He wondered if she were flirting with him or being sarcastic in a cutesy way, as though she knew something he didn't.

He watched as her buggy moved on down the line and turned at the H&R stable, which took her out of sight. Seeing the livery sign hanging from the barn loft reminded him that he needed to check on Slater's horse.

When he reached the big livery barn, he asked the day manager, a portly and unkempt man named Ragsdale, if he knew anything about Slater's horse. Ragsdale said the horse had been lodged in a stall but had been checked out for some period of time.

Gray asked if he knew if Slater had personally checked his horse out or perhaps someone else.

Ragsdale said the night man informed him that he noticed the horse missing around seven o'clock that night, but the bill had been paid by money in an envelope that had the name Tim Slater written on it. He let the matter go since envelope had the correct amount of money. He figured it was business as usual and thought no more about it.

Ragsdale, seeing Braxton Gray's unusual interest in Slater's horse, added, "The night man also informed me that Cut Worm Weaver had checked out a short-bed wagon, and he had seen both Slater and Cut Worm leaving town, headed toward the old Plantation Road." Ragsdale paused and added, "He said it was gettin' dark when they left."

Ragsdale went on to say that the night man had written in his rental log that Cut Worm had returned, alone, around two in the morning with two dirty horses and a buckboard with mud-mired wheels. Ragsdale recounted that the night man had said Slater was not with Cut Worm. But since Slater's horse stall and maintenance had been paid for, even with the horse missing, he had just assumed he had returned earlier and left.

Gray thoughtfully stroked his chin. He now knew Cut Worm had been with Slater. That answered an irritating question. Now, it was imperative that he contact Cut Worm. He feared that Cut Worm might have knowledge through Slater that he, Gray, might be involved in a plot against Cornelia Benson. He could not have that particular problem hanging over his head. He realized he needed to pick Cut Worm's brain fast.

As he exited the large barn, he fortuitously caught sight of Cut Worm exiting the hotel, two buildings down; he watched as Cut Worm directed his steps toward a pushcart street vendor and bought a fried peach pie.

Gray stopped dead in his tracks, made a hard left, and walked toward the slender man in question.

At that moment, Cut Worm had just taken a sizeable bite of his fried peach pie and had turned toward one of the two long benches that fronted the hotel. As he was making ready to sit down, he peripherally caught sight of Gray walking toward him. Suddenly that peach pie did not taste so good.

He knew he was going to undergo a serious question-and-answer period about Tim Slater that he was not ready for. He decided to tell as much truth as possible and lie about things that could get him killed.

He knew better than pretend that he did not see Gray approaching, but he secretly wished he were an ostrich with its head buried in the sand. He took another large bite of his fried peach pie, hoping he could enjoy it before he had to face the inquisition he knew was coming.

He grittily bit the bullet, courage-wise, and turned his head, making eye contact with the dour man who now was standing near his bench. He could tell by the commissioner's face that he was galled and that he was getting ready to sit beside him.

Cut Worm scooted over and allowed Braxton Gray to sit. He placed his half-eaten fried peach pie to his left and then gripped the edge of the bench to keep his hands from shaking. For a moment, he wished he were back at the desolate Pipton Ranch.

Gray sat down heavily. It was an authoritarian sit-down: all stiffly business. He remained silent for a few seconds, with his narrowed eyes directed forward as though marshaling his thoughts. Finally, he relaxed his rigid posture and leaned back against the backrest. He gave a partial view of his face to the slender lackey.

"Cut Worm, I'm going to ask you some questions, and you had damn sure better not lie or cut corners." Not giving Cut Worm a chance to respond, he continued, "You and Slater went riding toward sundown. You came back and Slater didn't. Tell me what happened, and I want the truth."

Cut Worm sighed and said, "I'm not shore where to begin."

Gray looked at Cut Worm's bony profile and asked, "Did someone pay him or promise to pay him to kill Cornelia Benson?"

Cut Worm shook his head in the negative. Cut Worm reasoned since Gray knew Cornelia Benson was involved, he knew lying about that was out of the question. "Slater has been at odds with the widow lady for some time now. He made plans over a month ago to kill her." Cut Worm thought on Gray's question some more and added, "Ain't nobody I know of wanted to pay him to do it. Even before the Pipton Ranch failure, he took it all on his own to take care of the matter."

Gray's face did not show it, but he was greatly relieved. He was off the hook. He felt Cut Worm was telling the truth. But he still was curious about the fate of Slater. "Tell me what happened." After an uncomfortable pause, he added, "I don't want a bunch of lies to save your neck. If you tell me the straight of it, I can see to it that you still have a future with us." Gray's voice dropped to an ominous register. "But if you lie to me, you will be dead before sunset."

Cut Worm, shocked by the severity of his words, swallowed audibly and then began, "Slater told me back at the Pipton Ranch that he was goin' to kill the ol' gal for ruinin' his plans and everyone else's plans that were connected to Sheriff Lang.

"So, when we got here in Austin, he told me to rent a buckboard and we would go out to her house, and he would kill her and hide her body in somethin' called a hope chest."

"Go on."

Cut Worm knew the next part of his speech had better be well-crafted, or he was as good as dead. He also knew he was a poor liar. His memory or logic did not favor lying, and since he feared Gray more than Sheriff Lang, he decided to do something completely drastic: He decided to tell the truth.

Braxton Gray had prompted himself to be skeptical and look for errors in Cut Worm's tale but found himself surprised at the logical veracity of it all.

When Cut Worm got to the part of Slater sneaking around the house and the subsequent gunfire inside the house, he had Gray's undivided attention. He went on to tell in detail about Hubert Hicks climbing into the buckboard and making himself at home and later assisting him and Bennie Leonard in cramming the body into the hope chest. He mentioned that there were other men were present but didn't know who they were. He related that they were very closed-mouthed around him, but he had an idea they were working for the army officer, Lieutenant Bragg.

Cut Worm then described how Hicks and Bennie Leonard and he had loaded up the hope chest, serving as a coffin, with difficulty. He described how they went to the quicksand location in his rented buckboard with the two men's horses tied on the tailgate.

When Gray heard the name Hubert Hicks, it mentally shook him. He had been with Slater when he hired them sometime back. He realized now the enormity of their mistake and recognized more clearly the insidious subterfuge of the wily Lieutenant Bragg.

Gray had another nettling question: "How come they didn't kill you?"

Cut Worm sighed; he hated admitting it, but he confessed, "They figured since I was there at Mrs. Benson's place that I would incriminate myself if I was to tell. And I also helped in burying Slater. They knew I was in so deep that it probably was a waste of time killin' me, since they didn't figure I'd have the guts to tell."

Gray evaluated Cut Worm's tale and decided he was telling the truth. He sat stunned as he digested all this disturbing information, but didn't want Cut Worm to know that fact.

As Gray sat and stared straight ahead, he concluded that Slater had made known his plans to kill the widow Benson, and somehow others had overheard him and then passed this information on. It seemed like an ironic outcome that he was killed by divulging his motive and plans to others, when he had accused Cornelia Benson of doing the same thing.

Gray ended the conversation by slapping his knees with the palms of his hand and quickly rising. He glanced down at the still-seated Cut Worm. "Come over to my office in an hour, and bring those two gunfighters with you."

He said over his shoulder as he walked away, "I've got some money for you and the chance to make a whole lot more."

Cut Worm, surprised how the truth worked in his favor and Gray's positive reaction, grabbed his half-eaten fried peach pie and jumped to his feet. He gave a hearty, "Yes, sir," and quickly left to find Utah Jimmy Pruett and Memphis Mayford.

Braxton Gray was in his office with his eyes darting up at the regulator clock. He knew it was time for them to arrive. Seated in the dark corner of the office was Sheriff Lang's private secretary, a man named Horace Hewlitt, a wormy-looking individual with thick glasses and a choleric personality. Gray wanted him there for a witness against any pushback from Lang about what he was planning on doing. Horace was not liked by anyone, including his own wife, but he was greatly respected. Gray needed him as a credible witness of what he had planned.

The officious Horace jumped to his feet when he heard the knocks on the door. He swung the door wide open and stepped aside as Cut Worm, Jimmy Pruett, and Memphis Mayford entered. There were no other chairs besides Horace's in the corner, so all three men stood before Gray's desk, like schoolboys facing the headmaster.

Gray had a fake smile plastered on his face as he panned the three men's faces. "Boys, I got some plans for you." He paused and added with a more friendly tone, "Big plans."

He placed a cigar in the corner of his mouth and thumb-snapped a match. He lit his smoke, and after shaking out the match, he slowly reached down and pulled up two leather bags filled with greenbacks. He counted out three thousand dollars, placed a thousand dollars in front of each man, and then looked up to catch their reaction.

They seemed more confused than receptive, so he explained, "I want you three to go to the H&R stable and pick out a good packhorse and go to the Austin mercantile store and get you some supplies." He took another puff and added, "You're headed to south Texas to kill John Lee Johnson."

Before Cut Worm could shoot his hands down to gather up his thousand dollars, Jimmy Pruett broke in. "Make it fifteen hundred each, and we'll do it."

Gray gave a phony pained look. He shook his head in the negative as though Pruett had asked too much. But much to the surprise of Horace Hewlitt, watching intently from the corner of the room, Gray then slapped his hands down on his desk and agreed to Jimmy's demands, saying, "Okay, damn it."

Gray sighed and leaned back in his chair as though they had outfoxed him. "Get the job done, and I'll give you five thousand dollars to split among yourselves."

Jimmy Pruett looked back and forth at his cronies, who were giving him positive looks.

Gray counted out the correct amounts and shoved them to the three individuals. He then looked each one in the eyes and asked, "Do we got a deal or not?"

Utah Jimmy shot his hand over the desk and shook Braxton Gray's hand like Gray was an ambassador of God. "Give us two hours, and we'll be headin' to south Texas and shoot that big bastard dead."

Later in the H&R Livery barn, after purchasing a three-year-old sorrel mare for a packhorse, Cut Worm worriedly looked back and forth at Memphis Mayford and Utah Jimmy Pruett. "Chief Gray ain't goin' to like it one bit that you charged that mare to the sheriff's department."

Utah Jimmy shrugged and said, "Hell, Cut Worm, we're goin' to charge some more stuff at the Austin general store. Big cigars, coffee, and enough beef jerky for a squadron of soldiers."

Cut Worm exclaimed, "They'll just take it out of the five thousand dollars when we get back."

Utah Jimmy gave him a subtle but tolerant smile, and Memphis Mayford seemed totally indifferent to Cut Worm's worrisome words.

Cut Worm tilted his head this and that way, trying to figure out the two gunmen's enigmatic expressions and body language. Seeing that his words had little effect and catching the veiled looks between the two men, he suddenly had a revelation.

Cut Worm stepped back with a startled look on his face. That look quickly transitioned into a knowing expression. "You ain't goin' to south Texas and look for John Lee Johnson, are you?"

Both Utah Jimmy and Memphis Mayford gave Cut Worm a scornful look. Utah Jimmy placed a patronizing hand on Cut Worm's bony shoulder. "Do you think me and Memphis Mayford are really headed South to look for that big sumbitch?" Not giving Cut Worm a chance to reply, Jimmy continued, "There ain't no way in hell that I'm goin' to ride all the way there, accumulating all kind of saddle sores, just to be buried six feet deep in that hot, south Texas dirt.

"No, siree, Cut Worm, me and Memphis Mayford are headed to Utah. My uncle has a ranch he'll sell to me for three thousand dollars. Me and Memphis Mayford are goin' to pool our money and buy it."

Seeing he had Cut Worm's attention, Jimmy elaborated, "The spread's got a big ranch house with a two-sided porch. You can sit outside and cuss, drink, and smoke, while them damn cows multiply." Jimmy's eyes gleamed when he added the clincher: "And there ain't no damn John Lee Johnson."

Cut Worm thoughtfully rubbed his chin with his index finger and thumb, as the images Jimmy described wistfully passed through his mind. He dreamily repeated Pruett's words, "Ain't no damn John Lee Johnson."

Jimmy happily nodded, adding, "Not for over one thousand miles. That bastard will be working someone else's hindquarters over for a change."

Having said his piece, Jimmy removed his hand from Cut Worm's shoulder. He and Memphis Mayford abruptly turned from him and were heading to gather their new packhorse and mounts. As the two men were making ready to saddle up and visit the mercantile store, they both gave a quick two-finger salute of farewell to their comrade.

Cut Worm, feeling the effect of being left behind, shouted out, "Hey." The two gunmen turned to face him.

Cut Worm said, "You think the three of us could buy that ranch instead of just two? I think I would like sittin' on that porch."

Jimmy smiled and said, "And with no damn John Lee Johnson in sight." Jimmy looked over at Memphis Mayford's agreeable face and added, "Say hello to our new partner." Turning to Cut Worm, he said, "Throw you a saddle on that mangy roan of yours, and let's go charge some more stuff; after all, we are up-and-comin' cattlemen."

Back in Deputy Commissioner Gray's office, Horace Hewlitt had pushed his chair back to the front of Gray's desk. He took the seat, leaned forward over the desk, and asked, "Braxton, do you think it was wise to give those yahoos forty-five hundred dollars? Hell, that Cut Worm is average at best, and those two gunfighters failed the first time. They ain't likely to do it the second time."

Braxton Gray leaned back in his chair. "Best money I've ever spent, Horace." He leaned forward to meet the eyes of the meddlesome secretary. "There are some things you don't know, Horace, so trust me on this. Cut Worm may not even know it, but he has essentially played into Lieutenant's Bragg's hands. He would be passing along incriminating information on us for what they have over him." Gray's eyes took on a twinkle. "I would have had to hire a gunman to kill the bastard, and that costs money. As far as Utah Jimmy and Memphis Mayford, two run-of-the-mill gunfighters are now off the payroll. Not only that, they are going to take off to God knows where. They won't be around here, running their mouths. I can now take the money I was going to pay them and get some gunfighters who aren't scared out of their minds about facing John Lee Johnson." Gray took a serious puff off his cigar and repeated, "Best money I ever spent."

Horace leaned back in his own chair with an approving expression. "Someday, you just might be ruling Texas, Braxton."

Braxton did not reply to that remark. But that thought was in the back of his mind.

CHAPTER 9

IT WAS JULY THE FIRST. A SUNDAY. MIKE JONES AND THE LANKY JOE Carson were up by six o'clock. They had coffee over the small fire Tullis had made earlier. There was tension in the air among Pemberton's men; not much was being said. The whole group knew that on this very day, Mike Jones was putting his life on the line. He would either be successful or die. With this in mind, the conversations were terse and limited because anything spoken could be perceived as awkward or too forced. They remained silently pensive for the most part, but the California gunman received a lot of nonverbal support in the form of pats on the back and shoulders. Jones knew he had their support but inwardly regretted that he was the centerpiece of their tautened state of mind.

Jones drank one cup of coffee and nixed anything else. He didn't want any food that could trigger his heart spells. He had taken his medicine with his coffee and poured water on a bandana and wrapped it around his neck to keep him cooler. He had exchanged his California banking clothes for denim pants and a yellow buttonless shirt. If he were worried, he didn't show it; if anything, he seemed relieved to finally complete his mission, one way or another.

He had hidden some extra heart tablets in a small pocket on his dungarees. He asked Joe Carson for some extra canteens and received six. He had many eyes on him when he reached down and placed them on his gun belt; that action seemed to draw attention to the magnitude of his assignment and the short amount of time left.

The whole Pemberton unit gathered around him. They were suffering from the angst of the impending showdown. Not only did Jones's new associates like and respect him, but there was a sense of pride that he was not only California's finest, but was one of them.

When it was nine thirty, Joe Carson brought around the buggy. It was understood that Carson would take him to the site of Valley of the Sun's Aztec altar and have him there a half-hour early. It was also understood that Carson would drive back at one o'clock and retrieve Mike Jones or bury him, one way or another. None of this was verbalized. But the thought of it seemed to ratchet up the somber mood even more among Jones's supporters.

Mike climbed into the buggy and began sipping water. Carson snapped the reins, and they were off. After riding a while, Jones looked over at Carson, who was being stoically silent, and extended his hand. Carson, seeing the proffered hand, quickly took Jones's hand and shook it. That bonding handshake signified unity and friendship and brotherhood, with no words being spoken.

The two men passed a Catholic mission just a half-mile out of the small town. They could hear children singing "Ave Maria." Those young voices so innocent and beatific, contrasted so deeply with the dark violence ahead. Those childlike voices laid bare the two paths of life: God's way or the devil's way. Those conflicting views matched the feelings of the two men headed inexorably into the dreary Valley of the Sun.

In Temecula, Macro Cio held Alicia in his arms. She gave him a brave smile, placed a white carnation in the buttonhole of his tan coat, and said, "Kill John Lee Johnson and return to me, my love."

Macro Cio pulled her in for one more lusty kiss. After several minutes, he sighed as he withdrew. "Hold that thought."

She laughed lustfully, as he stepped back and mounted his new appaloosa horse with the ornate silver saddle. He smiled down at her and told her to wait for him at five at the bodega and order the red wine again. He then took on his no-nonsense gunfighter's face; gigging the beautiful mount, he did not look back as he galloped away to meet John Lee Johnson.

It was 11:25 a.m. when Joe Carson and Jones passed the altar of the sun, stacked heavily with wooden containers secured with tight metal bands. These heavy military-style trunks were filled with gold bullion. Their eyes were filled with awe at the rich but heavy treasure the winner would have, but that wonderous thought quickly evaporated into the sobering reality of the big showdown.

Their buggy passed the altar and pulled up to one of the mission's few remaining walls, which extended at least seven feet into the air. That was enough to create a sizeable shadow, even near noon.

Jones, still seated in the buggy, grabbed one of his canteens and removed his hat. He poured half the contents of the container over his head. The overflow settled on his shoulders and chest. Joe Carson, obviously concerned, handed him two more canteens and said, "Take 'em. It's better to have 'em and not use 'em than to need them and not have 'em."

Jones grabbed them and gave a nod to the angular Carson that he probably was correct. He stepped down from the buggy and immediately sought the shade from the uneven and fragmented partial wall.

Joe Carson gave him an evaluating look. Jones looked surprisingly alert with a particular strength that he had not had days prior. Satisfied that Jones was fit as he could be for the gunfight, Carson angled the buggy around and snapped the reins. He headed back to the small Mexican village.

Jones watched the departing buggy become a mere dot on the barren, yellowish horizon. He looked around, taking in the bleak and desolate countryside. He gave himself a mirthless smile as he panned the whole area from beneath the lifesaving shadows of the mission wall. This cheerless smile was spawned because he never knew, when he was eighteen, practicing his draw and perfecting his shooting skills, or even later in life, when he was the toast of California, that his destiny would be ending up in one of the most desolate places on earth, the Valley of the Sun, which looked very much to him like the Valley of Death.

He didn't dwell on that long as his smile transitioned into a thin line; his eyes picked up an appaloosa in the distance, cantering toward him. He knew it was not John Lee Johnson because the rider was coming from the south. He knew it had to be Macro Cio. Jones suddenly took on an impassive face. He felt no need to greet his nemesis with anything less than his true feelings.

He felt better than he had in a month. He had not felt his heart flutter all morning long, and he hoped providence would continue to smile favorably on him. He was glad Cio was coming in early. He knew the temperature would soon be unbearable. He decided to stay in the wall's shadows as long as possible. It was imperative that he face arrogant Cio early while he still was Mike Jones and not an aging man with a heart condition.

Macro Cio, as he rode in, had seen a buggy pass far to his left, going back toward the small village not far from Temecula. He knew that buggy had probably brought Mike Jones to the old mission. It irritated him that the intrusive gunfighter from California had involved himself in a gunfight that was not his fight.

He reasoned in his own mind to just kill Jones and get the pest out of the way. He had it mentally mapped out that after he killed Jones, he would in sequential order knock off John Lee Johnson and then eradicate Homer Timms, Johnson's second. He didn't plan on messing around. Since Jones had obviously been dropped off, it would be impossible to send him packing with his tail tucked between his legs. He felt it was a logistical necessity to rid himself of Jones as soon as possible.

Cio, having caught sight of Jones himself beside the ruined mission facade, chose to ride toward the jagged remnants of the wall where Jones was positioned. He coveted the shade that Jones was now occupying, making it even more necessary to brace him as soon as possible.

Another thing in Cio's mind was that he could not logically afford to face John Lee Johnson or Homer Timms and have a possible turncoat shoot him in the back after he had done all the heavy lifting, and then claiming the hundred thousand dollars as his own.

Cio scrutinized Jones from the edges of his eyes as he slowed his mount to a walk and rode up just four feet away from the California gunman. Their eyes met, and then Cio rode past him, dismounted, and tied off his horse, utilizing a gaping hole in the dilapidated rock wall.

The tense moment was accentuated by the scorching orange sun set high in the valley sky. Those heat filled rays illuminated and vivified the stark yellow sand and sparse weeds that grew in the infertile soil. An eagle's black, menacing silhouette was outlined against the fiery orange of the sun; it screeched out in the near distance as he hovered ominously, seeking a prey.

Other than the eagle, there were no other sounds, including the usually ubiquitous wind. It was as though time and nature had purposely chose to stand still. However, each sound was magnified: the silvery sound of the bridle bits of Cio's horse, the leathery sounds of the saddle and stirrups as

Cio dismounted. Jones could hear his own breathing and each spur jingle as Cio walked behind and around his horse and stood in the sun, facing him.

They sent evaluating looks to the other. Neither spoke for several minutes. Then Cio's eyes moved to an indistinct point above Jones's head. He asked in a disdainful tone. "Jones, is it?"

The Basque's eyes quickly leveled as he awaited Jones's response.

Jones gave a small nod but did not verbally reply.

Cio snorted as he shook his head side to side in a contemptuous manner. "You got my message about not showing up, right?"

"I got the message."

Cio's eyes widened as he scornfully added, "And yet, you showed up." Not waiting for a response, Cio continued, "You aren't too intelligent, Jones."

Jones gave Cio his quick dimpled smile. "You really are an ass."

Cio heard him but had never met anyone with the trepidation to speak to him in that manner. Cio thought on Jones's words and his deportment. With an exaggerated sneer, he said, "It's reported you are California's finest."

Jones drolly replied, "Some people do carry on."

Cio again shook his head, in disbelief that Jones had such a strong sense of confidence.

Cio gave a quick look to the south to see if he could catch sight of the Johnson party arriving. Seeing nothing, he looked once more into Jones's hazel eyes and said, "You realize I can't allow you to live."

Cio's eyes widened when he saw a smile move across Jones's face.

Jones nodded and widened his stance, adjusting his combative posture. "I was hoping you would say that."

Cio, at first, not comprehending nor recognizing Jones apparent fearlessness, snorted and continued shaking his head. "If you take off your gun belt and toss it in front of me, I'll let you walk; if not, you're minutes from death."

Jones's voice took on steel. "You can forget that toss-the-gun-belt idea. Listen, first of all, it's hot out here. Secondly, I don't like doing a whole lot of talking, and thirdly, I really don't like talking to you. What do you say if we end this silly parley and get down to business?"

Jones's vehement words and the passion he said them with caused Cio to pause. For the first time, it occurred to Cio that Jones was after him and even more so than the other way around.

Another factor passed through Cio's mind: It appeared on the surface that John Lee Johnson was not even in the equation in Jones's words or actions.

Cio quickly processed Jones's angry but confident words and the mixed look of hate and disgust that were directed toward him. He deduced correctly that Jones had been sent to kill him and not the big Texan. Those facts had eluded him earlier, but not now.

But at this point, Cio didn't give a damn. He figured it was too late and too damn hot to analyze the convoluted setup between the McGrew and California factions.

Cio was even more worried about the impending arrival of John Lee Johnson. Each minute created a shrinking time-frame. All in all, he knew that he and Jones needed to settle this matter now and not protract the inevitable.

Cio's calculating eyes again were focused on Jones, who seemed ready to accelerate the action.

Cio, filled with confidence, smirked and shrugged his shoulders indifferently, as he knew the moment was at hand.

He began backing up. Their eyes were locked into the others. The eagle's constant screeching was the only external sound as they stood facing each other, ten feet apart.

It was only seconds, but it seemed longer. It was as though they were mentally connected, as if they knew it was time; they simultaneously drew. It was an extraordinary display of speed. Both fired as one. In unison, their .44s emitted hot jets of wicked orange. The concurring gunshots sounded as one. An eerie wavering sound echoed out over the hot sand, moving along the horizon and tailing off into a haunting reverberation.

The two men stood still, with smoking .44s still in their hands. Jones looked down at the front of his yellow shirt. He saw no blood, but he felt weak. He was having trouble catching a full breath. He stumbled backwards, barely keeping his balance, looking around desperately for a canteen of water. He cussed to himself that he lost to the condescending man who was still standing.

Jones holstered and placed both hands on his chest to stop the infernal hammering. As he felt his strength quickly leaving him, he caught the strange sight of Macro Cio, weaving and staggering blindly across the yellow sand.

Jones, even in the painful throes of his heart beating out of rhythm, could see blood running out of the white carnation attached to Cio's coat. It came out in gushes and ran down the lapels of his tan coat. The Californian watched through his pained eyes as Cio fell to one knee and released a grievous cry into the heated Mexican sky. The Basque gunman reached toward Jones with his fingers gruesomely resembling claws and then collapsed onto his face, dead.

Jones dropped to his own knees and literally crawled back to the wall, grasping for a canteen and finding one, but not having the strength to uncork it. He curled up in a ball in frustration, trying to stay in the wall's shade as much as possible. He knew he was close to death. Mysteriously, he could vividly see the aeriform image of Marilla Urmacher and hear her voice in his hallucination telling him, "You must not fail me. You will not fail me; you are California's finest."

Those words were the last thing Jones thought about; the next moment, he passed out, with his body barely covered by the thin shadow of the wall beneath the unrelenting, near-noon sun.

Weeks earlier, traveling across the Chihuahua Desert, John Lee Johnson had told Homer Timms about the gunfighter named Mike Jones, as related to him by Jim Pemberton. He felt at that point it was no longer a breach of a promise that he not reveal his identity and purpose. John didn't mention Marilla Urmacher. There were somethings he would not discuss, and his unusual relationship with her was one of those things.

The matter of Mike Jones was discussed and understood but wasn't mentioned again.

But at the present, both John and Homer, deep in the Valley of the Sun, rode side-by-side as they approached the old house of God built centuries ago. Neither seemed worried or nervous about the coming showdown with Macro Cio.

When they were just a half-mile from their destination, they heard what sounded like one gunshot in the distance, rolling and echoing across the flat desert.

The two horsemen broke into an easy but determined gallop. They realized that either Jones or Cio was dead or perhaps both. They had no idea of what lie ahead, but they sure wanted to find out.

When John and Homer arrived at the mission, they saw the dead body of Macro Cio, sprawling facedown in the hot sand, with a circle of blood beneath his upper torso. Beneath the wall's jagged shadow, Mike Jones looked mortally wounded or dying, except his fingers were moving as if fighting to stay alive.

Before the two gunmen could dismount, off in the distance, they saw a buggy with four men approaching. There were two riders on each side of the rig.

John gave a quick look at Homer that reflected not only the odd timing of the men's arrival, but the possible danger of it as well. As Homer dismounted, John galloped toward the five men, who were about a quarter-mile away.

Homer led his horse to the wall and tied off next to the appaloosa; he looked closely at Macro Cio's corpse and then moved toward Mike Jones.

Homer could see Jones was barely alive. His eyes were fluttering and his fingers were moving as though he were willing himself to communicate. Homer then caught sight of the canteen next to his twitching hand. He knelt down and pulled Jones up, cradling his upper body. He grabbed the canteen and pulled the stopper out. He reached inside his coat for a handkerchief and splashed some water on it. He put the wet handkerchief on Jones's brow. Next, he removed the gunman's hat and poured more water on his hair.

Jones opened his eyes and looked up at the kind face peering down at him. He barely eked out the words, "Need water."

Homer gave him a light swallow, followed by a heavier drink. The Californian nodded when he had enough.

Homer could see that Jones was trying to speak but was having trouble mustering the strength. After a few minutes, he managed to ask, barely above a whisper, "Did I kill that bastard?"

Homer gave him a soft smile, nodded, and said, "You did your job, Jones. You killed that bastard."

Jones gave his trademark dimpled smile and indicated he needed more water. But then, something else hit Jones's mind, something mysteriously pressing. He moved his face from the proffered canteen and pulled up his yellow shirt, sending his trembling fingers toward an envelope wedged inside his belt. The letter seemed to weigh a ton, but he dislodged it and lifted it up to Homer. Jones, wielding as much strength as he could summon in his dying state, held onto the letter. His eyes looked imploringly into Homer's blue eyes. Jones could no longer talk, but his eyes said plenty. His eyes were searching for some response as though it were a secret code.

Realizing his message involved the letter, Homer looked at the envelope and saw John Lee Johnson's name scrawled in large elegant penmanship. He deduced the dying man's request, leaned in closer, and said, "I will give this letter to John Lee Johnson."

After Homer spoke, Jones's expression changed from desperation to one of calm, and he released the letter. It was as though the weight of the world was lifted from his shoulders.

Homer could see that Jones regarded this act as more important than his own personal need, in this particular case of delivering the letter more than slaking his own thirst.

Jones never spoke again. With his mission accomplished, he gave a faint smile and nodded softly. He then closed his eyes, and ten seconds later, he died in Homer Timms's arms.

John Lee Johnson rode up to the buggy facing the sweaty and anxious Pedro Morales. His gray eyes panned the four men, two on each side that guarded him.

As the big Texan sat on his horse, sweltering in the 100 degree heat, he seemed indomitable to the four guards mounted across from him.

They marveled at his physique, as though he had been chiseled from cut bronze. The dripping and glowing sweat from both his chest and face made him appear even more formidable.

Pedro gulped when he saw John Lee Johnson. He had no idea that a human being could look like that. He just wished he knew beforehand what he knew now. He never would have made a bet. In his best English, Pedro asked, "Cio, is he dead?"

John straightened in the saddle, not really sure of what reaction his response would bring. But he nodded in the affirmative.

Pedro flinched noticeably, and his eyes began to water. He was financially ruined. The four men who were riding with him were his guards at the mine. They were acquainted with his bet and the consequences if he lost. They saw the ominous nod of John Lee Johnson concerning Macro Cio. They also recognized the futility of going up against such an aberration of nature, especially for no reason. It was understood that if Macro was dead, they had no dog in the hunt.

Pedro Morales no longer had money. He no longer had influence. The four riders, seeing the futility of trying to gun down the giant across from them, turned their horses away from Pedro's buggy. Abandoning him, they rode off, leaving heavy trails of dust.

Pedro began to weep. He tried in vain to stifle his tears. His chubby fingers covered his pained face. He did not turn his head to watch his men leaving. He suddenly felt the weight of his opprobrium. Feeling the fall from privilege to being nobody caused him to keep his hands shielding his eyes.

Gathering courage, he look at John Lee Johnson and pleaded, "Will you kill me?"

John Lee Johnson walked his big black horse to the side of the buggy and looked at Pedro's grief-stricken face. The big Texan could see a Navy Colt that was lying fully cocked on the seat by Morales. It was obvious that if he didn't shoot the effete man, he would kill himself.

"No, I don't do killings by request."

John and Pedro's eyes locked; in a broken voice, Pedro proclaimed, "If you won't kill me, I'll do it myself." He paused and added. "I am now living in disgrace."

John listened and leaned forward with his massive hands on his saddle pommel. "You have children?"

Morales nodded and then emitted a soft, "Si."

"How many?"

"Five."

John looked off above Pedro's head and asked, "And you're goin' to kill yourself?"

Pedro nodded glumly and said, "I cannot live with myself and the shame I have brought."

John sighed with impatience, as he needed to get back to Homer and the matters around the old mission. "It seems to me that your children would rather have you alive livin' in disgrace than dead in disgrace."

Pedro shook his head in frustration. "I cannot stand myself."

The big man said firmly, "That's your trouble, senor; you keep thinkin' of yourself. Maybe you should stop and think about others, includin' your wife and children."

With that said, John Lee Johnson whirled his mount around and headed back toward the ruined church.

Pedro Morales watched the broad back of the Texan as he rode away and thought on John's words. He knew the big man was right. He uncocked his Navy Colt, slumped forward, and wiped his tears. Gathering his courage, he turned the buggy around and headed back to Temecula.

John rode up and saw Homer holding the dead body of Mike Jones. Homer tenderly placed the Californian back on the sandy soil. He stood and looked down admiringly at the fallen gunman.

John dismounted, tied off beside Homer's sorrel, and walked slowly to stand by his friend, peering down at Jones.

"Don't know much about him, but he has my respect." Homer went on to explain about what he thought took place during the gunfight. He pointed to a thin groove of reddish blood on the side of Jones's neck and said, "I think Macro was aiming for a throat shot, which I understand is his method of execution. He came mighty close." He paused and added, "Jones went for his heart, and he won." Homer shook his head and continued, "I'm no doctor, but it seems to me that Jones died of a heart attack.

"Another thing about this man: He wouldn't allow himself to die until he delivered this." Homer handed the envelope with the refined handwriting to John Lee Johnson.

John gave a surprised look. He reached over and took the envelope. Instinctively, he knew it was from Marilla Urmacher. He turned his body for some privacy and opened the flap. He pulled out the letter and saw his name written once more in the salutation. It read as follows:

> If you are reading this, it means you're alive. For that I am most grateful.
>
> Each night I go to my lonely bed, thinking and longing for the moment we will see each other again. Even though you belong to another, I love you still.

There is no power on this earth that can stop me from loving you. I yearn for the day in this life or the life to come when we can hold hands and sing "Shall We Gather at the River" once more.

You may not know it, John, but you belong to me.

Eternally, Marilla

Homer tried not to look at John as he read. He knew by his friend's body English that he was reading something that was affecting him and affecting him greatly. John walked toward the Aztec altar, stacked with containers of gold, and leaned against the heavy boxes to steady his weakened legs. He studied the missive and reread it. After a few minutes, he reluctantly folded up the letter, replaced it in the envelope, and slid it in his front pocket.

While he had a moment of privacy, he took the time to find a blank sheet of paper and a heavy stubbed pencil in his saddlebags. He thoughtfully wrote a response note to Marilla. He tightfully folded it, placing it carefully in his pant's pocket to later give to the Pemberton riders.

He returned to the curious Homer, pulled the Marilla envelope from his pocket, and handed it to him. He said, "It's too beautiful to destroy but too dangerous for me to read again."

Homer did not totally understand but placed the letter inside his coat pocket and gave a nod that indicated he would see to its security. He looked at his tall friend and could see that he was shaken. He wanted to ask more but knew it would be an infringement, so he let the matter go.

The moment passed, and the two wagons driven by their crew arrived. They backed the wagons up to the altar laden with the heavy boxes. It was soon obvious as they opened one of the boxes that the gold was in bullion form for a reason: bulky to load and heavy to transport.

They soon realized that they were one wagon short to carry this heavy load.

After loading what gold they could, Homer caught sight of Joe Carson approaching in a buggy with a line of riders on each side, headed toward the mission. His eyes brightened when he saw they were followed by a heavy-duty wagon pulled by mules.

When the Pemberton group heard the rumor that Auguste Maduro had placed the gold in bullion form, they donated their own wagon with four mules (and a spare mule tied on to the back).

When they came to where John and Homer and their friends were, they dismounted and removed their hats in respect to Mike Jones, whom they could see was dead. Tullis told Homer about Jones's heart condition, confirming Homer's suspicions about Jones dying of a heart attack.

Homer, seeing their sadness about Jones, explained how he thought the gunfight had gone down. Although there were a few smiles of pride at Jones's successful effort, most wore grieved faces that he had died.

Joe Carson pragmatically had brought a shovel in the back of his buggy, and the whole Pemberton guard unit took turns digging the grave in what would have been the nave of the original church. Each man would dig for a length of time and then, exhausted by the sun, hand off the shovel to the next man, who gladly took over.

While they were digging, Tullis, the unquestioned leader of the Pemberton outfit, asked Homer if he would write on the grave marker, since he seemed learned.

They handed him an oval piece of wood that had been the door to a small room where the Communion had been stored in the church. They had brought it in case they needed it, and unfortunately, they did.

Homer pulled out his knife and began carving on the smooth surface of the miniature door. As he did this, the grave digging continued, and the wagons were loaded with the gold.

By midafternoon, the three wagons had been loaded, the grave was dug, and Jones was buried.

John Lee Johnson and his men blended in with the Pembertons as they lined all four sides of the grave. They all deferred to John Lee Johnson, who became the de facto speaker by the esteem he held among all the men.

John stood at the end of the grave and surveyed all the faces looking back at him. He slowly removed his hat and held it over his chest. This respectful act was followed suit by the whole assembly.

John sighed and said, "I'm a rancher and not a speaker, but unlettered or not, I know enough to say thank you." He paused for a moment and continued, "Like most people, I have trouble distinguishing what is God's providence and what is coincidence. But either way, I am most grateful for the outcome. Good don't always win, bad sometimes has its day, but in the end, good seems to come through. You all may have saved my life, especially this man." He dipped his head downward at the grave. "I have spoken enough. May this man rest in peace, and may the rest of you go with God."

The Pemberton riders removed their Spencer rifles from their scabbards, made a military line, and fired a twenty-one-gun salute.

After that, they gathered once more around John Lee Johnson. It seemed as though they wanted more of his time. They also seemed both sad and joyful that their mission was over.

John could sense that they wanted him to say more. He turned to face the three gold-laden wagons. His eyes drifted over to the leathery Tullis and said, "Take the gold to Marilla Urmacher. If not for her, I might be dead." John knew she had been out tremendous expense. He also realized when McGrew discovered she now had his gold that it would scorch his liver. It just seemed the expedient thing to do.

The stunned Pembertons could scarcely believe their ears. Tullis took a step backwards, astonished at the largesse of the big man, and asked, "Are you sure?"

"I'm shore." With that said, he handed Tullis the handwritten note addressed to Marilla. "See to it that she gets this."

That done, John Lee Johnson turned away and started walking toward Homer Timms and his men, but as he ambled along, he stopped and looked once more at the grave marker that beamed in the late afternoon sun. The words, carved and beautifully crafted by Homer Timms, read:

Here lies Mike Jones—died 1866.
He did what he thought was right.

John Lee Johnson nodded at the grave in appreciation, approached his horse, and mounted up. Jones's death and the effects of Marilla's letter had made him more emotional. He did not fault himself for having a heart; he did not fault himself for feeling sad, but he knew he had to recapture his rational mind for the long journey ahead.

Hobie, Van Edwards, and Fud had tethered all the horseflesh they had accumulated, including Macro's appaloosa. They seemed anxious to rid themselves of this dreadful place.

Homer rode up beside John and gave him a sideways look. "Proud of you, John Lee. Not many men I know could turn down a hundred thousand dollars. But you are you, and I'm glad we are partners."

John gave a friendly nod to Homer. They rode out of the Valley of the Sun and eventually across the Chihuahua Desert. It was a happy ride of sorts. There were no roaming bandits, and they ate well. They made faster time without the wagons.

When they got to Gandy, John bid Homer and his friends farewell. They extended his departure as long as possible, but they knew the big man needed to get home to Baileysboro.

John's solitary ride home allowed stormy thoughts to foment in his mind. He accepted those thoughts, knowing when he arrived at his home, the clouds would break, and he would see the sun of optimism once more. That driving force kept him on his usual breakneck pace.

Twice on the journey, bandits tried to attack his campsite in the middle of the night. Each time, John left broken or mangled bodies in his wake. The survivors all swore to stop thievery and possibly give their lives to Jesus.

John's spirits rose as he rode down the road to his ranch. He felt even better when he saw his house in the distance. Minutes later, he saw his beautiful wife Martha, standing on the porch, just like he knew she would.

Martha had sensed he was close. When she saw the black horse and the broad shoulders of her man down the road, she placed her hands to the side of her head and ran down the steps, crying for joy.

He made a running dismount, and they met in the front yard in a long and desperate hug. John Lee Johnson cried. Their tears and kisses were renewals of true love. He realized this was where he wanted to be and needed to be.

When the Mexican bullion was delivered to Marilla Urmacher, she had it assayed, and it came to $120,000; she invested it all in the Central Pacific Railroad and placed it in John Lee Johnson's name.

On Saturday, September 15, Marilla did as she was instructed in the note she had received from John Lee Johnson almost a month earlier. She had her clock set by the best timekeeper in San Francisco, and at the exact stroke of noon, she opened the door to her balcony deck, walked outside, and faced east. She began singing "Shall We Gather at the River" in a beautiful soprano voice. Her words seemed to soar, not only in sound but in conviction. She sang every line with tears streaming from her obsidian eyes. She knew he was doing the same because he gave his word. His word meant something. He was John Lee Johnson.

Over a thousand miles away, in a secluded grove of trees near Baileysboro, at exactly the same time, John Lee Johnson stood facing west and began singing the same hymn. His deep bass voice boomed out over the horizon in a haunting emotional tone. He remembered Marilla's soprano voice from two years back. He also had wet eyes when he finished.

After this special time ended, John mounted up and rode away, not knowing whether what he just did was sublime or not, but he felt better. He had kept his word and knew she had also. He felt that an ethereal love was best kept an ethereal love and never acted on. But even an impossible love needed nurturing.

The emotionally drained Frank McGrew was slumped over his desk in Philadelphia. In front of him was the telegram that informed him that John Lee Johnson was still alive and the Macro Cio was dead. He realized he lost a hundred thousand dollars. That amount stung and would cause his accountant concern. He also realized that he had been played by Marilla Urmacher. He now knew she sent a number of men to support John Lee Johnson instead of killing him. It scunnered him further that she now had his gold.

He sighed and leaned back in his leather chair. As he was mulling over what tack he might use against John Lee Johnson and Marilla Urmacher, he caught sight of the new dark-headed housemaid as she waved flirtatiously from the doorway. She was very pretty and engaging. He liked how she filled out her servant's dress. He momentarily forget about revenge and was overcome by a surge of lust.

The pretty housemaid's name was Janet Lincoln. She had been working for Frank McGrew for over a week now. What McGrew did not know was that she had banked ten thousand dollars recently, a check from Marilla Urmacher. Janet Lincoln's real name was Judith Levy. She was actually an assassin and had been paid to kill Frank McGrew. She took her craft very seriously.

EPILOGUE

1. Fud went to work for Van Edwards in Gandy and eventually became half-owner of the livery stable. Later that year, he married a heavy-set gal north of town.

2. Utah Jimmy Pruett, Memphis Mayford, and Cut Worm Weaver bought a ranch in Utah. To everyone's surprise, it turned out to be a viable success.

3. Hobie was hired by Homer Timms to be a foreman on one of his ranches. He became one of the best cattlemen in central Texas.

4. Braxton Gray became Frank McGrew's main man in Texas, replacing the lost and missing Robert Lang. In August, he married Cornelia Benson. He felt surely she would keep his secrets.

5. Cornelia Benson continued to communicate with Lieutenant Bragg, both sharing her bank lock box.

6. Pedro Morales did not commit suicide. He chose not to pay his bet debt and kept his mine.

7. Alicia Ruiz, upon hearing that her beloved Cio had been killed, ran back to her husband's arms, claiming she had been held hostage and ravaged. Her husband bought it. A few months after her name was placed on all his holdings as half-owner and beneficiary, he mysteriously died.

Printed in the United States
by Baker & Taylor Publisher Services